HUNTER'S WAR

Judson Gray

A SIGNET BOOK

SIGNET
Published by the Penguin Group
Penguin Putnam Inc., 375 Hudson Street,
New York, New York 10014, U.S.A.
Penguin Books Ltd, 27 Wrights Lane,
London W8 5TZ, England
Penguin Books Australia Ltd,
Ringwood, Victoria, Australia
Penguin Books Canada Ltd, 10 Alcorn Avenue,
Toronto, Ontario, Canada M4V 3B2
Penguin Books (N.Z.) Ltd, 182–190 Wairau Road,
Auckland 10, New Zealand

Penguin Books Ltd, Registered Offices:
Harmondsworth, Middlesex, England

First published by Signet, an imprint of Dutton NAL,
a member of Penguin Putnam Inc.

First Printing, December, 1998
10 9 8 7 6 5 4 3 2 1

Preface

His name is Kanati Porterfell, and he is on the run, as both the hunter and the hunted.

The son of a Cherokee mother he loved dearly and a white father he has never known, Kane carries in his mind the memorized contents of several secret encoded letters, pieces of a puzzle that purports to lead to a legendary treasure of unsurpassed value, lost years before in a violent Civil War. The treasure also involved one William Porterfell, the father Kane Porterfell until recently thought was long dead.

Only one final piece of the puzzle does Kane not possess: the contents of one last letter, existing now only in the mind of William Porterfell.

Though Kane was kidnapped by the ruthless Robert Blessed, an old wartime associate of William Porterfell's and a man who will stop at nothing to gain the lost jewel and restore his own faded wealth, he has escaped and now flees across the American West of 1885, seeking his father while trying to evade Robert Blessed and his merciless hired agents.

He had been helped along the way by an old black

Mississippi River dweller named Cypress Washington and his son, Lewis, as well as by a traveling magician named Frederick Railey and his beautiful daughter, Carolina. She, like Kane, has both white and Cherokee blood flowing through her veins.

Now Cypress and Lewis Washington are dead, Kane has narrowly escaped the clutches of Robert Blessed and his agents, and with Frederick and Carolina Railey, he is traveling into legendary Dodge City, Kansas, where he believes he will at last find his father.

Kane dares to hope that the threat of pursuit by Robert Blessed is now past, but he enters Dodge knowing that he can assume nothing except a continuing danger that stalks him like a shadow. In reality, a new and greater adventure looms just ahead . . .

A NEW QUEST

"I put your father on a train bound for Colorado, and as far as I know, that's where he is now. Part of my brother's private army."

"So he's safe, at least," Kane said.

At this, Flanagan looked troubled indeed. "Well . . . I don't think 'safe' is quite the word. Things have gotten worse at Three Mile. I've been following it in the newspapers and have heard a thing or two from business associates who've come out of Colorado. That strike is something terrible, Kane. There's fear of serious violence before it's through. I'm afraid I sent your father right into the midst of a very dangerous situation."

"Then that's all the more reason I have to go find him."

When he heard that, Flanagan looked up quickly at Kane, knitting his brows. Kane could see that his statement had sparked something in Flanagan's mind.

"Kane, indeed you do need to go to Three Mile. You can find your father and tell him to come back here with you. Try to talk him away from Three Mile and that cursed miners' war. And let me know—a wire, a letter—what happens. Will you do that?"

Those were terms Kane could accept. "Indeed I will."

Chapter 1

He had coppery skin and long black hair, and he stood in the middle of the road, as stiff and heedless as a statue, staring southward. The big painted wagon drew near him, slowed, then stopped.

"Pardon me, sir," called the wagon's driver, a broad and bearded showman named Frederick Railey. "Might you step aside enough to allow us to pass?"

The man in the road remained remarkably still, unresponsive. His hair blew slightly in the late-afternoon breeze. He was in his mid-twenties, with a hooked nose and flat cheekbones. His eyes were unmoving, riveted upon a level horizon that boasted no spectacle worthy of such rapt attention.

Railey glanced at the younger man perched beside him on the shotgun side of the driver's seat. "I don't think he's aware of us, Kane."

Kanati Porterfell replied, "I think you're right. Deaf, maybe?"

"Maybe . . . though even then he ought to be seeing

7

us from the corner of his eye. Judging from the look of him—an Indian, you think?"

"So he appears to me." Kanati began to clamber down from the wagon. Railey threw the brake and did the same.

They approached the standing man slowly. Still he did not seem aware of them.

"Sir?" Kanati said. "Sir, are you well?"

The Indian continued to stare southward.

"Not even blinking," Railey said.

"Sir?" Kane said again, fruitlessly. "Do you hear us, sir?"

Railey stepped directly in front of the Indian, who was a muscular, weathered young fellow with a firm, clenched jaw. The Indian's gaze meshed with Railey's, but the impression was strong that he did not really see Railey at all and was staring, as it were, *through* the man rather than *at* him.

Railey lifted a hand and waved it slowly in front of the Indian's face. No response. He thrust it forward suddenly, as if to flatten the Indian's nose. Not so much as a blink resulted.

"I'll be!" Railey declared, lowering his hand slowly. "Cataleptic!"

"What?"

"Cataleptic . . . a kind of fit, if you will. This fellow is basically in a stupor, or trance. And not the kind that Carolina and I simulate during our stage performances. An authentic, spontaneous trance!"

"So he doesn't see us?"

"Nor hear us."

"Will he stay this way?"

"No. No, from what I've read, it's a recurring sort of thing, coming and going abruptly. Rather pitifully victimizes those afflicted with it. Can you imagine walking across a crowded street, only to be seized by a state in which you were aware of nothing around you, frozen in place, your senses cut off . . ."

"But why, and how, could such a condition come to—"

Kane's question went unfinished. Something swept across the standing man, abruptly animating him. He blinked twice, three times, sucked in a hard breath, and gaped at Railey before him. He twisted his head and saw Kane, then with a startling yell he ran at Railey, shoving him back with both hands and rushing past him, across the rolling landscape toward the horizon at which he'd been staring so intently. He quickly disappeared from their sight behind a gentle swell of land.

"That was indeed the oddest thing I've witnessed in quite some time," Railey said, gently rubbing his chest where the Indian had pushed him.

Carolina Railey called to them from the wagon, which was little more than a large roofed box on wheels with the stage names of Railey and Carolina—"Lord Faust" and the "Indian Princess"—garishly emblazoned on the side panels, along with other teasers about the traveling magic show. She had been resting inside for the last several miles. "Who was that, Papa?"

"We don't really know, dear. A young Indian man. He was standing in the middle of the road, cataleptic. But he came out of it."

"Cataleptic? Truly?"

"He wasn't so much as blinking, and hardly breathing. I've never encountered an authentic case of it before. Odd indeed! I wonder what made him pull out of it so quickly?" He mulled over the mystery for a moment, sighed, then glanced at the sky. "The day is fast waning, my dear hearts. So let's get on into town before dark, hmm?"

They reached the outskirts of Dodge City about dusk. Lights were just beginning to blink to life in windows here and there as the day relinquished its hold on the midwestern landscape and crawled to the other side of the world.

Kane looked to the right and left as the wagon rolled ostentatiously down Front Street, drawing, as Railey intended, quite a lot of attention from the citizens on the boardwalks. But Kane noticed, with a little mystification and more than a little concern, that many of the eyes that turned toward them focused more on him than on the flamboyant wagon. Given the adventure he'd survived—barely—before becoming the Raileys' traveling companion, and given that even now he might still be under pursuit, he had good reason not to want a lot of public attention. He wouldn't bring up his concern with Railey just yet, however, fearing that his imagination was exaggerating his perceptions.

He asked a question instead. "Is this city as wicked as people say?"

"Not so much as a few years back," Railey replied authoritatively. At the town limits he had suddenly taken on a faux British accent, part of his Lord Faust persona that he had dropped on the trip from Wichita, but now adopted again to get himself back in character. "You see here a town deeply affected by the temperance movement. In addition, Texas fever is causing a major turning away of the cattle trade that built both this town's economy and its reputation. So what you have right now in Dodge City is a wildcat that's been substantially declawed."

"Have you performed here before?"

"Several times. Most recently . . . let me see . . . two years ago, during the cattle season. Some wonderful response, some good money made. My only problem was keeping some of the more amorous young cowboys away from Carolina. But even then I could tell that the town wasn't quite the wild place it had been a few years before. Ah, the calming and civilizing effects of time!"

Kane looked at the faces of the people staring at the wagon—or were they staring at *him*? "I wonder if one of them is my father? I wonder if he's watching us right now?"

"It could be, Kane. Or, it may take us some time to locate him. Either way, if William Porterfell is here, we'll find him. We'll do whatever it takes."

"I do appreciate it, sir. I appreciate you and Carolina both, more than you know." Kane meant every word, but he left a further and darker thought unspoken: his hope that the Raileys would see no harm come their way because of their involvement with him. The last two people who had made his quest their own had wound up slain by the men who pursued him.

The wagon rolled on to its destination, a big, rough

stable, where the liveryman, an aging, transplanted Mexican with only one good eye, enthusiastically greeted Railey, whom he obviously remembered, though he called him by his stage name, Faust. Railey, pumping his false British accent to obnoxious heights, delivered a miniature performance on the spot, pulling a coin from the Mexican's ear, making a handkerchief disappear and reappear, tearing a paper apart and restoring it. The Mexican clapped and nodded and grinned and seemed content even though Railey gave him no gratuity for his services. *Clever man, that Faust,* Kane thought. *Tricks instead of tips. Good way to stretch a traveling showman's limited budget.*

They removed their baggage from the wagon and made their way through town to the three-story Excelsior, one of Dodge's newest hotels, built adjacent to the Pearl Dance Hall and Medicinal Dispensary, the venue where Lord Faust and his Indian Princess were scheduled to perform for two weeks beginning the next night. In return, they would receive cut-rate winter pay, with free lodging at the hotel thrown in.

"What's the meaning of the 'Medicinal Dispensary' part of the name?" Kane asked as he set the Raileys' baggage in the corner of the big room that the father and daughter would share, Railey taking the bed and Carolina the trundle. Kane's own room, smaller than this one, was down the hall, rented for him at Railey's expense and over Kane's protest. They'd argued it out on the way from the livery, and Railey had won, betraying a generous streak that his cheating of the liveryman had belied.

"The law in Dodge these days is no saloons," Railey explained. "Part of this sweeping temperance effort, you see. But the law allows vendors of drink for 'medicinal' purposes. Which explains why every tavern and dance hall you see in Dodge these days is calling itself an 'apothecary' or whatever else. The temperance law did little to close down any saloons, but it bolstered the sign-painting business considerably and changed a lot of business names on the town registers."

"So whiskey is 'medicine' now?"

"Has it ever really been anything else?" Railey grinned and began brushing out his beard at the mirror.

Stomachs were empty, and supper called. Railey was in a good mood, ready to buy. Oddly, however, considering his hunger, Kane didn't find much appealing about the prospect of visiting a restaurant. He'd been through a lot just to reach Dodge, and he was tired and not very sociably minded. He admitted as much to the Raileys.

Carolina said, "If you'd like, we could bring food back to you. Let you dine in your room, or in here, if you wish, in peace and quiet."

Kane smiled. "That sounds good. Thank you."

She smiled, too. Kane had never seen anything more beautiful.

"Excellent idea, Carolina! Ripping! We'll bring you back a thick Delmonico's steak," Frederick Railey said, with his usual enthusiasm and fake accent. "And you'll never have so marvelous a meal, I assure you, Kane. There's no finer steak to be had in this nation than that which Delmonico's delivers up."

"I look forward to it."

"And perhaps, later on, we can talk over something that I think needs discussing. These letters that you've committed to memory . . . do you think that perhaps they should be written down before they slip your mind?"

Had that suggestion come from anyone else, Kane would have suspected a possible ulterior motive. But Railey he trusted. And he understood, too, why Railey would find the letters so intriguing, written, as they apparently were, using a code similar to that employed by performers to transmit hidden clues from the prompter to the "mind reader." Railey and Carolina performed just such an act, and Railey was itching to try decoding those letters.

"I don't think I want to write them out just yet, Mr. Railey," Kane said. "Though I'd trust you with those letters as much as I trust myself, this is a case in which knowledge means potential danger. If you had copies of them, you and Carolina might become targets of Robert Blessed as much as I am already. And, frankly, the fact that only I know what those letters say and that copies of most of them don't exist is protection for me. It gives Blessed a reason to keep me alive if ever he gets his hands on me. Without me, he has no letters, no hope of tracking down his treasure."

"I see, and I agree. But perhaps, if we find that Blessed is dead or if this whole business somehow comes to an end . . . maybe then we can write them down again . . . you think?"

"Definitely."

When father and daughter were on their way to Delmonico's, Kane walked down the hall to his room. He entered it, thinking of lying down and relaxing, but as soon as he was inside he realized he didn't really want to be here at all, and wished he'd gone with the Raileys. Every time he closed his eyes he relived the recent terrifying battle that had played out atop a moving train and the deadly result of it, not only for the hired gunman who had tried to capture him, but also for poor Lewis Washington.

Suddenly feeling enclosed by the walls around him, Kane decided he would join the Raileys after all. He locked the door of his room and pocketed the key, then turned down the hall toward the landing that overlooked the hotel lobby. When he'd descended one level, he heard the voices of two men engaged in conversation in the lobby. What he heard made him pause and listen, then move closer to hear better.

". . . and there they found him, just as the train pulled into the station for water," one man was saying. "Dead as stone, this colored fellow was, right atop the train. He'd been shot. And the brakeman was missing. They found him lying back up the track a couple of miles with a broken leg, but otherwise well enough. He couldn't tell them what had happened—he'd been so disturbed by it all that he couldn't recall it."

"And there was another body on the track, too, wasn't there?" the second conversationalist asked. "I heard there was."

"It's true. There was another dead man. Or what was left of him. They found him a mile or two back up the track from where the train stopped. He'd obviously been run over. That train absolutely chewed him up and spat him out like Jonah from the whale's belly. They could tell this one was a white man, but they don't know that they'll ever be able to figure out who he was, nor who the colored one on top of the train was, for that matter."

Kane moved quickly back up to the third floor to his room. He unlocked the door, yanked it open, and closed himself inside. He leaned back against the wall and sank slowly to a seated position on the floor, breathing hard. Panic and a deep, overwhelming anguish filled him. All the tensions and sorrows of the ordeal that had brought him here now flooded in painfully. The very room suddenly seemed ominous, the patterns of its wallpaper masking eyes that watched him, unseen but knowing.

He came to his feet with a great effort of will. No! He would not give in to irrational panic. He had endured much, escaped, and perhaps thrown off his pursuers forever. One of them, Jason Wyrick, he'd blinded in a fight; Wyrick now lived impotently in endless darkness back in St. Louis. The worse of the pair, the heartless Blessed, was quite possibly dead, having leaped or fallen from the same train atop which Lewis Washington had died.

Remembering the advice of his childhood Cherokee mentor, Toko, Kane drew in several deep breaths and concentrated his attention on his panic as an objective thing, apart from himself. He examined it, studied it like a specimen, analyzing the feelings it brought, the physical effect it had on him. In so doing, he took power over his fear and willed it away.

Rising slowly, Kane glanced at his reflection in the mirror and smiled wanly. It had probably been inevitable that such an attack of panic would come, considering what he had endured. He promised his reflected image that he'd not allow such a thing to happen again, though. He had to be in control now. He was in Dodge City to find the father he'd never known. Nothing was to be gained by letting fear take over.

Kane straightened his clothing, combed his hair, and stared at his reflection in the mirror until he was content with what he saw. He opened the door and stepped out into the hall.

Chapter 2

Kane wasn't sure that he would be able to catch up with the Raileys before they reached the restaurant. If not, he could simply join them when he got there.

He walked down the stairs into the lobby, glancing toward the two men whose conversation he'd overheard. They looked back at him, and something in their eyes changed. Kane strode quickly across the lobby, feeling their gaze following him. It was surprising and unnerving.

He exited onto the street and looked about, trying to spot his traveling companions, but he saw no sign of them. Darkness had fallen and the wind was colder. What was that restaurant Railey had named? Delmonico's. Kane set out to look for it.

Three women talking outside a clothing store paused to stare at him as he drew near. The closest of them backed away a couple of steps as he passed by them. Across the street, he saw a man gaping at him, but the fellow looked away as soon as their eyes met.

What was going on here? Why was he stirring this kind of interest merely by walking down the street?

Finally Kane saw the Raileys ahead, just rounding a corner. He increased his pace and made the same turn as they entered a restaurant with "Delmonico's" emblazoned on its sign.

Just inside, the host of the establishment, in a black suit, encountered Kane. His eyes got bigger, as did Kane's sense of disquiet.

"May I help you?" the man asked in a cautious tone.

"Yes. I'm here to join a couple of your patrons . . . there they are, sitting down at that table."

The host glanced at the Raileys. "Very well."

Frederick Railey greeted Kane jovially. But as the young man sat down and looked around at the other patrons, he saw heads turning away, eyes shifting quickly downward.

"Glad you decided to join us after all, Kane," Railey said.

"I'm not sure I should have. I've never been stared at so . . . strangely. I'm beginning to think I've sprouted horns."

"Hmm," said Railey, having himself just taken note of the attention Kane was getting. "Odd."

"Is it because I'm Indian?"

"I doubt it. Carolina is as Cherokee as you, and she hasn't drawn such a response."

Kane hunkered low in his chair. "I don't like it."

"Most likely you bear a resemblance to some well-known person," Railey speculated as he picked up his menu.

Forty-five minutes later, when they were all engaged in cleaning the last of their food from their plates, Kane was beginning to feel not merely puzzled by the stares, but outright angry. One man in particular, who sat alone at the opposite side of the cafe, seemed especially preoccupied with him.

"I've got half a mind to walk over there to that table and ask that fat man with the whiskers what's so blasted fascinating about me," Kane said. "He's stared more than anyone else."

"I hope you won't do that," Railey said over the rim of his coffee cup. He drained the last of it, then raised the cup to catch the waiter's attention. "In Dodge, I've found, it's best to leave strangers be. And perhaps your imagination is exaggerating the significance of this just a little. After all, a few stares never hurt anyone."

The waiter approached with a steaming carafe in hand. He poured Railey's cup full again, his eyes shifting all the while toward Kane.

That was it.

"Excuse me, sir," Kane said, resisting the impulse to rise and put himself right in the man's face. "Might I ask for an explanation of why you just looked at me the way you did? And why everyone else in this town seems to be doing the same?"

The waiter blanched. "Sir, I'm sure I don't know what you mean." He turned and scurried off.

"Well, that settles it," Kane said. "It's not my imagination."

"No," Railey mumbled. "I suppose not."

"Kane," Carolina whispered, "there's a man who just came in, talking to the fat man with the big whiskers. And they've glanced this way three times now."

Kane pushed his plate away, his appetite gone.

"Perhaps we should head back to the hotel," Railey suggested.

They walked through the town together, not speaking. Eyes followed them all the way, all drawn, it seemed, to Kane. Kane's annoyance grew. By the time they reached the hotel, he was seething, and he declined to go in.

"If everyone here intends to stare at me, then I'll give them every opportunity," he said. "I'm going to take a walk."

"I wouldn't mind a turn about town myself," Railey said. "Would you mind if Carolina and I—"

Carolina touched her father's arm. "Papa, I think Kane wants to be alone just now."

"Oh. Yes. Indeed."

Kane flashed a quick, subtle grin at Carolina. What she'd said was only partly correct. He really didn't fancy parading around Dodge with the flamboyant Frederick Railey at the moment, but Carolina's company was welcome at any time.

"I'll be back soon," he said.

Five minutes later he was striding up famous Front Street, reading broadsides and shingles and window signs . . . and becoming aware, all at once, that he was being followed. The Raileys? He glanced back. Several people were in sight, but the Raileys were not among them.

Kane quickened his pace, fighting the impulse to run. Better to slow down and see if he could solve this little mystery. He halted and pretended to read a poster hanging on the porch post of a store. In doing so he turned just enough to allow himself a glance at his follower. A thin but well-muscled man with largish ears and close-set eyes. A mustache covered his upper lip.

Kane began walking again, whistling softly to himself. He turned in the next alley out of sight, backing against the wall to await the man who trailed him.

Seconds passed. No man appeared. A minute went by. Still no one. Maybe the man really hadn't been following him at all. Curiosity got the better of him, and Kane thrust his head out just far enough to glance back down the boardwalk. Empty. The man must have turned away or entered a doorway somewhere back along the way.

Kane decided that his imagination was overwrought. Not at all unlikely, if he was honest about it. The things that had happened to him lately were enough to rouse paranoia in anyone.

He heard something behind him. Turning, he stared into the face of the man who had been following him. He'd come up from the other end of the alley, circling around after seeing Kane duck off the boardwalk.

For a moment the two stared at one another, unspeaking.

"Howdy," the man said at last, his rather homely face breaking into a warm, disarming smile. "My name's Sughrue."

"Can I help you, Mister Sughrue?"

"Why, yes, you can. Yes, indeedy. I'm the sheriff of this county, you see. I'd like a few moments to welcome you to Dodge City . . . and after that, I believe you and me need to have us a little talk."

For a moment Kane thought it all was undone. Somehow the law knew everything and was after him, even though he'd done nothing wrong. Blessed was surely behind this! Somehow he'd gotten to the law at Dodge and—

Kane forced himself to snap off this new surge of panic.

"Why do we need to talk?"

"You talk your English mighty good, young man."

"Why wouldn't I?"

"A lot of Indians don't."

"You think I'm an Indian?"

"I can see that you are."

"I'm not."

Sughrue laughed. "I know an Indian when I see one."

"I'm only half Indian."

"See there? You *are* an Indian."

"Given that the mix is the same either way, couldn't you just as easily say I was a white man? And you still haven't said why you want to talk to me."

Sughrue seemed to find the verbal cat-and-mouse amusing. He grinned patiently. "Listen here, young man—white, Indian, or whatever you want to call yourself—I've got a right to ask you whatever questions I need to when it's the public safety we're talking about."

"Am I a threat to the public safety?"

"Maybe so. Maybe so. Who are you?"

Kane's immediate impulse was to lie, but he knew that to do so would be counterproductive. He'd come to Dodge to search for his father, which would inevitably require openness about who he was. "My name is Kanati Porterfell."

"Uh-huh. How long you been about Dodge?"

"Got here today. I came in with a traveling show that's going to be performing at the Pearl Saloon."

"It's a dance hall and medicinal dispensary, in case you ain't noticed. Dodge hasn't got no more saloons. Just apothecary shops and vendors of healthy beverages." Sughrue had a certain twinkle in his eye as he said this.

"I noticed."

"You been in Dodge before this?"

"No."

"Where'd you come from?"

"I was in St. Louis not long ago." True enough. Kane saw no merit in adding the further fact that he'd been in St. Louis first as a kidnapping victim, then as a fugitive on the run for his life.

"So you're a showman."

"No. I just came here with some people who are."

"Why'd you come to Dodge?"

"Would I get into trouble asking again why you're so curious about me?"

"I'll answer your questions once you answer mine."

Kane paused, and then took a further step into the dangerous arena of honesty. "I came to Dodge to look for my father."

"Who is he?"

24

"His name's William Porterfell. Do you know him?"

"Can't say I do. He lives here?"

"I was told he'd come here from Wichita."

"Does he know you're looking for him?"

"No. The truth is, he don't know me."

"Your own father don't know you?"

"Listen, Sheriff Sughrue, I'd appreciate knowing why I'm so interesting to you."

"One more question. Are you prone to fits that render you still and quiet and stiff, like a statue?"

Suddenly it was all clear. Now, Kane understood. He was being mistaken for that very Indian he and the Raileys had met on the road today! It made sense. One young Indian man would look like any other to many whites. And he was willing to bet that the cataleptic Indian had some crimes on his list of life achievements. No wonder people had been staring! They thought a criminal was parading himself blatantly in their midst!

"I'm prone to fits of no kind, Sheriff, other than fits of irritation at being falsely accused. But I did see an Indian on the road today, as we were coming into Dodge, who was standing still as a tree, not seeming to either hear or see us when we spoke to him."

Sughrue said nothing for a time. Kane could feel the man sizing him up, evaluating his words, the impression he made. "Come with me," Sughrue said at last. "Let's go meet a fellow who maybe can clear this up right away. He's the one who put me to following you to start with."

The sheriff walked with Kane back up the street to where a man stood waiting at the end of the next alley.

It was the same big-whiskered man who had stared so curiously at Kane in Delmonico's.

"Mr. Billy Seers, is this the Indian who stole your horse?"

The man frowned and looked Kane up and down, carefully avoiding his eyes. "I think maybe it is."

Wonderful, Kane thought. *Just wonderful as can be.*

"Maybe, you say? You need to do better than maybe, Billy. I don't like locking people up on maybes."

Locking people up? Kane swallowed hard.

"Well . . . it surely looks like him. He's cut his hair shorter, though. Kind of makes it harder to know him."

Kane raised a hand in protest. "Wait just a minute— I've done nothing! I've robbed nobody! I've not even been around Dodge long enough to have committed any kind of crime, even if I wanted to. This man obviously has no idea whether he's seen me before—which he hasn't."

Kane's protests only seemed to bolster his accuser's conviction. "Sheriff, he *is* the one. The more I look, the more sure I am."

"You'd swear to that in a court of law?"

A pause. "I would."

Kane protested again. "Hold on, Sheriff. Before you go dragging me off to some jail, you'd best go look up Mr. Frederick Railey and his daughter, Carolina. They're the performers I came into town with. They can tell you that I've been with them for days and I've committed no crimes."

"We'll go find them right now, then."

But when Kane and Sughrue, trailed by the increasingly belligerent and accusative Billy Whiskers, as Kane had mentally tagged him, reached the hotel, they found the Raileys gone. Kane felt like sinking into the earth. Probably the pair of them had taken off for a walk of their own after Kane left them.

"I'm sure they'll be back soon, Sheriff."

Sughrue scratched his jaw. "Well, Mr. Porterfell, I don't have time to stand about waiting for them. And that leaves me in a bit of a predicament about just what to do with you. I've got me a good citizen swearing you to be a robber, and you've got no verifiable alibi. Looks to me like I have no recourse but to lock you up."

"But the Raileys can back up everything I say!"

"Unfortunately, the Raileys ain't here. And them being show people ... there might be some question about just how reliable their testimony would be. When I can, I prefer getting my evidence from folks I know. We may have to do some further investigating." He turned to Billy Whiskers. "Billy, you're *sure* this is the Indian who robbed you?"

"Absolutely certain, Sheriff. He's the one."

Kane suddenly felt very tired indeed, and he saw that this particular battle wasn't one he was going to win. With a sigh, he nodded, and Sughrue led him away, Billy Whiskers looking on with smug satisfaction.

"Don't worry, son," Sughrue said. "It ain't that bad. Not another soul is locked up just now, so you'll be comfortable, not crowded. And if Billy's wrong and you're innocent, we ought to be able to verify that soon enough."

Kane mentally surrendered, too weary to fight.

It was remarkable. In Dodge City for only a few hours, and now he was bound for jail, suspected of a crime he hadn't committed.

The jail was more like a dungeon. Located beneath the county courthouse, it was dank, dark, and as utterly unappealing a place as Kane could have hoped never to see. He bit off what he knew would be a futile protest as he was ushered into the little hole of a prison, while through his mind passed words first spoken by the black-skinned father of the late Lewis Washington: *The law is a white man.* Indeed. He bitterly doubted that a white man would be treated as he was right now, being locked up on the word of a man who had obviously not been at all sure of his identification until he'd argued himself into it.

"How long do you think I'll be in here?" Kane asked the sheriff as the door clanged shut behind him.

"Depends on a lot of different things."

"Sheriff, I think it was very clear that the man who identified me wasn't at all sure of himself."

"Seemed the same to me. Which is why we'll be doing some further question-asking with other folks."

"You've got the wrong man. I told you—I saw the Indian you're after on the road today."

"Mighty convenient sighting. What are the odds of that happening, huh?"

"You doubt my word?"

"A man in my position has to doubt the word of everyone, young fellow. Nothing personal, you understand."

Kane had much more to say, but prudence told him

to be quiet. He sat on the edge of the hard and dirty cot, sullen, hating Dodge City, Sughrue, Billy Seers, and even that cursed cataleptic Indian, just for the mess they were all conspiring to make of his life.

Chapter 3

The jail's outer door opened and a heavyset man in a battered gray hat entered. A deputy's badge glittered dully in the gap of his open overcoat. He looked straight at Kane.

"That him, Sheriff?"

"So Billy Seers would have us believe."

The deputy walked up to the bars and stared through them at Kane, as if he were an unusual beast in a cage. "Has he froze up yet?"

"No."

Froze up? Kane was puzzled, then realized this was a reference to the catalepsy afflicting the *real* criminal Indian, for whom he was being mistaken.

"Is Billy sure it's him? He don't look like what Joe Franks described."

"Billy says he's sure. But it took him a minute or two to come around to it. I'm going to want to know a lot more before we go making official charges."

Kane was glad to hear that, anyway.

The deputy turned away from the cell. "Any further word in about the dead colored man on that train?"

Kane looked up sharply, then regretted it, for Sughrue happened to be looking his way when it happened. The sheriff squinted one eye thoughtfully, then answered his deputy without taking his eyes off Kane.

"Nothing except that they still ain't been able to figure out who he is."

"Well, I been thinking," the deputy said. "There's got to be some tie-in between the dead colored man on the train and the dead white man who was spread over the tracks back behind."

"I think everybody's assumed that, Kenneth."

"Well," the deputy went on, "I figure it this way: The colored man and the white man was on top the train together, you see, fighting or something. The white man shoots the colored one, bang!, and the colored man falls down and dies on top of the train. And the white man falls off the train and gets down under the wheels, and that's it." The deputy smiled like a schoolboy at the end of a successful bit of classroom oratory.

"Fine theory, Kenneth. Maybe you got it right. Not that it tells us what they were fighting about or who they were. But it don't matter to us here, anyhow—it ain't a Ford County concern. Nothing to do with our jurisdiction." Sughrue eyed Kane again. "Not as far as I know, anyway."

"Wish it was our case. I'd be interested in poking about in it."

"We've got situations enough of our own."

"Want me to stay around the jail and watch our redskin?"

"No, you go on out and make some rounds. I believe I'll talk some more with Mr. Porterfell here, private."

"Porterfell? That ain't much of a redskin name."

"He's half white."

"Oh." The deputy looked Kane over one more time, then left.

Sughrue walked over to the bars and peered through them at Kane. "Maybe this talk we need to have ought to be about more than just Billy Seers's accusations against you."

"What do you mean?"

"I think you know something about that dead colored fellow on the train top."

"Why would you think that?"

"I saw you react when Kenneth mentioned it. That was one of my deputies, Kenneth Rimes. Simple fellow but honest and reliable. So tell me, Mr. Porterfell, what do you know?"

"Nothing. All I know is that I've done nothing but come into this town, then find myself stared at by everybody, locked up for crimes I never did . . . and now you're talking about dead men on trains . . ."

Sughrue grinned. "You *do* know something. I can tell."

"Why don't you tell me what it is I'm supposed to know about?"

"Fair enough. The other day, a train bound for here pulled into a station west of Wichita for water. While it was stopped, a corpse was found atop the train. A Negro man, shot to death. The brakeman was gone, but before long he was found back down the track. Busted leg, addled in the head, no good explanation of what had happened. Besides him, there was a corpse on the track. Spread over a good hundred feet. White man. He'd obviously gotten chewed up under the train."

"Who was he?"

"Nobody knows. Nor the identity of the dead Negro. Big mystery, big mystery. Has all this part of Kansas talking and wondering. But as I said, it didn't happen in my county, and it ain't this office's concern."

"Where's the dead man now?"

"They scraped him off the tracks and turned him over to the coroner."

"No . . . the black man, I mean."

"Him they're trying to get identified before burial, in that he's got a face left and the white man didn't. What they usually do in such cases is salt the body down to preserve it, then hold it for a time until it can be identified."

"What happens if he isn't identified?"

"Pauper's grave. Unmarked. Best that can be done."

Kane stared through the bars at the far wall. A pauper's grave for Lewis Washington . . . that wouldn't be right. Lewis had been too good a man for that. If not for Lewis and his father, Kane would probably have been recaptured, even killed, by the kidnappers he had escaped.

"What are you thinking on, young man?"

"Just thinking it would be a shame to die and not have anybody know who you were."

"I'm playing a hunch here, but sometimes hunches win card games. You know who that colored man is, I believe. Maybe who the white one is, too."

Kane debated about whether to answer truthfully. Would he betray anything hurtful to himself if he did? Perhaps not, especially if he did a slight revision job on the truth. "Yes," he said, "I think maybe I do. The colored man, I mean. Not the white one." The last statement was a lie, but Kane felt no regret. McGrath the murderer didn't deserve to be honored with a name on a gravestone.

"How so?"

"There was a fellow I knew in Wichita. Colored man, named Lewis Washington. He had a tendency to drink a little and ride the rails. He told me he was going to ride a train into Dodge, sneaking onto a boxcar, and he tried to get me to do the same. I wouldn't, and he went on alone. So naturally, when I heard your deputy say a colored man had been found dead atop a train bound for Dodge, I had to wonder if it was Lewis."

"Which accounts for why you reacted the way you did when Rimes spoke."

"Yes."

"Mr. Porterfell, it may indeed be that this man is this Lewis Washington. You'd know his face?"

"Yes."

Sughrue scratched his chin. "Well, even though it's not a Ford County affair, still I suppose the law in one county owes it to other law to help out when it can. Mr. Porterfell, I want to take you on a train ride with me. And I want you to take a look at this body and see if you can identify him."

A train ride? Back in the very direction he'd come

from? Kane felt an explosion of frustration. He had come to Dodge to find his father, not to be diverted by faulty arrests, false accusations, and the necessity of identifying a body whose identity he already knew full well anyway!

Then again, if he declined, Sughrue might hold it against him, whereas a cooperative spirit might earn him some favor. Besides, and most important, there was Lewis to think about. He deserved to have his burying place marked with his name, and Kane was uniquely positioned to make that possible for him.

"When would we go?" he asked Sughrue.

"I expect we could catch a train tomorrow."

"Very well. I'll go."

Sughrue gave a curt nod, no more, but Kane felt a warming of the sheriff's favor toward him and knew at once he had done the right thing.

So he felt it diplomatically safe to ask a needed question: "Sheriff, how long will it take for me to prove I'm not this Indian thief you've been looking for?"

Sughrue squinted one eye at him, as he was wont to do when thinking. "What the devil, son, I may as well be honest with you. I don't believe you're our bird. Billy Seers is a good fellow, but not very reliable. His identification don't carry a lot of weight with me. I need to bring in another man to look you over. I fully expect he'll tell me you're not our man, and you'll be free to go."

"Can't you go find him now?"

"Afraid not. Out of town at present. We'll have to wait for him to get back."

"But if you already don't believe I'm the one, can't you let me go free in the meantime?"

"The fact still remains that I've got a crime victim who swears you are the criminal. And you want to know the truth, son? Half the town's been here squawking at me since you showed up in Dodge. Even if I don't think you're the right man, a lot of people do. You're safer in here just now."

Time passed, the hour growing late, then later. Kane resigned himself to a night in jail, closed his eyes, and in moments slept deeply. No dreams at first, but then he suddenly was atop that moving train again, Lewis Washington fighting for survival, the wicked McGrath tormenting him. In the dream, Kane himself was tripped up by Lewis and fell beneath the wheels, the train jolting as it ran across his body . . .

Kane jerked awake and sat up. He really *had* felt a jolt. The cell door had opened and closed with a bang. Kane blinked and stared at the stranger who had just been shoved into the cell with him. Sughrue, outside, said, "Mr. Kane Porterfell, meet Mr. Pete Rampling. Your new cell mate."

Kane looked blankly at the sullen Rampling, a disheveled auburn-haired fellow with fresh bruises forming on his swollen face. Rampling glowered at him, his standoffish manner silently daring him to speak—a dare Kane had no desire to take. Rampling threw himself onto the empty bunk on the other side of the little cell, turned his back to Kane, and curled his legs up into a nearly fetal posture.

Kane laid down again, closed his eyes, and let himself fall back to sleep.

"So . . . are you that crazy Indian who's been robbing folks?"

Kane opened his eyes, confused. Though it was hard to tell in this dismal cellar jail, he knew it was morning.

"Hey, did you hear me?"

Kane sat up and looked out of the cell, trying to figure out where the voice was coming from. It wasn't the deputy Rimes, who snored at the desk. Then he remembered his fellow prisoner and looked to the left. The fellow was glowering from the corner of his bunk, swollen, black-eyed, and obviously still a little drunk.

Kane finger-combed his hair and sat up slowly, swinging his legs to the floor. "No. It isn't me."

"Then why are you in here?" The voice was slurred and slightly nasal.

"Because white folks think every Indian looks like every other Indian."

"You are an Indian, then?"

"Half. My father was a white man, my mother a Cherokee."

"Huh. Makes you Indian in my book. You take a clear puddle and fill it halfway with dirt, and you don't have a half-clean, half-dirty puddle. You got a dirty puddle through and through."

Kane took great offense to that analogy, but now didn't seem to be the time to make an issue of the man's attitude . . . which was, after all, the same kind of attitude a man of Kane's heritage found almost everywhere he turned. "What was your name again?"

"Pete Rampling." Rampling groaned and seized his head with a grimace. "Oh, Lord. Somebody just shoot me and be done with it."

"Who'd you fight with? The sheriff?"

"No. A couple of fellows I was drinking with. Fellows I worked with a little while over on the Flanagan house."

"What's that?"

"Big old mansion going up just west of town. Texan named Ben Flanagan, rich as hell, building it. Cattleman. I worked as a carpenter there until I got into a row with a fellow and got myself fired. I do that a lot—get into rows with folks, and it's always me who pays the price for it." Rampling grimaced again and groaned loudly.

"Your whole face is bruised," Kane told him.

"I can feel it. Bet I'm black as a cotton field hand. Do I know your name, Indian?"

"The sheriff said it last night, but I doubt you really heard it. I'm Porterfell. Kane Porterfell."

Rampling squinted at Kane. "Porterfell? Really?"

"Yes."

"I'll be! I worked with a man name of Porterfell, before I lost my position."

Kane grew very alert all at once. "William Porterfell, maybe?"

"Yeah! Bill Porterfell! Good fellow, that Bill. Mighty skilled carpenter, too."

Kane came to his feet, his heart rising to his throat. "Bill Porterfell is my father."

"What? *Bill?* I be shot! So old Bill's got him a squaw somewhere! Fathered him a little Injun boy! I'll be! I'd never have figured him for that!" He laughed hoarsely.

"Are you telling me that my father is a carpenter at the Flanagan house?"

"He is, indeed. Assuming it's the same Bill Porterfell."

Kane felt weak, and sank back down to his bunk. His throat was suddenly quite dry.

"You feeling all right, boy?"

"I'm fine. Just . . . surprised. Well, no, not surprised, for I'd been told my father had come to Dodge. I'm . . . overwhelmed."

"What's the story here? Does Bill not know you're coming?"

"Bill Porterfell has never laid eyes on me."

"No! How'd that happen?"

"It's a long story. My mother raised me back in the Indian Nations, without my father. I thought he was dead until very recently."

"And you've come here to find him?"

"That's right."

"That's going to be one big surprise for Bill, when he sees you."

"Yes, I'm sure it will be."

Kane stared up at the ceiling, listening to his heart hammering. He was dumbfounded and awed by a feeling that destiny had its hand on him in bringing him to this jail and Pete Rampling to this cell. He might have searched for days to find his father and failed, but now the facts he needed had been laid right into his hands.

He had to get out of here, right away, and find that mansion. And his father.

The outer door opened and Sughrue walked in, the morning light silhouetting him for a moment until the door closed behind him.

"Good morning, gentlemen. Your breakfast will be here in a little while. Then, Mr. Porterfell, you need to be ready to go. I've made the arrangements. There's a morning train pulling out eastbound in just over an hour, and you and me are going to be on it."

Chapter 4

Kane shifted on the hard seat and glanced again at Sughrue, who slouched across from him in the passenger compartment, legs sprawled wide apart, hat pulled over his eyes, his arms folded. His chest moved up and down in rhythm with the train, but Kane wasn't sure he was really asleep.

"What are you doing, Sheriff?" he asked. "Trying to see if the desperate Indian thief makes a break for it while you're sleeping?"

Sughrue drew in a deep, slow breath, scratched his nose, and said from beneath the hat, "I don't figure you're going nowhere."

"Maybe I will, just to surprise you."

"Nah. You got no reason to run. You're innocent."

"How do you know?"

"Intuition, son. Intuition."

"You always believe in your intuitions?"

"Yep."

"Ever been wrong?"

"Nope."

Silence took over. Kane watched the level Kansas landscape slide past his window. Sughrue continued in his slouch, maybe sleeping, maybe not. The train rumbled and swayed very slightly, creating quite a lulling sensation.

"Sheriff?"

Another scratch of the nose. "Hmmm?"

"That Rampling fellow in the cell with me . . . do you know him?"

"A little."

"Is he reliable?"

"Well, I reckon. Generally so." Sughrue lifted the hat back onto the crown of his head and shoved himself up in the seat a little. "Why?"

"He told me he'd worked with my father, building some big house."

"Yeah, that cattleman's mansion. Flanagan. Quite a sight to see. Tell me something, son—how'd you and your daddy come to be apart?"

"His choice, I guess. He was an old soldier who had a liking for Indian women. He fathered me, but never stayed around to raise me."

"Why do you want to find him?"

"Because until recently I never even knew he was alive. When I found out that he was, I knew I had to see his face, talk to him." There was more that could have been said but Kane chose not to.

"Reckon he'll want to see you?"

"I don't know. I hope so." Kane wondered why he was talking about such personal matters with a near-stranger, and an officer of the law at that.

Sughrue pursed his lips and shifted them from side to side, brows lowering into a thoughtful glower. "Tell you what, son," he said abruptly. "Once we get back, how about I go over to the Flanagan house and bring your pap in to see you?"

Kane blinked, surprised by the offer. "Well . . . kind of you, but no. I'd as soon not meet him in a jail, you know."

Sughrue grinned. "I see. Don't blame you on that one."

Kane looked out the window. Sughrue studied him quietly for a while.

"Bet you've got some interesting stories to tell, Mr. Porterfell," he said, pulling a thin cigar out from under his vest.

"Another intuition of yours?"

"Maybe."

Kane shrugged. "I don't know. Until lately my life hasn't been much to talk about. Growing up in the Nations. Never much money or possessions."

"Your mother's still there?"

Kane felt an intense stab of grief. His mother . . . murdered. Taken from him without warning, and himself so preoccupied with trying merely to stay alive, ever since, that he'd hardly had time even to really comprehend that she was gone. "She died recently."

"Mighty sorry." It sounded like he meant it.

Suddenly Kane wanted to tell it all, to take this man of the law into his confidence and reveal the entire, terrible ordeal he'd been through. He ached to seek protection, friendship if Sughrue would give it, and to lay down the burden of worry that weighed so heavily on him.

But he couldn't. Too much had happened, too many fights, too many deaths . . . he couldn't risk telling the full truth to a man who wore a badge. The law, after all, was a white man.

So all he did was turn back to the window and try to force down the wrenching emotions that begged now to rise.

It wasn't much easier when the moment came to identify Lewis Washington's body. Standing in a shed that made do as a temporary morgue, Kane choked back tears as he saw the dark, graying face exposed, the black skin flecked with the salt cast around the corpse to preserve it from decay.

Kane nodded quickly and turned away. "Yes. That's Lewis Washington."

Sughrue muttered to the coroner and motioned for the tarpaulin to be pulled up across the unmoving, sunken face again. Sughrue and Kane exited the shed as fast as possible; salt and cold weather hadn't been enough to stop the beginning of the corpse's decay.

"Lewis Washington, then. That's how we'll record him," the coroner said as he joined the pair outside the shed. "Do you know anything of his kin? Wife, parents?"

"His father died recently," Kane said, once again speaking a truth conveniently lacking in details. "He had no wife."

"Where was his place of residence?"

"At one time he lived south of St. Louis. More recently he lived with an uncle at the Two Snakes Ranch, near Wichita. The uncle's name is Lemuel Washington. Used to be a cook on trail drives."

The coroner brought out a pencil and pad, licked the lead, and laboriously recorded the relevant names in big block letters. "Reckon they'd want to bury him on the Two Snakes?"

"You'd need to ask his uncle."

"Well, we'll have to do it fast, or find some more salt. Or ice. Or something. He's going down fast."

Kane was glad he'd identified his late benefactor and saved him from anonymous burial, but now that his duty there was done, he was ready to move on and get back to his original quest: finding his father.

"When will we go back to Dodge?" he asked Sughrue.

"Soon as a train runs. Meanwhile, there's a fine little cafe in yonder train station. I'm buying."

Kane didn't expect to have much appetite, considering the sight and smell of Lewis's corpse. The food was good, however, and he ate far more, and more readily, than he'd anticipated he would. It was a fine meal, but it was made somewhat uncomfortable by the way Sughrue looked studyingly at him throughout.

After he'd wiped his lips clean on a checked napkin, Sughrue leaned back with another of his little cigars.

Kane fiddled with his fork, ready now to leave. He didn't look forward to being back in that dismal dungeon jail in Dodge, but it wasn't much more uncomfortable than this conversation.

Sughrue asked, "Any notion of who killed this Lewis Washington?"

"If I had to guess, I'd agree with Kenneth Rimes and say that man they found chewed up on the railroad track was the one."

"We'll probably never know."

"Probably not." Kane did know, of course, but there was nothing to be gained in the telling that he could see, unless he wanted to get himself embroiled in endless tangles with the law of the land. He kept his eyes focused on the tines of his fork until Sughrue finished his cigar.

On the train ride back to Dodge City the silence was rarely broken. At sunset, sheriff and prisoner walked through the town, back toward the jail, Kane asking Sughrue if they might send word to the Raileys of where he had been, for they were surely worried by now.

The truth of this was proved when they reached the courthouse and found a distraught Frederick Railey pacing back and forth, muttering to himself and generally giving a strong impression of a madman.

Sughrue eyed the man wildly. "Who the devil . . ."

"That's Frederick Railey, alias Lord Faust, magician," Kane said. He looked about for Carolina and didn't see her.

Railey spotted Kane and sent up a loud hoot. Sughrue looked even more askance and appeared ready to reach for his pistol. Railey trotted up to Kane and embraced him.

"Kane, thank God! Carolina and I have been so worried!"

Kane had to grin at the almost matronly way Railey

treated him. But he was glad to be reunited with his friend.

"Where have you been, son?"

Son. The word rang with unexpected sweetness in the ear of a young man who had never known a father. "I've been under arrest," Kane said.

Sughrue cleared his throat. "Not exactly. Jailed on suspicion."

"And who are you, sir?" Railey asked the sheriff, who introduced himself, then explained, "Mr. Porterfell here has been identified as being a certain Indian who's committed some robberies upon several local citizens in the last two months."

"I can assure you that you have the wrong man," Railey said. "Kane hasn't even been in this community until he arrived here with my daughter and I." Railey told the sheriff who he was and why he was in town.

Sughrue heard him out patiently. "Mr. Porterfell has already given me the same facts, and thus what you say backs up his story. Unfortunately, we've still got a victim who's ready to swear under oath that Mr. Porterfell robbed him. At the moment I'm awaiting the chance to let some of the other victims of this Indian robber take a look at him and see what their view of the matter is."

"This is injustice!" Railey bellowed. "My word should be sufficient to set him free."

Conversation flew back and forth, Kane largely left out of it, with Railey and the sheriff vying for ascendance. Kane waited to ask where Carolina was, but he never found the opportunity.

So he looked around, eyeing the men who passed on the far boardwalk or rode down the middle of the street, and thought about his father. He scanned the horizon, wondering if the Flanagan house was visible from where he stood. It wasn't.

Rimes the deputy emerged from the courthouse door. "Sheriff, glad you're back," he said. "Joe Franks is back in town."

"Well!" Sughrue said, turning a grin on Kane and Railey. "Maybe we can settle this matter right away. Joe Franks is the very man I've been waiting for! He also was robbed by this Indian I've been looking for, Mr. Railey. And if he says Mr. Porterfell ain't our man, as far as I'm concerned he's free to go. I'd take the word of Joe Franks over Billy Seers any day. Come on inside. Deputy, do us all a favor. Go out and bring in Mr. Franks. Let's get this question answered right away, and maybe we can have some peace."

Two hours later, after Railey had gone back to the hotel to rejoin Carolina, who had been camped out there to keep a lookout for the missing Kane, Kane still was lodged in the jail, and both Sughrue and Rimes were apologetic—Sughrue for Kane's continued incarceration and Rimes for his failure to find the much-needed Joe Franks.

"I've got half a mind to let you go, Mr. Porterfell, even without Joe's identification," Sughrue said.

"Best not do that, Sheriff," Rimes said. "You remember last month, when you let Charlie Nickels go free

and he turned around and tried to rob that cowboy outside the Long Branch, and half the county was ready to
lynch you for letting him out early?"

"You think I'd forget that?"

"No . . . just reminding, that's all." Rimes glanced at
Kane. "Sorry."

Kane cast himself down on his bunk, anticipating
one more night in this jail. It seemed fortune was determined to turn against him and throw every conceivable
kind of bad luck his way.

He hoped that his father really was at the Flanagan
mansion and that he'd somehow be able to crawl out of
this jail before the man got restless or spooked and ran
off again.

Kane closed his eyes, though he knew he was far too
restless to sleep.

But sleep he did, and his awakening was sudden and
startling.

"Up from there, men!"

Kane opened his eyes.

"Up! We need you."

Kane sat up in the darkness. Sheriff Sughrue was
there, standing in the open door of the cell. On the other
bunk, Pete Rampling rose on his elbows, grunting and
confused, then rubbed his face and swung his feet to
the floor.

"What the devil's this?" Rampling asked Sughrue.

"I'm letting you fellows go free," Sughrue said. "But
for a reason. There's a fire, and we need able-bodied
men to help fight it."

Kane sneezed, once, twice, then realized the air carried a definite tang of smoke. He came to his feet, brushing back his hair with his hands and looking around for his boots.

"You mean to tell me we can just walk out of here?" Rampling asked.

"That's right—as long as you go straight over to the Excelsior and give a hand to the fire crew."

"The Excelsior?" Kane said. "Good Lord—that's where the Raileys are playing. Sheriff, is the hotel—"

"Burning like a house of reeds, Mr. Porterfell. And not everyone is out just yet."

Carolina. Kane put on his boots as fast as he could, and without another word pushed past the sheriff and out the door into the night.

It was a night heavy with smoke, and with an eerie, flickering glow that at first seemed to come from nowhere in particular. But as Kane raced toward the Excelsior he saw with horror the flames that cast that weird light. They poured out of the windows of the upper levels of the structure, gushing a heat he could feel from far away.

Phantom, fleeting black figures rushed about at the base of the hotel: citizens, refugees from the hotel, firemen. Kane ran hard, looking for the Raileys among the crowd, studying faces illuminated by firelight.

He did not see them. His heart pounded harder, faster. A sense of desperation, combined with the choking, endless smoke, made his throat feel tight and his chest strain for air. He prayed hard: *Don't let her be in there, don't let her be in there . . .*

He saw Rampling reach the fire crew. Taking up an axe, he joined a band of firemen who were quickly demolishing a shed that, if it caught fire, would pose a threat to the safety of an adjacent saloon-turned-apothecary. Even in his terror for the Raileys' safety, Kane actually felt proud of Rampling. He'd figured the man would simply turn tail and flee the moment Sughrue let them go.

A woman in the crowd screamed and pointed up. A collective gasp and cry arose from the crowd as they saw what she was looking at: A man had appeared at the corner of the flame-shrouded roof, cringing and trying to protect himself from the wall of flame that whipped toward the place he was, the only spot on the roof not already fully engaged.

Firemen yelled to the man, "Stay put! We'll get you!" But it was obvious that the man couldn't stay put, that the fire would reach him long before any fireman's ladder could be wrangled into place. Kane thought, *He'll not hope to make it even long enough for the fire to reach him. The heat will cook him alive.*

The man, no doubt aware of the same facts, let out a mournful, wailing cry and moved to the edge of the roof. There he tottered, outlined against the leaping and growing flames, and spread his arms.

"He's going to jump!" someone yelled. "For God's sake, catch him!"

Though many of the crowd stayed frozen in place, watching in horror the seemingly doomed man three stories up, others ran to the place where it seemed he would fall if in fact he did leap. Kane was rather surprised to find himself among them. He'd not come planning any heroics . . . but he could not stand by and let a man jump to his own death.

He wondered, with a thrill of dread, if Carolina and Frederick Railey might be inside, as trapped as this poor fellow. Maybe even dead. The fact that he himself would have been inside that burning hotel if not for his unjustified incarceration did not escape him, nor did the obvious sense of irony it brought about.

Just then the man leaped. His body arched out into space, arms flailing, legs kicking, and he plunged, face down, toward the gathered men below. With no time to find a blanket or another makeshift catch-basket, all they could do was thrust up their arms and try to catch him as best they could.

To Kane's astonishment, it actually worked! The man hit hard, but the arms that caught him were strong and many, and he was lowered gently to the ground, where he lay for a moment, weeping, then laughing, then weeping again. Finally he got to his feet, his face streaked with tears, ash, and dirt, to embrace and thank those who had saved him from an ignoble death. Two of the men hurried him off into the crowd.

More screams rose from onlookers. "Look there! Oh, somebody help the poor girl!"

Kane looked up. A woman was leaning out of one of the windows in a top-floor section of the hotel that hadn't yet caught fire, but that had flame both above, on the roof, and below it. Kane knew that in minutes that fire-encompassed room would become an oven, then burst explosively into full flame, and the young woman in the window would die . . .

And he could not stand for that, for the young woman was Carolina Railey.

Chapter 5

For a few moments Kane could not move. He stood rooted to the spot, staring almost dumbly up at Carolina, who waved her arms, called for help . . . and something about her father. Had she said he was hurt? Unconscious? Kane couldn't make it all out, but it didn't matter. He broke through whatever paralysis held him and darted toward the door.

"Don't you go in there!" one of the firemen yelled, but his voice was an unheeded blur in Kane's ears. He was inside the hotel in moments.

Smoke swirled through the lobby. He lifted a hand to his mouth and nose and ran on, up the stairs, where the smoke thickened, rushing down in choking, almost liquid currents. Kane felt a rush of cool wind—a broken window at the end of the hall—and ran to it, sucking in a lungful of fresh air.

He turned and plunged into the roiling smoke, back to the stairs, then up again. His eyes burned and stung, but still he climbed, holding his nose closed, his mouth clamped shut, his eyes open only to the width of slits. He prayed that no one was still on this floor; survival would be unlikely for any such unfortunate at this point. This was surely the floor on which the fire had started and on which its merciless heart still was.

He stopped for a moment . . . had he heard a groan, somewhere in that boiling hell of black smoke? He listened but heard nothing more, except the crackling of flame and the whistle of heated air being driven by fans of fire.

Kane climbed on, beginning to feel weak, longing for air but knowing that there was no air here fit to breathe. But the smoke cleared a little as he mounted the next landing, turned, and reached the floor where his own room was—never slept in by him and now, obviously, destined to remain so—and that of the Raileys.

The air was very smoky here, but he was able to breathe just enough to get by, though the grit in the atmosphere made him cough.

He stopped, shocked, as he saw that down the hall, in front of the Raileys' door, the smoke was far thicker, boiling up through the floorboards. He clamped his hand over his face again and advanced cautiously. The floor was growing hotter beneath his feet—fire just below threatened to break through. The closer he got to the Raileys' room, the hotter the floor became. Almost unbearably hot, in fact, roasting his feet through his boot soles.

He pounded on the Raileys' door. "Carolina! Carolina!"

On the other side of the door he heard movement, footsteps on the floor, coming toward him . . .

In the corner of the hallway, flames appeared, piercing through steadily blackening, widening cracks between the floorboards. Some of the smoke caught fire and turned to flame, bursting toward the ceiling.

The latch was rattling and moving. Paint on the door began to peel, and Kane found he could not now breathe at all. Some basic instinct for survival told him to turn and run, back the way he'd come, down the stairs and out. He fought it. He'd not leave this place without taking the Raileys with him—especially Carolina.

The door opened. Kane burst inside and slammed it shut behind him. He embraced Carolina quickly.

"Where's your father?"

"He was downstairs . . . he tried to help a man there, and he didn't come out again! I tried to find him, but the smoke and the heat drove me back, up here!"

"Downstairs . . . the floor just below?"

"Yes!"

Oh, no. Lord, don't let it be. If Frederick Railey was trapped on that floor, he was surely dead, or soon to be so.

"We have to find him, Kane."

"First we have to get you out of here."

"I'll go, but only to the floor below, to search for my father. I'm ashamed of myself, Kane. I shouldn't have come back up here and left him. I should have stayed until I found him."

"You would have choked on the smoke if you had." Kane looked around. "Have you any towels, water?"

"Yes, at the basin . . ."

"Soak the towels. We'll put them around our mouths and noses, to filter the smoke."

Heavy smoke was pouring under the door now. Straining, crackling sounds from the other side of it spoke of new and growing flames.

"We must get out, now, or we'll not get out at all, unless we leap from the window," Kane said.

"I'll not leap—I'll not leave this building at all without my father!"

"Then be prepared," he said as he put his hand to the doorknob. "There may be too much flame for us to leave this room."

"We *must* leave! I have to find my father!"

They wrapped the dampened towels around their faces, gave one another one more quick embrace, and then Kane opened the door. Flames roared at him like deadly, startled beasts. But there remained still a part of the floor not yet destroyed by the fire. Kane pointed at it and stepped onto it, followed quickly by Carolina. They ducked low, into the clearer air, and ran down the hall toward the stairs.

Kane saw smoke rising fast up past the landing and worried that the flames on the more heavily engaged floor below had reached the stairwell and rendered it unusable. If so, no option remained but to return to the room and . . .

He glanced back and saw that even that option no longer existed. Flames now licked up every inch of the door through which they'd just exited. There was no going back . . . and maybe no going forward.

Holding hands to avoid any chance of separation in this increasingly smoky, toxic atmosphere, Kane and Carolina reached the stairwell. A glance over the rail showed, to their relief, that the fire hadn't yet reached this end of the lower hall. They trotted down the stairs together, then paused.

Smoke was black and terrible and malignant back in that dark passage . . . yet it wasn't a fully dark passage, for the flames consuming the structure at the other end cast a filtered but hellish light through the boiling, gaseous poison.

"Papa is in there!" Carolina said, speaking loudly above the roaring of fire and the rushing of heated air. Her voice was slightly muffled by the damp towel around her face. She tugged her hand away from Kane and was about to plunge into the hall, but Kane grasped her and pulled her back toward him.

"No . . . you can't go . . . too much smoke."

"It's my father, Kane! Let me go!"

"Carolina, it's too dangerous. You go on, out . . . I'll go see if I can find him."

"He's *my* father, Kane! I'll not leave without him!" She jerked her hand free. "You go on . . . there's no need for both of us to take the risk."

"You'll never carry him alone," Kane said. "Come on . . . we'll find him together."

It took every exertion of will to go into the perdition that was that flaming, smoking hallway. In moments, vision became a mere memory, and Kane could hardly bear even to open his eyes at all. His skin seared; he actually feared his hair might catch afire.

They located Railey more by feel than by vision. Squinting, Kane saw Carolina on her knees beside a supine, burly male form.

"He's alive!" she said.

Kane reached out a hand and closed it around an ankle. "Are you sure it's him?"

"Yes! I can just see his face! We've got to pull him out of here, quickly!"

They worked together, each holding one of the feet and pulling. It was slow going, though, Railey being a heavy man and Carolina and Kane both being weakened by the heavy smoke and lack of breathable air.

Suddenly it was all very much worse. A great explosion of heat burst upon them, almost knocking them down. Kane lifted his eyes and watched a vision of hell bearing down on them.

It was a huge, rolling ball of gaseous fire, fed by the burning wall, ceiling, and floor. It rushed toward them at frightening speed, threatening to overtake them.

"Quick, Carolina, quick!"

Carolina answered him, but her voice was lost in the roar of hot air that pushed ahead of the rolling fire.

They pulled hard, but it was maddeningly slow.

Kane lifted his eyes and saw that the ball of flame was bigger and almost upon them. . . .

They pulled even harder, finding strength from somewhere, and in a moment were at the landing. They dragged Railey down the stairs roughly, not at all concerned at this point about the physical battering to his back and head. They wanted only to escape that rushing, roiling wall of fire coming down the hallway. They both knew that when it hit the landing, it would without question shoot upward, but perhaps downward, too, and if so, it might reach them even in the lobby below.

They made it to the lobby, now filled with heavy black smoke. The front door, barely visible through the smoke, was still open. Kane felt pain, looked down, and saw that one of his trousers legs was on fire. He beat it out quickly, hardly feeling the heat of it on his hand.

Carolina was dragging her father alone now. Kane saw her moving through the smoke and admired her courage, her strength, and her willingness to risk her life for the sake of her father. Even in the desperation of the situation he felt a burst of envy. He wished he could have had a relationship with his own father as rich and heartfelt as that between Carolina and Frederick Railey.

Kane joined Carolina, and together they moved Railey's still body to the main door, where firemen emerged from the smoke like phantoms, seized him, and pulled him and Carolina outside. Kane was about to follow when a sound reached him . . . a human voice, lost in the blackness, the faintest of groans, masculine and deep, and then a whimper that was definitely not a man but a child.

Kane pulled away from the hand of the fireman who was reaching for him and turned back into the dark, toxic hotel interior. He heard the fireman yell for him, but paid him no mind.

He thought not at all about what he was doing. He was moved to action now by the same spirit that had caused Carolina to go to her helpless father despite the danger.

Feeling faint, starving for air, Kane pushed on, reaching the huge, dark desk of the hotel, feeling his way along it. He rounded the end and came in behind, and there, in a little pocket of somewhat cleaner air, he dimly saw the form of a man, lying on his back, and a child collapsed upon his chest.

He went for the child first, a boy, no more than six or seven years old. Kane carried him through the smoke and heat and out the door.

The crowd had grown since Kane had entered the building. First a collective gasp rose from it, then cheers and applause. Kane didn't even hear it. He laid the child on the ground at the feet of a fireman, turned, and plunged back into the burning building.

Moments later he reappeared at the door, dragging the man who had been behind the desk. More cheers, louder this time—but interrupted by a yell of warning from one of the firemen. Kane looked up and saw burning timbers, dislodged from the upper part of the wall, tumbling toward him and the man he had saved. With a yell and a heave he somehow managed to pull the man and himself out of the way just in time. The timbers crashed to the ground with a terrible crackling thud, showering hot sparks over a wide area. But Kane was not hurt, nor was the man whom he had dragged from the death chamber, back to life.

He felt hands slapping him suddenly and looked down to see that some of his clothing was afire again. He didn't even feel the flames . . . he was numb, listless, suddenly very, very tired.

And dizzy. Coughing abruptly, hacking up black soot that filled his mouth and throat with the most horrendous of tastes, he felt the earth suddenly spin beneath his feet. He collapsed, crumpling into an unmoving, un-hearing, unseeing heap.

His next awareness was of lying on a bed in a white-walled room where the air was fresh and pure and cool. He felt pain, the sting of burns on his body, and looked down to see that he was unclothed except for a pair of soft trousers with the legs cut short. He saw burns, several of them, here and there about his form, but they looked rather innocuous. He lowered his head again into the soft pillow.

"You're going to be all right, the doc says," a voice from somewhere beside him said. "Your burns are so minor they didn't even bandage them. Doc said they'd heal that much faster if you just let the air get to them."

He looked over and saw Sughrue grinning at him. Beside him was a stranger who gave Kane a faint smile as Kane stared deeply at him.

"Father?" Kane tried to say, but his voice failed him and his whisper came out as a raspy noise.

"You played quite the hero, Mr. Porterfell," Sughrue said, the smile growing to a beam now, lighting the lawman's rather homely face until it actually looked a little bit handsome.

Kane tried to speak again. Still no voice. His throat was dry, hot, raw.

"I wouldn't try to talk," Sughrue said. "You sucked a lot of smoke and heat down that gullet of yours. But thanks to you, there's three people alive who'd be dead if you hadn't done what you done. Your friend Mr. Railey is going to survive, it appears, and so are the Flanagan brothers."

Flanagan . . . the same name as the wealthy Texan on whose house Bill Porterfell was reportedly working. Kane eyed the stranger at Sughrue's side again and wondered, with a heart pounding faster by the moment . . .

Kane's wild hope, however, was dashed when Sughrue addressed the stranger. "Mr. Franks, is this the Indian who robbed you?"

Franks, a red-haired man with a sweeping mustache, looked at Kane with one squinted eye and shook his head. "Not a bit of it. Don't even look remotely the same."

"Billy Seers says it is the same one."

"Well," Franks said with a knowing roll of the eyes, "you know how Billy is."

Sughrue grinned. "Indeed I do." He directed his next words to Kane. "You're a prisoner no more, young man, for I'm as confident as a man can be that you're not the redskin we've been looking for. And I apologize to you for the time that you've been locked up. I know now that we were in the wrong to do it."

Kane nodded slightly and closed his eyes.

A free man again . . . free to go find his father. But at the moment the thought of doing that, or anything else, was simply overwhelming. He had only enough strength to lie there and seek the wonderful release of sleep.

He felt much better the next day, though his burns stung more and sometimes itched. He found out at last where he was: a room in a small second house owned by a local doctor, sometimes rented out to tenants, but other times, as now, used as a recuperation clinic for patients.

The doctor visited Kane and examined his burns, informing him that he was a fortunate young man to have escaped such a major fire without serious injury. His thick clothing had saved him. Even though it had caught fire, the flames had been beaten out before the fire could burn through the fabric and directly touch his skin.

The doctor rather sternly told him that he'd been foolish to take the risks he had, running into the midst of such a conflagration when even the firemen were holding back. Then his face softened, and he smiled, and Kane again heard the word "hero."

He would hear it several times over the course of that day. People came by just to look at him, shake his hand, and tell him what a great young man he was, even if he did look rather like that Indian thief everybody had been worrying about.

In reference to that very matter, Sughrue visited with news of an arrest. None other than Rimes had brought in an Indian he'd found standing like a statue outside of town. Franks had positively identified him as the robber Indian, and even Billy Seers had concurred, admitting that he'd been wrong to identify Kane as the robber, trying to imply, to Sughrue's amusement, that the sheriff had pushed him into it.

But the best visitor of all was Carolina. She was burned too, but only on her left arm, which was bandaged. That didn't seem to be bothering her nearly as much as the fact that her hair had been singed badly on the left side and had to be cut away. The other side, of course, had to be cut equally short to match, and she was concerned about the effect this would have on her performance as the Indian Princess. Who would believe an Indian Princess with short hair?

Carolina's voice, like Kane's, was raw and hoarse as a result of inhaled smoke. Their conversation was a raspy whisper passed back and forth.

"How's your father?" Kane asked.

"He's very weak, but he'll live. Thank you, Kane, for helping me get him out."

Kane shook his head solemnly. "I have to confess something, Carolina. I was more worried about you than Mr. Railey. If it had been up to me, I might have gotten you out first and worried about your father later. And that might have killed him. I feel guilty that I could have thought that way. It was because I care so much about—"

She put her hand to his lips, quieting him. "We both did what we had to do. And what was done was done well. We need think nor say no more about it. My father is alive because you helped me, and we're alive, and I've got no feelings but deep thankfulness."

Kane smiled, and just then he was sure he was looking at the most marvelous piece of creation he'd ever seen in human form.

"There's going to be a reward in this for you, you know," Carolina said.

"What?"

"The town's talking of it. Those last two you rescued

were named Flanagan. Two brothers, one nearly a man, the other maybe ten years old. They'd been at the hotel visiting someone when the fire broke out. But the point is that their father is a very wealthy man, has plans to see you and thank you, and according to what everyone is saying, give you some sort of reward."

Kane didn't know what to say. He mulled it over. "It's for Flanagan that my father works," Kane said. "A man in the jail with me told me that." He paused. "Carolina . . . do you think that all this talk about me has reached my father? Do you think maybe he's heard my name and knows who I am and that I'm here?"

"Maybe so," she said. "Isn't that an exciting thought! I suppose you'll know soon enough."

"He might come visit me . . . he might walk through that very door."

"Oh, Kane, wouldn't that be wonderful!"

Kane swallowed. It made his throat hurt worse. "I guess it would . . . but it scares me to death at the same time."

"It's going to be all right," Carolina said. "I know it will be."

"I hope so. I really do." He reached over and took her hand.

Chapter 6

When Carolina returned to visit Kane that evening, she found him out of bed, restless. No visit from his father had come about. Kane paced back and forth, fuming, nervous, declaring one moment that his father, if he was indeed in Dodge, surely would come, then the next moment fatalistically declaring that of course he wouldn't. Why should Bill Porterfell repent now of a lifetime's worth of ignoring his son?

"It may be that he simply doesn't know who you are," Carolina reminded him. "For heaven's sake, Kane, you're hardly the only young man in the world with the last name of Porterfell."

Kane drew in a deep breath and admitted that she was right. He turned and faced her quickly. "You know, I'm tired of being in here, Carolina. Where's Mr. Railey? I might like to go visit him."

"Does the doctor want you out and around this soon?"

"It doesn't matter. All I've got is a few burns, and a little bit of cough and shortness of breath. The quicker I get out and work it out of my system, the sooner I'll be better."

"All right, then. It's really interesting where Father's staying. There's an old traveling magician living in town—he left the road long ago and became a merchant here until his health made him close up shop and retire. When he found out what Father's profession was, he sent word to have him come and stay with him until he was well."

Kane grinned. "Very handy!"

"Indeed." A flicker of worry showed in Carolina's eyes. "Especially now that we're suddenly without winter employment."

Kane hadn't thought about that. Indeed, the Raileys were in a tough situation, for the very venue that was to provide their work through the lean season now was nothing but a heap of smoldering, ashen rubble.

"What will you do?" he asked.

"Get by, somehow," she said, forcing a smile. "We've always survived, Father and I. And Dodge isn't the only town there is. We'll just move on somewhere else."

"Once Mr. Railey is well enough, you mean."

"Yes."

"How long will that be?"

Again the dark flicker. "I don't know. A while, I think. He's very weak."

Kane reached for his coat. "Let's go visit him."

The walk across town winded Kane considerably. His lungs, coated with smoke residue, felt tight and simply couldn't supply him the oxygen he needed. He and Carolina had to pause several times for him to stop and cough and wheeze. It was quite embarrassing to him, especially in that Carolina had also taken lungs full of smoke, and she wasn't nearly in such weakened shape.

When he admitted this to her, she said, "You've got to remember that you went back into the smoke after I was already out, to save those Flanagan brothers. You breathed in much more smoke than I did."

When they reached their destination—and along the way Kane received many salutes and hails of congratulations, praise, and general veneration as the newest hero of Dodge, from complete strangers who must have seen him in action at the fire—Kane was surprised and distressed to see Railey's state of health.

The man looked simply terrible. His hair and beard had been badly scorched, so Carolina had shaved him bare, head and face, making him look like a virtual stranger to Kane. But the smile that flashed at once as he saw his daughter and again when he saw Kane was the same bright one Kane had come to know in his relatively brief association with these good people.

Railey was not now making his pretense of a British accent. His voice was weak, but not as muted from smoke inhalation as Kane had anticipated. "Kane! Good to see you, son." Railey struggled to lift a hand toward him. "I want to thank you, so much . . . Carolina told me she never would have gotten me out of that hallway without your help."

Kane shook Railey's hand and smiled. "And I couldn't have done it without her. How do you feel?"

"Weak . . . very weak. Like a sickly baby."

"No performances for a while, eh?"

"I hardly think so. The only trick I want to pull right

now is regaining my strength and getting out of this bed."

"You'll be up and around in no time."

"Yes. And meanwhile, Carolina will be looking out for me. A good nurse, she is, as well as a fine rescuer!"

"She's fine in every way, sir. As are you."

"You look a bit scorched, Kane."

"I'm not hurt badly at all. Really. It's remarkable how well I came through."

"Oh, you did more than come through. As I understand it from my fine host—did Carolina tell you about Mr. Swindell, an old hand at the conjuring trade himself? Yes? Good!—anyway, as Mr. Swindell tells it, you're being talked up all around Dodge as the hero of the hour. And deservedly so!"

"I'm getting more credit than I deserve. Carolina did as much."

"Carolina did her share, no question, but this return into the pit of hell, as it were, to rescue those two Flanagans—that's made your name legend here."

Kane, not knowing how to respond to such a statement, merely shrugged uncomfortably.

They talked further, as long as Railey felt strong enough. Kane heard again what Carolina had already said about the intention of the Flanagan brothers' wealthy father to reward him.

"You know, Kane, I expect that the spreading of your name based on this incident has surely reached your father's ears, if he really is in Dodge. By now even the church mouse has surely heard of you."

"Carolina and I have already talked about that."

"He may well look you up."

Carolina cut in. "It may be, Papa, that Mr. Porterfell won't realize that Kane is related to him. He may think it's just a chance coincidence of surnames."

"Be that as it may, this hero status you've attained is bound to help you get off to a good start with your father, whenever and however you find him," Railey said. "No man could be anything but proud to have a son who performed like such a champion." He put out his hand to Kane again, and a tear formed in his eye. "I'd be proud to claim you as my own son, if another didn't already have that privilege."

Kane, moved, was threatened by tears of his own. He wasn't comfortable with emotional displays. "Thank you, sir. Though I have to note that my father may not consider it a privilege to claim me . . . considering that he never has."

"Kane, don't become bitter. You may be on the verge of a grand meeting with a man who'll prove to be all you ever hoped to have in a father. Don't poison water that might prove fresh."

"You have quite a way with words, Mr. Railey."

"Bosh! Just melodramatic patter. Showmanship . . . the only valuable thing I have in my life, other than my Carolina." He gripped Kane's hand harder. "And my friendship with you." He let his hand drop away and seemed more weary. His voice was softer as he went on, shifting topics slightly. "Of course, this new notoriety of yours, I suppose, might have a negative side."

"If Robert Blessed is still alive and pursuing me, you mean."

"Yes. It might help him track you down."

"I know. But probably it would make little difference. He knew already that I was coming to Dodge. Still, if there was some way to keep my name out of the Dodge newspapers . . ."

"You can forget that, I'm afraid," Railey said. "It's just too grand a story for them to ignore: A jailbird, falsely accused as a criminal because of his partial Indian heritage, becomes instead a hero among the very people who mistrusted him. Your name may be spread far and wide by a story such as that."

"Right to the ears of Robert Blessed."

"*If* he's alive. The man did jump off a moving train, after all."

"Have they found his body?"

"Not that I've heard. They haven't found his accomplice, Wilson, either. But out in the grasslands a corpse could molder for years and never be seen, even a few yards from an active railroad."

"That's true," Carolina agreed. "Maybe your pursuers are gone, Kane."

"I hope so."

Kane visited with Railey only a few minutes more, then left. Carolina remained with her weary father. Kane walked slowly through the town, meandering over to where the fire had destroyed the dance hall and hotel, examining the smoking heap with a feeling of both horror and deep gratitude at having escaped. One of his visitors had told him the blaze apparently started in the dance hall, at the rear, where a woodstove had been overloaded and left insufficiently attended.

In the few minutes he spent at the site of the fire, he was approached and greeted by no fewer than five Dodge Citians, all declaring themselves proud that such a fine young man had come into their city. He recognized with some amusement that two of the faces belonged to the same people who had eyed him with mistrust and fear when he'd walked through the Dodge streets to join the Raileys for supper at Delmonico's. Humanity indeed was a fickle breed.

That evening, Kane returned to the Raileys' lodgings, bearing news.

Railey looked stronger than he had earlier in the day, and was propped up, eating supper from a tray.

"I received a visitor today," Kane said. "A man named Grossett. He's a personal assistant to Mr. Ben Flanagan, and he told me that Mr. Flanagan wants me to come see him tomorrow morning. He's sending around a carriage to pick me up. Ten o'clock."

"The reward, Kane!" Carolina said, beaming. "That's surely what it is."

"Probably," Kane replied. "I feel odd about it. I didn't go back in there to rescue that pair for the sake of some reward."

"Which is exactly why you deserve one," Railey said. "There may be good times ahead for you, son. A reward, maybe a rich one, and the chance to meet your father at last. If he's working for Flanagan, he's bound to be there."

"I know," Kane said. "And I have to admit, I'm scared to death."

"About meeting Flanagan?"

"No. About meeting my father. And wondering if he will even be glad to see me."

Kane stopped by a general store after he left the Raileys and bought himself a fresh shirt and a pair of trousers. The storekeeper had been just about to lock up for the evening when Kane arrived, but he gladly extended his hours by a few minutes when he discovered that his late caller was Dodge's newest hero. He even gave Kane a discount, over his obligatory protest. Kane was secretly glad for it, for he knew he would have to stretch what money he had to last heaven only knew how long.

Bearing his new garments in a sack, he made his way back to his own quarters—quarters he was beginning to feel he didn't have the right to occupy, since he was obviously regaining his strength at top speed. On the street Kane again was greeted and praised by several citizens. It gave him the strangest, warmest feeling, and he began thinking it might not be bad to live in a town such as this, where everyone admired him. Where he was somebody, not just a nameless, unknown half-breed from the Indian Nations.

He glanced toward a trio of men across the street, talking to one another over cigars, and froze.

The face of one of them, in profile, made Kane's heart jump into his throat.

Robert Blessed.

Kane sucked in his breath and took three steps back in sheer surprise. Terror overwhelmed him for an instant; he tried to shake it off, but it held on. Blessed, en-grossed in making some point to one of the other men, turned his head slightly . . .

It *wasn't* Blessed. From this new angle, the man didn't look like him at all. Just a trick of the light.

Relief inundated Kane. *Thank God!* His heartbeat slowed to something closer to a normal pace.

As he walked into his temporary residence, though, he thought about what had just happened. The mere sight of someone he had taken to be Blessed had been almost enough to knock him off his feet.

Though this fellow hadn't been Blessed, the *real* Robert Blessed might be out there, still searching for him, still as wicked and murderous as ever. If he was, then it would be only a matter of time until their paths crossed again.

His fleeting notion of perhaps making his residence in this town and enjoying the wide favor he'd gained suddenly seemed absurd. Of course he couldn't settle here, or anywhere. Not until he knew for certain what had happened to Robert Blessed. Not until his quest, and his pursuit, were truly and finally over.

He sat up late, staring out the window into the dark, both anticipating and dreading the next day.

Though he'd had only four hours' sleep at most, Kane felt quite refreshed and generally much brighter and more optimistic when the morning came. He dressed in his new clothes and waited outside for the promised carriage. The sky was clear, almost cloudless, the sun brilliant and crystalline. A very cold wind was the only negative feature of the day's weather, but even that was bracing. Kane paced back and forth, coughing some but not feeling nearly as raw in throat and lungs as he had the day before. He felt stronger, and the melancholy broodings of the night no longer weighed upon his mind.

A carriage rumbled into view, turning a corner and coming toward him. On the seat was Grossett, a tall, gangling man, nicely dressed and groomed, but not preeningly so. Kane had already detected from Grossett's way of speaking that he was an educated man. His speech patterns, in fact, interested Kane: Grossett spoke with the clipped authority of a highly educated New Englander but somehow managed to sound a little bit Texan, too.

Grossett hopped down from the driver's seat and greeted Kane warmly. "Glad to see you ready to go," he said. "Mr. Flanagan places much store in punctuality."

"I'm eager to meet him."

"No more, I can assure you, than Mr. Flanagan is to meet you."

"Is that the only person I'll be meeting . . . Mr. Flanagan?"

"Why, yes. Were you expecting someone else?"

That answered one question, anyway. Kane had spun out in his mind the possibility that part of his reward might be a Flanagan-hosted meeting with his father, if the latter had surmised, from all the momentary town gossip about the "hero" half-breed, that his never-claimed son was in town. Clearly this wasn't to be. "No, I wasn't. I just didn't know what to expect."

"Expect good things, young man. Good things. Now, shall we get aboard and on our way?"

Kane climbed in and settled back. A posh, comfortable seat. What an oddity! Being driven through a town for a meeting with a wealthy man bent on doing him good . . .

For a moment, he felt a vestigial panic. This situation was remarkably reminiscent of the scenario that had first brought him to Robert Blessed and abundant misfortune. He'd ridden to Blessed's St. Louis doorstep in a horse-drawn rockaway, with promises of great things coming his way. Lies, all lies. The fabrications of kidnappers luring their prey.

This meeting would be different, of course. This one he would gladly see through.

The carriage rattled down the street and out of town, heading west.

Chapter 7

HUNTER'S WAR

The carriage rolled to a stop in front of what was perhaps the finest dwelling Kane had ever seen. It stood three stories tall, had more gables than a man could count on two hands, and put out a wonderful scent of fresh wood that had Kane sniffing the air appreciatively. He glanced around, looking for signs of workmen, one of whom might well be his father. But he saw no one.

Grossett was off his seat and opening the door almost before Kane could begin to make his exit.

As Kane climbed out and looked the place over, he said, "I'd heard the house was still being built, but it looks finished."

"Fine structure, eh? Mr. Flanagan is justly proud of it. And no, it isn't finished. The exterior is done, except for some painting, and a good part of the interior, but there's still plenty of work to be done on the rest. The third-floor interior, for example, isn't finished at all yet. Most of that floor will be taken up by a ballroom. Mr. Flanagan plans to host some marvelous parties once the house is complete."

"So . . . you still have carpenters and so on working about the place?"

"Yes, and masons, and various other craftsmen."

"All the same ones you've had from the beginning?"

Grossett gave Kane a curious look. Kane hated himself for asking such bizarre-sounding questions. He wished he could find it in himself to ask straight out about William Porterfell, but he couldn't bring himself to do it.

"Well, not all the same workers. Some of the rough carpenters, by which I mean the framing and exterior men, have moved on." Grossett paused, and his brows arched up. "Come to think of it, we had a carpenter here named Porterfell. Is that why you're asking about the workers? Has a relative of yours been among us?"

Had a carpenter . . . Kane's heart fell, and maybe his countenance, too, for Grossett moved quickly toward him as if to catch him if he fainted. "Mr. Porterfell, are you sick?"

Kane steadied himself, embarrassed. He was discovering a little more every day just how much emotion he'd invested in this matter of meeting his father. "No . . . I'm fine. Just a little weak from all the smoke I breathed."

"Do you need to rest?"

"No, no, I'm fine."

"Good. Let's go on in, shall we?"

The question Grossett had asked Kane had slipped by unanswered, and Kane was glad to leave it that way for now.

Had a carpenter. It could only mean that Bill Porterfell was no longer here. Suddenly this meeting with

Flanagan didn't seem nearly as important, even with that talk of reward.

Kane looked around as they entered the edifice. A truly fine house this was, though its unfinished state was far more evident inside than out. The ceilings lacked moldings, the floors had no rugs, the walls needed a second coat of paint, and the spiral staircase wanted a railing on one side. Even so, the wealth that was behind the place was quite evident.

Grossett pointed up the staircase. "Mr. Flanagan's sons, James and Elwin, Elwin being the younger, have rooms upstairs. They're laid away in bed just now and will be for many days to come, I think. They were very nearly done in by that fire. Would have been if not for you. Thank God they weren't burned, though. Merely smoked very thoroughly, inside and out."

Kane coughed, deeply and violently and unexpectedly, then cleared his throat. "I know how they must feel."

Grossett smiled. "Indeed." He gestured toward a closed door to Kane's right. "Mr. Flanagan will be meeting you in there. Would you like a glass of water while you wait?"

"Please." Kane coughed again.

Grossett nodded and saw Kane into the indicated room. Unlike the rest of the house, it was completed—thick rugs on the floor, excellently crafted woodwork throughout, paintings on the papered, rich-looking walls. A huge and obviously valuable light fixture hung from the center of the ceiling. Even so, the room lacked the stuffiness of a formal parlor. On one wall the wide-spreading horns of a Longhorn were mounted decoratively, and upon a more careful examination, Kane realized that the pictures depicted frontier scenes of Texas. He studied the one closest to him, a rendering of the famous chapel in the Alamo, bathed in a rich sunset light.

All in all, it was a very masculine room, Kane thought. He wondered if there was a Mrs. Flanagan around the place, and he asked Grossett.

"Sadly, no," Grossett replied, shaking his head and looking sad in a way that seemed practiced, though not necessarily insincere. He'd probably answered the same question countless times. "Mrs. Flanagan passed away five years ago. Mr. Flanagan still grieves deeply for her. A fine woman she was." He waved a hand toward the several overstuffed chairs around the walls. "Please, have a seat. Do you like this room?"

"It's quite a place."

"Yes. Mr. Flanagan loves the better things in life. Yet he's as authentic and earthy a man, in the best sense, as you'll ever hope to find."

Kane settled himself in one of the chairs. As he'd thought—fine leather. He'd never sat in such an excellent chair before, and he nestled comfortably into it.

"I'll bring you your water," Grossett said.

Kane tried to relax as he sat there. He drew in several long, deep breaths, then stopped the exercise when he found it only made him more prone to cough. He hoped he wouldn't hack and choke his way through the meeting with Flanagan.

His father . . . here at one time, now obviously gone. It deflated him every time he thought about it. So he tried to put it out of his mind, not wanting to present a grim exterior when Flanagan came in.

Grossett returned with the glass of water and presented it to Kane, along with a full pitcher in case he needed more. He gave a sort of quick lecture in passing on the origin of one of the paintings he thought was particularly good, then left with the practiced flourish of a man accustomed to the diplomacy of business and meetings and hostmanship.

Knowing the reputation of rich and powerful men who were accustomed to being waited upon rather than waiting themselves, Kane settled back for what he anticipated would be an interval of at least several minutes. He was quite surprised when less than a minute later, a door at the other end of the room opened with a bang, and a big, broad, florid-faced man burst into the room. He wore boots, denims, and the plainest of shirts . . . but he wore them well, lending to them an elegance that they would have never possessed on a less imposing figure. Kane started when the door opened, then rose hurriedly as the man came rushing toward him, hand out. To Kane's chagrin, when he stood he tipped over the water glass and drenched the leather chair.

"Mr. Porterfell! Sir! I'm so pleased, so abundantly pleased, to meet you! My name is Ben Flanagan, and I'll not hear you call me anything but Ben!"

Kane smiled nervously and put out his hand to take Flanagan's, as he thought Flanagan expected him to do, but Flanagan bypassed the proffered hand, threw his bearish arms around Kane's neck, and hugged him like

a long-lost son. The embrace was strong, almost choking. When Flanagan at last released him and pulled
back to look Kane in the face, Kane was surprised to see
a film of tears over the man's blue eyes.

"You, young sir, are a stranger to me, but as beloved
as a family member! You've saved the lives of my two
boys, and for that you have my gratitude, unendingly."
He still had hold of Kane's shoulders, but now he patted those shoulders firmly with his broad hands and released them. He waved back toward the door through
which he'd entered.

"Normally I receive guests out here, but in your case,
I'd like you to come into my own sanctum," Flanagan
said. Kane noticed that the man had a Texas drawl. He
hadn't perceived it before because Flanagan, like Grossett, managed to be well spoken despite it.

"Thank you, sir," Kane said. "I'm honored, Mister . . .
I mean, Ben. I'm sorry about spilling that water."

"Water dries! Forget about it!"

Flanagan led Kane into his private office, which was
actually not as formally fancy as the room they'd just
left. The walls here were covered less with paintings
and more with relics of a cattleman's life: spurs, whips,
ropes, another huge, spreading Longhorn rack (upon
one prong of which hung a big and battered hat), and
various ancient firearms. A locked case in one corner
held at least a dozen other firearms, these much newer.

In the center of the room was a desk that had obviously been around for quite a long time. Its finish was
worn away completely on the top, and the legs and
paneled sides bore the scuffs and scratches of countless

encounters with boot toes, other furniture, and maybe the gnawing teeth of a family dog or two.

A fire blazed in a big fireplace on the opposite side of the room, and before it, sure enough, lay a big, old dog that had put the enthusiasms of puppyhood behind it many, many years before. It didn't even raise its head to look at Kane, merely studying him sidewise out of one watery eye.

"That's my old friend Tavish lying there. And I do mean old. He was due for the hole-in-the-ground half a decade back, but he's like me, he just holds on. I dread the day I lose him. Have a seat, Mr. Porterfell."

"Please . . . if I'm to call you Ben, call me Kane."

"Very well, Kane." Flanagan sat down heavily in a plain, creaking chair behind the desk. He scooted back, propped one boot on the desktop, and looked just past it at Kane, who perched himself on an equally battered chair at the front of the desk. "Kane . . . is that short for something?"

"Kanati, sir. I'm half Cherokee." Kane waited for a reaction, not sure whether Flanagan had realized that fact about him. If it was news to the man, it apparently wasn't significant in his mind, for nothing about his look or manner changed.

"Kanati . . . let me see if I can remember. 'Hunter,' I think."

" 'Lucky Hunter,' to be exact. You speak Cherokee?"

"Lands, no, son, not much of it, anyway. Had me a couple of good friends who were Cherokee, though. Good cattle workers, both of them. We rode the cattle trails up and down together more times than old Tavish over there can pass his wind in an hour! One of them spoke the language fluently, and I picked up a trace of it from him. Interesting language, the Cherokee. Really quite a beautiful lingo."

"Yes, sir."

"Forget that 'sir' nonsense! It's Ben. Ben!"

"Sorry. I was always raised to speak formally to . . . people."

"To white people, you mean."

"Yes, sir. Ben."

"That carries no weight with me, I'll tell you! I've always held the startling belief that a man is a man is a man. I don't care what color his wrapper is or whether his grandpappy dined on beefsteak or dogmeat. I find the attitudes of most people toward such things to be infuriating. Did you know that in some of the mining towns there are ordinances against Chinamen even setting foot in the town? Terrible! It's just plain wrong."

"I agree with you, Mister . . . Ben."

"There you go! Starting to get it now."

Kane found himself relaxing, liking this cordial man.

"So, Kane, were you born in the Nations?"

"No, sir. North Carolina."

"Is that right? My father was born and raised there. He was a fine man. Looks more like my brother than me, though. I got this size of mine from my mother, God rest her. Big woman, big woman. Big heart, too. I miss her often. And worst of all, I miss my late wife. That's her picture there." He pointed to a framed picture on his desk and looked wistful. Kane studied the portrait and nodded.

"I'm sorry you lost her."

"Yes. She was a fine woman. A true lady. As was my mother. You're not married, are you, Kane?"

"No."

"Is your mother living?"

"My mother died recently."

"I am sorry. Your father?"

Here it was. The chance to find out where Bill Porterfell might have gone, if Flanagan even knew. But as he opened his mouth to speak, another coughing fit struck, robbing him of speech. He leaned forward, hacking terribly.

Flanagan bounded out of his chair, lifted a finger to Kane to indicate he'd be right back, and left the office for the front room. He came back with the glass and pitcher, pouring Kane a drink. Kane got it down and quieted his cough, thanked Flanagan, and was about to enter into the topic of his father again, when Flanagan moved on and spoke first.

"Kane, I called you here for more reason than to say 'Much obliged.' I'm a man who prefers to show his gratitude in tangible ways . . . and fortunately, I'm well situated to do it. I want to give you something . . . you may think it a large gift, but compared to what you did, it's not even enough."

Kane had never been a greedy type, but Flanagan's words stirred him. He sat up a little higher in his seat and tried not to look too eager.

Flanagan went to a safe in his wall, opened it, and came back with a prepared envelope that he handed to Kane.

"Look inside," Flanagan said. "Tell me if that's sufficient and don't hesitate to say if it isn't."

"Sir . . . Ben, I must tell you that this is unnecessary. I didn't pull your sons out of that fire for reward."

"I know. But I can afford to give proper rewards, and hang it, I will. Now, look inside."

Kane opened the envelope and stared at a stack of hundred-dollar bills. Fifteen of them.

He raised a stunned expression toward Flanagan. "Sir . . . this is a fortune. Far too much . . ."

Flanagan grinned with satisfaction. "If you think it's far too much, then it's just the right amount." He gave Kane a solid, jovial pound on the shoulder. "Take it and use it to do whatever you need to make a good start in life for yourself. And know that every cent comes to you with my gratitude."

Kane blinked, fighting tears. He'd never even held such an amount of money in his hands, much less actually possessed it. He thanked Flanagan softly, the best voice he could muster just then.

"But it's just too much."

"If you say that again, I'll give you even more for spite."

Kane smiled at the generous man. "You're a good man, Mr. Flanagan."

"No better than most—just more blessed with worldly wealth, which enables me to bless others in turn."

The mood changed quickly once the giving of the reward was done. Flanagan seemed relieved of a burden and eager for some celebration.

"I'm not a drinking man myself, other than tea," he said. "People think that's downright odd, but I quit worrying long ago about what people think. Got some fine English breakfast tea on hand—care for some?"

"Gladly."

The tea, brewed up by Flanagan himself and served hot and sweet, was delicious—a drink that, despite its commonality, Kane had seldom tasted.

Flanagan, no sipper, drained his cup quite quickly and poured another. "You know, Kane, we had a workman here named Porterfell. A good carpenter. Not all that common a name, Porterfell. Any chance of a relation?"

Kane set his cup back in its saucer. "Yes. In fact, I think that he might be my father."

Flanagan looked at Kane in surprise, then laughed. "You are joking with me, I take it?"

"No. No, I mean it. My father's name is William Porterfell, and I came to Dodge to find him."

Flanagan set his cup on the desk and leaned forward. "Find him? You've been separated in some way?"

"I've never met the man."

Flanagan looked surprised. "Never met your own father?"

"No, sir."

"Are you sure we're talking about the same Bill Porterfell? I got to know our carpenter Bill some, and he never mentioned a son."

"He never claimed me that I know of. In fact, I believed him dead until very recently. When I found out he was alive, I decided to come looking for him. I tracked him this far, and then I found out from Mr.

Grossett, while we were coming in, that he's no longer here."

Oddly, Flanagan suddenly looked troubled. "No. He isn't." He dropped his gaze to the scarred desktop. "Your father! I'll be!" After a few moments of silence, he yanked open a drawer and pulled out a pipe and tobacco, then packed the latter into the former as the troubled look deepened.

"Ben, where is my father now?"

Flanagan stiffened at the question, then got up hurriedly, puffing the pipe and turning his back to Kane, who was growing very concerned by this sudden change in Flanagan.

"Ben, please tell me. Even if it's something I don't want to hear . . . let me know *everything*."

Flanagan let out a long, slow sigh, then turned to face Kane. "Your father is in Colorado, Kane. And, I'm afraid, quite possibly in the midst of trouble. And I'm very sorry that he is, because I feel responsible. I'm the one, you see, who sent him there."

Chapter 8

Ben Flanagan paced for a few moments, obviously ill at ease, then sat on the edge of the desk, balancing himself with the heels of his hands. All at once he had become a different man. No more hearty joviality. He stared at the floor between Kane's feet and spoke in a soft, almost monotone voice.

"I have an older brother, Kane. His name is Eiler Flanagan. Maybe you've heard of him . . . no? Well, he and I are different in many ways. From our appearances to our attitudes to the ways we chose to make our way in the world. But there's one similarity: Eiler and I have both been very successful in whatever we've taken on. We've both been blessed with wealth.

"Eiler is a mine owner in the town of Three Mile, Colorado. A remote, beautiful, mountainous place . . . well, beautiful until they started tearing the mountains apart, smelting silver out of everything they could dig. It's been one of the true boomtowns of the decade, though, and Eiler, my ever-successful brother, has been at the heart of it all. His mine is one of the biggest and richest in the history of Colorado." Flanagan paused and chuckled. "It really fits Eiler that he's a mine owner. He's always had an obsession with wealth, whether in the form of silver or gold or jewels. Jewels most of all.

"But to get back on track, everything hasn't gone smoothly for Eiler and his mining ventures. For the last several months, there's been labor strife at his chief mine, Flanagan Hill. Sometime back it evolved into an outright strike. An increasingly ugly one. Eiler became afraid of sabotage, violence. He worried that there might even be an effort to assassinate him. So he began hiring men, sort of a private army, if you will, to protect the mine, his home, himself.

"I'd known for a good while about the strike, the general trouble, but not about Eiler's worries for his own safety or his hired guns. Not, at least, until he wrote me. We've never been close, Eiler and I, so I was surprised to hear from him. He told me about threats against him and about how he was to hire men willing to defend the mine itself, as well as some particularly skilled men to serve as personal bodyguards. He knew that I've had many men hired over the years—cowboys, ranch hands, even the men who built this house. Wanted me to send him someone, if I could.

"It seemed an odd request, but I didn't really think much about it. And besides, I didn't have anybody in mind to fill the kind of role Eiler was wanting played. I'm not in the business of supplying soldiers of fortune, not even for my own kin.

"So I forgot the matter. But then, suddenly, Bill Porterfell comes in to see me. Tells me he needs to be moving on but won't say why. He seemed, I don't know, upset.

Nervous. Like he was feeling something breathing down his neck. He said a few things, implied he was in some sort of trouble, maybe even danger. But he wouldn't clarify himself, even when I pressed him a little, being worried about him, you know.

"I told him that whatever his problems, I didn't want him to leave. He was one of my best carpenters, and a steady, hard worker. A lot of the best features of this house are there because of him. I told him I'd help him any way I could if he'd stay on with me.

"But he was resolute. Had to go, and soon. What he wanted from me was any information I might have about where he could find some other work. I suppose he was secretly hoping that I'd have something for him in Texas, where I come from. He mentioned something about Texas, how a man could easily go to a place that big and vanish. But I couldn't help him on that one. I've cut my ties with Texas, moved all my enterprises north.

"So I stood here, right by this desk, telling him I had nothing for him, and then my eye happened to fall on Eiler's letter. Well, without much thought, and maybe against my best judgment, I told him that my brother in Colorado was looking for men willing to bear arms to protect him and his mine during the strike.

"Didn't figure that Bill would have the slightest interest—but he did. He was ready to take the job on the spot. It was odd, Kane—he seemed to like the idea of joining an armed band. Safety in numbers, perhaps.

"And so that's what happened. He wanted to go, I wanted to help him, and my brother wanted good men. I wired Eiler, told him I had an old soldier named Bill

Porterfell—Bill had told me some about his war experience with Patrick's Raiders, you see—who was willing to come help him out if he wanted him. He wired back almost at once that he did. Seemed unusually eager to have him. So I put Bill on a train bound for Colorado, and as far as I know, that's where he is now. Part of my brother's private army."

"So he's safe, at least," Kane said.

At this, Flanagan looked troubled indeed. "Well . . . I don't think 'safe' is quite the word. Things have gotten worse at Three Mile. I've been following it in the newspapers and have heard a thing or two from business associates who've come out of Colorado. That strike is something terrible, Kane. There's fear of serious violence before it's through. I'm afraid I sent your father right into the midst of a very dangerous situation."

Kane could have told Flanagan that his father had already been in a dangerous situation, that it was this dangerous situation that had surely prompted him to want to move on from here to begin with. William Porterfell was a prize as much sought after by Robert Blessed as was Kane himself. "I suppose, then, that I'll be going to Three Mile," Kane said, mostly to himself.

"I wish you wouldn't. I've already sent one good man into a bad circumstance. I'd hate to turn around and drop his son in the same hole right after him. They're starting to call that strike a 'war,' Kane. That's how fierce things are getting. There's some Irishman leading the miners' side, somebody Tobin—I can't recall the exact name. And Eiler, oh, I know Eiler—you push him, he pushes back harder. Got a fierce temper, he does, and he's ruthless. Hate to say that about my own brother, but it's true." Flanagan paused. "Kane, let me be honest with you. The more I hear about this strike, or war, or whatever it is, the less confidence I feel that Eiler is even on the right side of this thing. I've read the various complaints and demands of the miners, and to me they all seem quite justified—and Eiler's stubbornness seems completely wrongheaded and greedy. I've even thought about trying to persuade him . . . but it would be no use. The man's never listened to me in his life." Flanagan pursed his lips and slowly shook his head. "I'm afraid I've sent your father off to fight for the wrong army, if you want to think of it that way."

"Then that's all the more reason I have to go find him."

When he heard that, Flanagan looked up quickly at Kane, knitting his brows. Kane could see that his statement had sparked something in Flanagan's mind.

"Find him . . . and if you can, bring him back!" Flanagan said. "Get him out of there before something happens." His manner became instantly lively; his idea was animating him. He stood and walked to the fire, thinking and nodding. "Yes, that's it. Bring him back. I've felt a deep sense of responsibility for getting him involved in that mess. Well, maybe I—maybe *we* can do something about it!"

Flanagan strode over to Kane, who was a little befuddled by this sudden enthusiasm. "Kane, indeed you do need to go to Three Mile. You can find your father and tell him to come back here with you. Whatever problems he's been running from, I'll help him out. I like the man, have good instincts about him. And given that he's the father of the young hero who saved my sons' lives, well, that's all the more reason to give him whatever hand I can. Right? Right! So . . . we'll send you on! On a mission—a quest, as it were."

Kane was momentarily dumbstruck. A quest? He had a quest already! He wanted to find his father for his own reasons, not Flanagan's. And he could hardly afford to obligate himself to return to Dodge later on. What if Robert Blessed or one of his hired toughs showed up? No, this quest must remain Kane's, and Kane's alone—but how could he say that to a man who had just handed him fifteen hundred dollars?

He struggled a moment for words, then found them. "Ben . . . don't misunderstand me, but I can't promise I can bring my father back. I don't know that he'd want to come back, for one thing. And I don't know that I'd have any power to persuade him, or any influence over him at all. I do want to find him . . . but for my own reasons, and without a lot of strings attached to the situation."

Flanagan took that in, and for a moment Kane wondered if he'd offended him. But a smile broke out on his face. "Of course! You're right. I won't insist that you bring him back. But I do ask that you try to talk him away from Three Mile and that cursed miners' war. And let me know—a wire, a letter—what happens. Will you do that?"

Those were terms Kane could accept. "Indeed I will."

He touched the pocket in which the cash he'd received was now safely lodged. "Thanks to your generosity, it will be all the easier to make the journey and the search."

Flanagan was almost boisterous now. "Let's see if I can't smooth the path for you a little more! Let me wire my brother and tell him that you're coming. I'll tell him that you're Bill Porterfell's son and that you want to meet your father. He can arrange to have Bill ready for you. Of course, we'll say nothing to him of our desire to talk Bill away from that dangerous place."

"Thanks . . . but I'd rather not have my father know I'm coming."

Kane saw that Flanagan was quite puzzled to hear that. But how could he tell Flanagan that he didn't even know if his father would *want* to see him? How could he say that to forewarn William Porterfell about the arrival of a son whom he'd never bothered even to acknowledge all his life might do no more than send the man running away, never to be tracked down again? And there was also the possibility that William Porterfell might simply think the wire was some sort of trick by Robert Blessed to throw him off his guard until he could take him captive.

"I don't understand why you wouldn't want to let your father know you were coming, Kane. Not my business, I know . . . but wouldn't you want him to have at least some notion of what was to come?"

"I can't really explain it, sir . . . Ben. There are reasons. Private ones."

"Say no more, say no more. As I said, it's not my business. But let me suggest a compromise proposal. Would you object if I wired my brother privately, told him you are Bill Porterfell's son and wish to come see him, but as a surprise? I'll emphasize to him that your father must know *nothing* in advance about your coming. That way Eiler could at the very least tell us if Bill Porterfell is still there. After all, for all we know, he might have moved on already, if he didn't find being a private mercenary to his liking. And who would, in such a pit of turmoil as Three Mile is these days?"

Kane considered it. "I think that would be fine. Thank you."

"So it will be done, then!" Flanagan said brightly. "So it will be done!" He knocked his pipe empty at the fireplace and refilled it.

Kane sat down again, feeling the weight of the money in his pocket.

A stray thought came from nowhere: *Fifteen hundred dollars is a lot of money, but mere pennies compared to the worth of what Robert Blessed is after . . . what, maybe, my father and I together could actually hope to find.*

This was the first time since his adventure began that Kane had seriously thought about the fact that his father and he each possessed pieces of a puzzle that, when fully put together, could lead to a treasure so valuable that whoever possessed it would be rich for the rest of his days. So far all of Kane's ambitions had been small in scope: escape Blessed's clutches, evade this pursuer or that, stay alive until tomorrow, and with luck, in the end, find the father he had never known.

Kane hadn't thought much beyond that. He'd allowed himself to ask what would happen if his father rejected him and fled, but what if he didn't reject him? What if he welcomed his son? And what if Robert Blessed and his agent, Wilson, really were dead and the pursuit really was over? What if, together, Kane and William Porterfell could complete the puzzle of coded letters and find that treasure for themselves?

The thought so engrossed Kane that he didn't realize for a moment that Flanagan was talking to him again.

". . . and I'll have Mr. Grossett make your travel arrangements. We'll get you on the first available train to Three Mile. I'll handle the wire to Eiler personally, and let me assure you again, I'll be sure he knows not to alert your father that you're coming. Can't quite cipher out your reasons for that, I admit, but it's your affair and not mine. And in the meantime, do you have a place to stay?"

"I've been staying at a house owned by the doctor who's been treating me. He uses it as a kind of ward for his patients. But I'm well enough now that I don't quite feel right staying there. I'm hardly an invalid."

"Indeed not, and so you'll stay here. And we'll begin making the arrangements for you to go to Three Mile at once."

Kane was stunned by this man's seemingly unending generosity. "Thank you. I hardly know what to say."

"My friend, you needn't say anything. You've given me my sons back, and I'll do all I can for you. Speaking of my sons, are you up to a visit? I'd like you to meet them—*really* meet them, while they aren't unconscious!" Flanagan laughed.

He led Kane out of his office, out of the front room, and back into the hall. "Careful of the staircase—you can see it has only one rail," he said. "Follow me . . . my sons are upstairs."

That evening, back in Dodge, Kane and Carolina sat across from one another in a little cafe, Carolina staring in astonishment at what Kane had just handed her, tucked into an envelope.

"Kane . . . I can't take this! It's far too much! Seven hundred dollars!"

"Please, I want you to have it," he said. "It's a godsend, can't you see? Now you and your father won't have to worry because your winter's work is gone."

"But it's just too much!"

"Carolina, I have eight hundred dollars left from what Mr. Flanagan gave me, not counting what money I had before that. If anything, I'm giving you too little. I'm only taking as much as I am because I don't know what's ahead for me once I reach Three Mile. I want to be ready for anything. Thanks to Ben Flanagan, I think I will be." He reached over and patted her hand. "Now you and your father will, too."

"Kane . . . thank you."

"Don't thank me. Thank Mr. Flanagan."

"He must be a good man."

"I think he is. He seems eager to help me. And he likes my father! Speaks well of him. It makes me want all that much more to meet him."

"But doesn't it . . . you know, maybe frighten you a little?"

"It frightens me a lot."

She looked at Kane silently for a couple of seconds. "I almost envy you. What you'll do will at least be a lot more interesting than what my winter is going to be. I believe it will take Papa more time than he thinks to recover. I'll be playing nursemaid for some time to come."

"I'm just thankful he's alive."

"Me, too."

Kane squeezed her hand and stood up. "I need to get back to the Flanagan house now."

She stood, too, securing the envelope with the money underneath her shawl. "When will you leave?"

"Tomorrow. In the meantime, Mr. Flanagan is expecting a telegram back from his brother. Perhaps it's come by now . . . I hope so. And I hope it says that William Porterfell is still there, still safe and sound. Because then I'll know I truly can find him."

"I wish you well, Kane. And please . . . be careful. Just in case Robert Blessed is still out there somewhere."

"You be careful, too. Remember that he knows your face and who you are. And if he thinks he can use you to get his hands on me, he's the kind that would do it."

"I'll watch out." She smiled. "I'm going to miss you, you know."

"I'll be back. I don't know just when, or under what circumstances. But we'll see each other again. I promise."

When Kane reentered the Flanagan house that night and made his way up to one of the guest rooms on the second floor, he did so with the warm taste of Carolina Railey's kiss on his lips.

Indeed he would see her again. He had to. A man had no other choice when he was falling in love.

Chapter 9

Kane had never slept in a more comfortable bed. He awakened slowly, full of serenity, and stretched deliciously beneath the cool covers. Plumping his pillow, he propped himself up, hands behind his head, and looked up at the ceiling.

What a fine house! And what a kind and wonderful man Ben Flanagan was! Kane felt safe. Content. Wealthy, when he thought about the money Flanagan had given him. And as daunting as it was to consider traveling all the way to Colorado to find a man who might not want even to meet him, it wasn't too overwhelming when he remembered that Ben Flanagan was backing him.

Kane sent up a prayer to the Great Creator, giving thanks for those who had helped him make it this far—Cypress and Lewis Washington, the Raileys, and now Ben Flanagan. There were wicked men in the world, the Robert Blesseds who cared only for their own gain at any cost, but there were plenty of good people to counter them. Kane had never before fully realized just how true this was.

He had almost drifted back into a shallow but relaxing sleep when he heard a knock at his door. He rose, rubbing his face, and threw on a robe he'd found in the closet. He walked on bare feet across the luxuriant buffalo-skin rug and opened the door.

A smiling servant stood there, bearing a tray that exuded enticing scents from beneath a checked cloth. "Your breakfast, sir. Would you like to take it now, or should I leave it here beside the door until you are ready?"

Kane was astonished. Never in his life had he been served breakfast in bed. He nodded his thanks, took the tray, and closed the door.

Sitting up in bed, he ate slowly, thinking how easy it would be to grow accustomed to a lifestyle such as this. Of course, this wasn't to last. Later this very day he would be boarding a train, heading for Colorado. To his surprise, he was more eager than nervous about the prospect.

He got up, washed at the basin, and dressed. He'd just stepped out into the hall when he heard footsteps on the staircase. Flanagan came up around the spiral, a paper in his hand.

"Kane! I was just coming to see you! I've got something you'll be interested in." He waved the paper Kane's way. "Eiler has answered the telegram I sent him yesterday."

"Good news?"

"Good news."

Kane took the paper and read it. It *was* good news: Eiler Flanagan's wire reported that William Porterfell was still in Three Mile, still employed by Flanagan, and it would be no problem at all for Kane to meet his father in whatever circumstances Kane thought best, once he arrived. The telegram further instructed Ben Flanagan to wire back with news of exactly when Kane would be arriving at the Three Mile station. Eiler Flanagan would have someone there to meet him and bring him to his house, where arrangements for a private meeting with Bill Porterfell would be made.

Kane read the wire, then read it again. It was hard not to laugh out loud. He could scarcely believe how well it was all coming together.

Before Kane would leave there was time for two important last errands in Dodge: another visit to the Raileys, where farewells were said and best wishes extended—and where Kane received another kiss from Carolina—and then a stop to purchase a small Colt revolver and ammunition, along with a hideaway holster so he could wear the pistol, unseen, beneath his coat. He didn't anticipate having to use a weapon, but until he knew for sure that Robert Blessed was gone, he didn't want to be unarmed.

He didn't let Flanagan know about the pistol when he returned to the big mansion for lunch and farewell. He was to find that Flanagan had extended even more generosity to him while he'd been in town. Grossett had awaiting him a new carpetbag containing three or four changes of clothing, various personal goods, and nonperishable foods.

"Mr. Flanagan likes to be sure his guests are sent off with everything they could possibly need," Grossett explained. "You'll even find a couple of small novels in there, in case you enjoy reading. Have you read *Huckle-berry Finn*? A new novel by Mr. Mark Twain. A delightful book. You'll enjoy it."

"Mr. Flanagan is exceptionally generous."

"And you, if I might be allowed to return the compliment on Mr. Flanagan's behalf, are exceptional in many ways. Not only for what you did, but also in your manner, your well-spokenness . . . quite remarkable, if I may say so, for a young man raised in humble circumstances in the Indian Nations."

"My mother always insisted that I speak English well and read well. She always had hope for me making a success of myself, and she believed a good command of the English language was necessary. An unusual attitude for an Indian woman, I suppose, but that was what she believed."

"A wise woman." Grossett shook Kane's hand. "I wish you well in your quest. Now, Mr. Flanagan would like to see you in his office before you go, and his sons also would like to tell you farewell. When all that's done, I'll have the carriage awaiting you on the front drive."

Thirty minutes later, Kane disembarked at the Dodge City train station. He shook Grossett's hand, grinned, expressed for perhaps the hundredth time the depth of his gratitude to Ben Flanagan, then turned to the waiting train and climbed aboard.

When the train began to roll slowly out of the station, he looked out the sooty window of his compartment and saw Carolina running onto the platform, smiling at him and waving. He waved back, regretting he had missed the chance for one more embrace and kiss. She shouted something at him, smiling, and though he couldn't hear her, he read her lips: "Good luck."

The train left the station behind and picked up speed. Kane sat back against the hard seat, the carpetbag under his feet.

He was bound for Colorado at last, where, this time, he was sure he really would succeed in finding his father.

Time passed slowly on the train. Kane kept his mind busy by repeating to himself the contents of the coded letters. He struggled at a spot or two, but by using the old memory tricks he'd learned from the wise Toko in his youth, he successfully got through them all and was pleased.

The train rumbled on. Kane read, dozed, watched the landscape outside the window, and went through the standard train-travel rigors of scrambling for food and public conveniences at the various station stops along the way.

The farther he traveled, the more the landscape changed. Kane began to feel a steadily growing peace of mind. Despite all of Ben Flanagan's warnings about the strife currently afflicting Three Mile, Kane couldn't help but feel he would be far safer there than he was when Robert Blessed and his hired devils had pursued him all the way from St. Louis to that last fateful encounter on the Dodge City–bound train.

Here alone in this compartment, going to a new place where Robert Blessed, if he was living, could probably never track him down, Kane began to allow himself to think the ordeal really was over. A fearful time, a squeeze as if through the neck of a bottle, and suddenly in the clear. That's the way things often go in life, old Toko once had told him. Maybe that was the case here. He was out of the bottleneck and into the open. He could relax.

He discovered he wasn't as relaxed as he thought when a hand touched his shoulder and he very nearly yelled and leaped right out of his seat. He jerked around and looked up to see Pete Rampling's bruised face grinning down at him.

"Startle you there, Kane?"

Kane let out his breath. "You certainly did."

"I'm surprised to see you on this train."

"I'm surprised to see you, too."

"Reckon I could set here, talk with you a spell? There's something I feel the need to say."

Kane waved him to the opposite seat, though not enthusiastically. He knew from the things that Rampling had said in the cell that the man had no regard for Indians, and therefore Kane could hardly have much regard for him. But he could endure him for a time. Right now he felt he could endure anything.

Rampling settled himself into the opposite seat, then looked back at Kane rather uncomfortably.

"First thing," he said, "I want to tell you how I admire the way you did such good things fighting that fire."

"Just did what I had to. I saw you doing the same."

"Yeah, but not nearly so good as you. I never set foot inside the building once. And to tell you the truth, what

I did I did mostly in hopes that the sheriff would smile kindly on me and sort of forget about that row that got me jailed in the first place."

"The impression I had was that he'd already put that behind, anyway. I don't think he'd have let you go if he'd intended to keep you. All you'd done was get into a brawl."

"Reckon?" Rampling puzzled that one over. "Maybe I fought that fire for nothing, then. And maybe I'm scooting out of town, running when maybe I don't have to." He pondered this for a while, then shrugged. "What the hell. Tired of Dodge anyway."

High moral fellow, this one. Kane wondered sometimes if the world was populated entirely with self-centered scoundrels. But of course he couldn't really keep thinking that when he considered such people as the Raileys, or the late Washingtons.

"Anyway," Rampling went on, "I do want you to know I admired you doing such hero kinds of things. And most of all, I want to tell you how sorry I am for talking so bad about Indians while we were locked up together. You see, I was a little bit drunk at the time."

"I knew you were."

"I was raised to despise redskins, you see. My pap, he hated 'em. You're lucky it wasn't him you was locked up with. He'd probably have killed you as quick as look at you."

"Maybe I'd have killed him first."

"You probably could have. He'd most likely have been passed-out drunk." Rampling grinned. "Anyhow, no hard feelings, I hope."

Kane repeated something Toko had told him several times in boyhood moments when he was angry over some offense or another. "Anger is a torch that burns only the one who bears it."

Rampling seemed confused by that, but shrugged and grinned. "So you're saying there's no hard feelings?"

"No hard feelings." *And now,* Kane thought, *you can leave.*

But Rampling didn't leave. He settled back in a manner that suggested he was there for the long haul—and a long haul it would be before they reached Colorado. Kane could only hope that the man had no plans to travel farther than the next station.

"So . . ." Kane said, hoping to prompt Rampling to tell his plans, "you decided to get out of town, did you?"

"Yeah, yeah." Rampling began rubbing some old food remnants off a back tooth with his finger. His voice was muffled and distorted as he did so. "Bought myself a train ticket to Colorado."

"How far into Colorado are you going?"

"Three Mile. Booming silver town."

Oh, no, Kane thought. "I've heard of it. Going there myself, in fact."

"No! You got kin?"

"My father's there."

"Bill went to Colorado? I thought he was still working for Flanagan."

"No. He left. Got some new work in Three Mile."

"I'll bet Flanagan was sore to lose him. You could tell the old man liked Bill. And Bill did him some good work."

"That's what Mr. Flanagan told me."

"You talked to him? Oh, yeah . . . I suppose you would, considering it was his sons you pulled out of the fire. Did you read the story about it in the newspaper?"

"No."

"Played you up mighty big as the hero."

Kane had a thought: Rampling might actually be useful to him in Colorado. After all, he did know Bill Porterfell and could point him out. He decided to exercise a little self-serving patience with this rather unlikable man. "I don't consider myself a hero," he said.

"Hey . . . did Flanagan reward you?"

Kane knew better than to fully answer that question. If a man like Rampling got an inkling that he had a significant amount of money, Kane would find himself either robbed or stuck with an unwanted, mooching companion for days to come. "He gave me that carpetbag down there and some new clothes, and he bought me a train ticket to Three Mile when he found out I was looking for my father."

"No money, huh? Ain't that the way with the rich! Save their boys' damn useless lives, and they give you a damn carpetbag and a train ticket! Hell, he could have afforded to give you a small fortune, if he'd wanted!"

Kane smiled faintly. *If only Rampling knew!* "I didn't do it for reward, so I'm satisfied."

"You're a better man than me. Not that being a better man than me is any great challenge." Rampling leaned back, belched loudly, yawned, and stretched.

He then went on to roll himself a cigarette and soon had the compartment choked with bluish smoke. "Three

Mile! I'll tell you, I wouldn't be going there if not for having kin. Three Mile ain't the kind of place a man wants to be right now. I can't figure why old Bill would have gone there."

"Are you thinking about the miners' strike?"

"Yep. You know about that, do you?"

"Some."

"Hell of a thing, that war. Wickedness against righteousness, pure and simple. Good against evil."

"Which side is the evil?"

"It ain't so much which side as which person. And the evil in this case is Mr. Eiler Flanagan, the very brother of your own Flanagan back in Dodge."

"So Eiler Flanagan is outright evil, eh?" Kane voiced this skeptically, his perception of the Flanagan family being quite positive at the moment, though he did recall that Ben Flanagan talked about his brother in a tone of concern, particularly about his stance in the miners' strike.

"You ain't far from the truth, from what my brother tells me."

"What's he do that's so bad?"

"How about folks who cross him, including his own miners, disappearing and not being heard from again? How about letting his miners work in the worst kind of conditions? How about him stealing away the women and daughters of his own employees?"

"He does all that?"

"Yes, sir."

"This comes from your brother?"

"Yep. And he should know, being a miner himself."

"One of Flanagan's miners?"

"Works deep in the bowels of the Flanagan Hill Mine. Or he did until the strike commenced."

"Any chance he's blowing up his stories about Eiler Flanagan a little?"

Rampling the offensive was suddenly Rampling the offended. "My brother *ain't* a liar."

"I wasn't trying to say he is . . . just maybe that the stories going around get blown up some in the natural course of things when you have folks angry at one another."

Rampling aimed a finger at Kane's nose. "You just wait until you get there. You'll find that Ben Flanagan got all the share of goodness in that family, and his brother only the wickeness."

The conversation drifted to other topics, then became a rambling monologue by Rampling that might have been titled "The World and All That Is Contained Therein," then faded into silence as Rampling fell asleep. All the while Kane continued to think about what the man had said about Eiler Flanagan. What if he really was wicked enough to do the kinds of things Rampling had said? Was William Porterfell the kind of man to bear arms for such a villain?

The train came to a stop at another station, and Kane got out to buy himself a sandwich at the food stand. He returned to his compartment and was pleased to find Rampling no longer there. Maybe he'd returned to his original seat elsewhere on the train. But when Kane awakened from a brief nap Rampling was seated across from him once more, asleep again, snorting and muttering as the train bumped along.

It seemed he'd found a companion, like it or not. Kane sighed and decided to make the best of it. Surely he'd shake the man off eventually.

After many miles and much time, when the train's progress had made Kansas but a memory, Kane was enjoying a certain settlement of mind concerning the intrusive Pete Rampling and his disturbing commentary on the moral balance of the town of Three Mile.

In short, he'd persuaded himself that Rampling was little more than a fool. What was he but a drifter who both found and made trouble? Who was he to be taken seriously, especially about matters of which he possessed only secondhand knowledge? Rampling had obviously been fed an abundance of slanted information, presenting Eiler Flanagan in the darkest of terms. Surely the man wasn't really so bad.

Kane's reassurance soon lost steam, however, thanks to a newspaper he picked up at a station near the base of the mountains. While the train climbed and Rampling dozed—he seemed capable of sleeping endlessly—Kane idly flipped through the newspaper, hardly noticing what he read, until he came upon a lengthy story detailing the most recent developments in the strike at Three Mile.

Kane read with interest, expecting to see his suspicion that Rampling was distorting the truth about Eiler Flanagan vindicated.

But when he finished the story he was frowning and

distressed. Everything it reported tended to back Rampling's claims. Allegations about the character and crimes of Eiler Flanagan were rampant throughout the story, and this despite the fact that the writer had clearly made an effort to present a fair accounting. Kane looked for a byline but found none, other than a note that the story had been reprinted from another newspaper, the *Three Mile Standard*.

He tossed the newspaper aside grumpily. Maybe the *Standard* was just some miners' rag, labor propaganda cleverly disguised as news.

But if not, if the allegations it made were accurate, then Eiler Flanagan truly was no less than a wicked man. Maybe a murderer, and certainly a pitiless scoundrel, not to be trusted.

He wished that William Porterfell could have found someone better than Eiler Flanagan with whom to cast his lot.

Chapter 10

It took Kane some time to ascertain just what was different and unsettling about this new mountainous environment.

The air. It was thin here, not rich and satisfying like the air he'd breathed all his life in the Nations. Here every lungful seemed to fall just a bit short, which gave him an edgy, nervous feeling that wouldn't go away.

But there was more to his frame of mind than that. The closer the train climbed to Three Mile, the louder an inner voice of warning clamored for Kane's attention. And what it told him, quite inconveniently, was that he should stay clear of Eiler Flanagan, at least until he knew more about the man and the situation at Three Mile.

A discerning man learns to listen to the quieter voice. More words from Toko, words that he'd already heeded a few times throughout this adventure, and in life before it, and he'd seldom found cause for regret when he did.

The "quieter voice" was guiding him to avoid Eiler Flanagan, but he wasn't sure whether he should listen to it this time. On the one hand, Flanagan was expecting him. He had promised to unite him at last with his father. And wouldn't it be something of a slap at Ben Flanagan's generosity and kindness not to follow through on arrangements that he'd set up?

Yet that inner warning kept sounding, and Kane had to admit there were some solid reasons to heed it. Ben Flanagan himself had said his brother was probably on the wrong side of the labor war involving his mine. Pete Rampling, though perhaps a questionable source, had said even more severe things about Eiler Flanagan. But it was that newspaper story that had stirred Kane's doubts about Eiler Flanagan the most.

Kane had not told Rampling any of the details of his coming meeting with his father. All Rampling knew was that Kane's father worked in some undescribed capacity in Three Mile and that Kane was coming to the town to meet him. A few times Kane had almost told Rampling that his father was working as a hired arms-bearer for Eiler Flanagan, just to see what kind of reaction that would receive, but he'd not gone through with it.

His decision about meeting Flanagan still hung fire as the train chugged along the last few difficult miles to the high-altitude city of Three Mile.

As usual, Pete Rampling was dozing in the seat across from Kane. The facial bruises that had so marred his appearance when he'd been tossed into that cell at Dodge were fast fading. He wasn't a bad-looking fellow, overall, though he seemed quite rough-edged and unrefined.

Despite the fact that Rampling had intruded himself

into Kane's life with not the slightest invitation, Kane didn't much mind it. Rampling had been friendly enough, informative, and had provided company and diversion. And anytime he'd threatened to become annoying, he'd always drifted off into another nap just in time to avoid wearing out his welcome.

Kane watched out the window as the train climbed higher into the mountains. And what spectacular mountains they were! The only significant mountains Kane had known until now had been the barely remembered misty, haunted, foggy ridges, peaks, and balds of North Carolina. He'd heard of the great Rockies but had not, until seeing them now for himself, fully grasped how stunning, vast, and humbling they were.

Soon features closer in began to attract his attention. He saw shacks, cabins, ramshackle structures built among the trees along the mountainsides. The air became smoky; a new smell mixed with that of the belchings of the locomotive chimney. Kane sniffed, trying to place it. He would not realize until later that what he was smelling was the stench of the smelters that ran around the clock in Three Mile.

The grade leveled off, and soon the train began a slow, wide swing along a curve that led out to a trestle. Craning his neck and clearing grime off the window, Kane caught his first glimpse of the town ahead.

Three Mile. His heart raced. Here it was . . . the town where his father was. He could only hope that Bill Porterfell hadn't moved on since Eiler Flanagan had sent his brother that telegram. Kane had already narrowly missed his father in Dodge but had been fortunate enough to pick up his track. He might not be so lucky if the trail were broken again.

Kane's excitement died away to a far more solemn feeling as the station platform came into view. His eyes were drawn at once to three men who stood waiting there—armed men, wearing pistols and stern expressions. Two also had rifles, and beneath the coat of the third Kane saw a shape that looked like a hidden short-barreled shotgun.

He knew, without knowing how he knew, that these men were waiting for *him*. Some of Eiler Flanagan's hired gunmen.

Might one of them even be his father, sent to await the arrival of a newcomer whose identity and relation to himself he had not been told?

Kane hoped not. He didn't like the looks of these men. They reminded him too much of McGrath and Wilson and Dukane, the hired agents of Robert Blessed who had made his life hell after he escaped Blessed's St. Louis house and began his westward flight.

The train slowed. The armed men stepped closer to the edge of the platform, squinting at the passenger cars.

Looking for him already. It made Kane's skin crawl. That quieter voice was now not quiet at all, and it told him what he must do.

He reached across and shook Rampling awake.

"Huh? What . . ."

"Rampling! Pete, listen to me. There's something I need you to do for me."

Rampling frowned at Kane, uncomprehending, then looked around. "I'll be! We're here!"

"Listen to me, Pete! There's not much time to explain. I need you to do a favor for me."

"What's that?"

"Out on the platform . . . you see those armed men?"

Rampling looked out the window. The train was screeching to a full halt now. "Yeah. What about them?"

"I think they're waiting for me."

Rampling looked first at Kane, then back at the men. "Rough-looking reception committee."

"They are. And I don't know that I want to meet them."

"So what do you want me to do about it?"

"I want you to meet them for me."

"What?" Rampling shook his head and waved his hand dismissively. "I don't think so! What kind of trouble are you in, anyway?"

"None. But I'm afraid that I might be if those men get their hands on me."

"Who are they?"

"I'm not sure . . . I couldn't even prove it's me they're waiting on. But . . . it is. I know it is."

"Listen, Kane, you're a fine fellow, right as rain, but I don't know that I want to . . ." He trailed off, looking at the money that Kane had just held out in front of his face. Fifty dollars!

"It's yours if you'll go out there, tell those men there's been a change of plans, and that the fellow they were to meet couldn't make the trip after all. Tell them he'll be along sometime later, you don't know just when."

Rampling stared at the money quite hungrily. "But

what if they won't believe me . . . or what if they cause me some kind of trouble?"

"They'll have no reason to cause you trouble. You're just a stranger bearing a message. It's me they're supposed to meet."

"I sure would like to know who they are before I talk to them."

Passengers were beginning to disembark, carrying baggage and umbrellas and assorted bundles. The gunmen on the platform studied the face of each person who filed out of the passenger cars.

Kane added another ten dollars to the offering.

Rampling licked his lips. "There might be danger in it . . ."

Another ten went into the stack.

Rampling grinned. "Man, if I'd knowed you was so well off, you and me would have become close and dear *compadres* long ago!"

"Please . . . just tell them there's a change of plans and there's no one for them to meet for now. That should be all there is to it."

"And what will you do?"

"Get off through that opposite door and keep the train between me and them until I can get out of sight."

"You *are* in some kind of trouble, ain't you?"

"I'm just following my instinct, that's all. I usually find it guides me right."

Rampling took the money with eyes twinkling, folded it, and pocketed it under his coat. "See you later, maybe? Maybe find some other jobs I can do for you?"

"This one here should be sufficient. Now go on, before they climb on the train and start looking."

"You sure they won't hurt me?"

"They've got no reason to. For that matter, they'd probably not hurt me, nor anybody else. I just don't want to meet them, that's all."

"Who sent them?"

Kane felt guilty at once. He knew Rampling would have second, third, and maybe fourth thoughts about approaching men affiliated with the wicked Eiler Flanagan. So he merely ignored the question. "Hurry, Pete! They're starting to come this way!"

Rampling headed down the aisle toward the door. Kane grabbed his carpetbag, checked to make sure his pistol was secure in its hidden holster under his coat, and turned down the aisle in the opposite direction. Just before he exited, he glanced back. Through the windows he saw Rampling meeting the men on the platform, talking to them with a big, disarming grin on his face, shrugging and coming across basically like a man trying too hard to be casual.

Kane left the train and trotted back along its length on the edge of the track. At the rear he doubled back to the same side the platform was on, though now he was well away from it. He looked back up alongside the train and was shocked to see that one of the gunmen had Rampling by the arm and was talking angrily right in his face. Rampling was shrinking back like a dog fearing a beating, and looking wildly around for Kane.

Kane felt he might melt into the ground. He'd not

had any idea that Rampling would be treated so. A deep regret filled him, and an even deeper terror. Though he wanted to do the right thing for Rampling's sake and present himself to these men, he felt rooted in place, unable to move or even to think.

"You, there! Away from the track!"

A railroad man, yelling at Kane. He turned. "What?"

"Away from the track! What are you doing back here?"

"I was a passenger. I got off the train."

"Through the wrong door, I take it."

"Maybe so. Sorry."

"Are you an Indian?"

"No." Kane would later feel ashamed that he'd said that. It had just come out, unplanned, a self-protective lie born of a hardening awareness that is was difficult to make it in a world that was run by white men unless one was a white man himself.

"You look it. You sure you ain't Indian?"

"I'm *not* an Indian." *Forgive me, Toko,* Kane thought. *Forgive me.*

"Well, then you've truly got no excuse for being at the wrong place. Your redskins and your niggers got no sense worthy of the name, but a white man ought to know how to get off a train right. Come on, get up that bank there and off the track."

Struggling against an impulse to introduce his fist to this fellow's teeth, Kane glanced back up at the platform.

The gunmen, and Rampling, were gone.

Kane scrambled up the indicated bank, hurrying so much that he almost fell back again. The railroad man cussed to himself softly and shook his head while Kane continued to scramble and finally made it up the bank.

He hefted his bag and ran back around toward the station, wildly looking for Rampling and the gunmen. Had they taken him away? Or had they merely gone their separate ways, Rampling running off somewhere?

Kane slowed as he neared the station house and looked cautiously around. Worried as he was about Rampling, and responsible as he felt for the trouble he'd brought upon the man, he still didn't want to be nabbed by those gunmen.

He wished he hadn't unwittingly done such a dirty deed to Rampling, but he was glad he'd heeded that "quieter voice" that warned him to steer clear of Flanagan and his gunmen.

Kane looked all around again but saw no sign of those he sought. He peered farther, watching the traffic along every street and avenue that was open to his sight at this angle. Still he saw nothing.

A high, rounded object on the far horizon of the town drew his eye. A tower, built somewhat like a gable or a loft and attached to a big house, most of which was hidden from his view. He could see enough to know that it was an impressive mansion of a place, not as big as the new Flanagan house in Dodge City ... but probably, Kane realized, also the dwelling of a Flanagan.

Who but Eiler Flanagan, owner of the Flanagan Hill Mine that formed the heart and soul of this boomtown, would own such a big house in a generally squalid, slapped-together place like Three Mile?

If that really was Flanagan's place, and if those gunmen had been Flanagan's flunkies . . . then maybe they were heading back to that house just now, to give word to Flanagan of what had happened.

Maybe they had Rampling with them.

Kane eyed the streets, which were twisted and vaguely defined dirt avenues, patternlessly criscrossing like the tendrils of a web spun by a drunken spider. Picking out what looked like a probable route toward the big house, he trotted that way, keeping an eye out for Rampling and the gunmen.

He was almost to the base of the low hill that held the mansion when he saw them. They were taking Rampling up the long drive toward the house, and he didn't look any too happy about it.

Kane winced, and prayed hard: *God, don't let them hurt him! Don't let them hurt a man who's in a dangerous situation only because I stupidly put him there!*

Kane felt sad, angry, questioning—all at once. Why did it have to be that anyone who had anything to do with him got themselves endangered, hurt, or even killed because of it?

Kane watched as the three gunmen and Rampling disappeared around the back of the house. He wondered why they had bothered to take Rampling with them, rather than just convey his message. It was an innocuous enough message, after all.

Kane walked over to a nearby grove of trees and sat down atop his well-stuffed carpetbag. For the first time, he noticed that the wind was bitterly cold. He'd been so preoccupied with what had happened that he'd only just now paid heed to the weather. He cinched his coat tighter around his middle and shivered, eyeing the Flanagan mansion and trying to figure out what to do.

Maybe he ought to just go up there, knock on the door, and present himself. He could simply admit that he'd gotten spooked by the sight of the gunmen on the platform and had conned his traveling companion into delivering the false message. He could take his chances with Flanagan and let Rampling get out of there.

After all, Rampling was probably up there spilling out the truth even now, showing them the money Kane had given him, telling them that the message he'd borne was false and that Kane really was in Three Mile after all.

Yes, that was what he should do. Go up there and meet Eiler Flanagan, just like the original plan had been. He stood, his eyes on the stone-slab footpath up the hill to the mansion door. Why had he done what he'd done, anyway? Right now it didn't make sense. A few rumors, a newspaper article, a feeling of fright at the sight of some stern-looking but probably entirely law-abiding gunmen, and he'd panicked. A result of all the trauma he'd suffered while fleeing Robert Blessed, probably. It was really quite embarrassing, and he dreaded having to face Flanagan—who was probably just as decent and bighearted a man as his brother in Dodge!

Kane picked up his carpetbag and took his first step toward the mansion. Then suddenly Rampling appeared. He was running around the back of the mansion and down the same drive they'd led him up. Kane froze and watched him descend. Rampling's face was pale and he looked like he'd been scared almost out of his wits. He was so attentive to his flight that he didn't even see Kane. Kane was about to hail him and ask what the devil had just gone on when shame stopped him.

After what he'd unwittingly done to Pete Rampling, it would be difficult to look the man in the eye again. He could imagine the thorough cussing Pete would give him. And Kane wouldn't blame him.

At least they had let Rampling go. Kane supposed the gunmen had dragged him up there, made him spill the message Kane had given him—or more likely, the truth of the matter—to Flanagan, and Flanagan had heard him out and let him go.

Kane was immensely relieved. Rampling had taken a good scare, but he was clearly well enough. And seventy dollars richer, besides.

Kane watched Rampling vanish into the heart of Three Mile, Colorado, and sighed. What to do now? With no Rampling left to be rescued, should he go on and meet Flanagan anyway? Or should he continue to heed that earlier inner warning telling him to steer clear?

Only a moment earlier he'd persuaded himself that his fear of Eiler Flanagan was probably groundless. But at that point he'd been trying to muster sufficient motivation to get himself up the hill and into the house for Rampling's sake.

What would Toko tell him to do if he were here? Kane mulled it over and quickly knew the answer. As always, Toko would tell him to trust that inner, "quieter" voice.

Kane shifted his carpetbag and turned away from the mansion, walking back into the jumbled, crowded, smelly farrago that was Three Mile, Colorado.

Chapter 11

Though Three Mile possessed many qualities, beauty was not among them.

The mountains were spectacular, but even their appearance had suffered in the area close to the town. As he walked, Kane studied them, noting how the slopes within relatively easy reach of the townsfolk, and of the miners who lived outside the town proper, had been substantially stripped of foliage.

What foliage remained was oddly colored and dirty-looking. A sniff of the powerful smelter stench that permeated the atmosphere made it easy to guess the cause of the discoloration. Kane coughed a few times, and it wasn't just from the aftermath of the Dodge City fire. The very air in this town was noxious and starved for oxygen.

Kane strode along on irregular boardwalk, which occasionally simply ceased to exist for a stretch, leaving him no choice but to tramp through mud. The streets were so bumpy and full of holes as to hardly justify themselves as true avenues of travel. No effort had been made to keep the streets clear of manure. Nor were there any decent crosswalks. The few corrugated walkways made of logs laid side by side had been trampled so deep into the mud by passing horses that they no longer served the purpose.

The buildings were mostly new, and only a few of them were painted. As a result, the town was for the most part the same color as wood one would see stacked in lumberyards, though the polluted air was steadily doing its part to transform the new-pine yellow into a dull, lifeless gray.

Canvas, it appeared, was almost as much in use as wood. Several structures that upon a first glance appeared to be houses revealed themselves as glorified tents upon a second. Kane examined one such structure built on a sturdy wooden frame, with a chimney, a front porch of sawmill slabs, and—as best he could tell from the outside appearance—a true wooden floor. Smoke poured out of the chimney, carrying the smell of cooking poultry. Kane's stomach, last filled at some nameless train station food bar many miles back down the mountains, rumbled loudly.

Fortunately, Three Mile presented more than enough dining options. Free enterprise showed its shining face on every hand. Signs offered meals, drinks, haircuts, dentistry, palm reading, tool sharpening, miners' supplies, farrier and blacksmith services, groceries, laundry, shoeshines, clothing, boots, fabrics, rooms for rent, tents, and legal services—abundant legal services, always in demand in mining towns, where conflicts over claims were inevitable, courts were ever busy, and lawyers thrived. There was even a books-for-rent library in a tent, and it was doing a brisk business, probably the brainchild of some entrepreneurial bookworm who'd hauled his supply of volumes up the mountain on the train. There were a few churches, most of them operating in tents. Protestants predominated, though there was one Catholic chapel built of unpainted pine.

There were saloons, too. Lots of them, and not disguised as they had been in Dodge. Drinks were available everywhere at the standard price of two bits per slug. Gambling halls abounded and appeared to be busy despite the early hour. Kane would later learn that the gambling halls ran around the clock.

All in all, Three Mile matched and perhaps exceeded Kane's previous conception of what a mining boomtown would be. But it was more jumbled than he'd expected, more dirty and crowded. And something else, too—something he hadn't yet defined—failed to match his expectations. His inability to put a finger on it created a certain mild sense of concern in the back of his mind.

His thoughts turned to lodging. It would be night before long, and he needed a place to stay. This thought rekindled the nagging concern about whether he'd been sensible in not going to Flanagan's as planned. The odds were good that Flanagan would have put him up for the night, free, in that big and obviously comfortable mansion.

Even so, he decided, he had done the right thing, at least for now, in not meeting Flanagan. That inner, quiet voice again, that seldom-failing instinct ... He told himself that he would be glad in the end that he'd paid attention to it.

A little time in Three Mile, and he could get a better perspective on this miners' war and which side of it held the higher moral ground, Flanagan or the strikers.

Suddenly he stopped in mid-stride on the boardwalk, having just figured out what that undefined something was that didn't feel quite right. Looking around, he could see it clearly now.

Just then a door opened in a boxlike wooden building standing across the street from him. Two burly men emerged, looking this way and that, their faces as grim as those of the gunmen who had awaited Kane at the station. They both wore gunbelts with Remington pistols, and one had a shotgun in hand. They examined their surroundings thoroughly before stepping away from the door.

A third man, average in height and neat but plain in clothing, exited at that point. The two burly men stayed close to him, blocking him from the street with their bodies. Kane caught only a glimpse of him, but that was enough. The man's looks were distinctive enough to imprint themselves on his mind very quickly. He was reddish-haired, the hue tending more toward auburn than orange, and fair-skinned. His mustache, neatly combed and sizable, covered most of his upper lip. His eyes moved quickly beneath small-framed spectacles. His face might have been that of a scholar or a librarian, but his build was muscled. Obviously a miner.

A fourth man, also bespectacled, appeared briefly at the door. He wore an apron, armband, and visor pushed up high on his brow—a printer or journalist, or both. He spoke briefly and cordially to the auburn-haired man, shook his hand, and stood in the doorway as the man departed, closely guarded by the stocky men with him. At last, the man in the apron went back inside and closed the door. Kane glanced at the sign on the wall above it: THE THREE MILE STANDARD: THE VOICE OF THE COMMON LABORING CITIZEN

Kane smiled to himself. He'd just stumbled across the same newspaper that had originally printed the story he'd read in reprint on the train. Maybe that fellow in the visor was the very man who'd written it.

He looked up the street and watched the two guards and their charge turn a corner and move out of sight. He noted that many people waved at the guarded man, tipping their hats, greeting him respectfully.

Kane wondered who the man was. Not that it mattered . . . the only man here that really mattered to him was Bill Porterfell.

He shifted his bag to the opposite hand and moved on, continuing his search for lodging.

At last he found a sort of flophouse, a big, part-wood, part-canvas place filled with bunks available for night-to-night rent at a cost of fifty cents a night, or forty cents if a man obligated to a full week. Most people, Kane included, seemed to be declining the discount. This didn't seem the kind of facility where one would remain for long. It catered mostly to new arrivals.

Kane locked his bag in one of several heavy, hand-made iron rental lockers in the place. He kept his money with him, however, not willing to leave it untended, even under lock and key.

He was ready for supper. As dusk settled like a slowly lowering cloud over the mountains, Kane strode down another boardwalk, in search now of a promising-looking cafe. He spotted one across the street, a multi-smokestacked building made of wood, with a real roof on it and a sign boasting THE LARGEST FLAPJACKS IN COLORADO. Flapjacks . . . sounded good to him.

Kane stepped off the boardwalk and was about to cross the street when a band of horsemen came around the corner at almost a trot.

Someone grabbed Kane's shoulder and held him back. Surprised, he looked around, into the face of a stranger.

"Best wait until that bunch gets past," the man said.

Kane looked at the riders. Seven of them, all carrying rifles propped with barrels pointed skyward but held in such a way that they could be dropped, aimed, and fired in half a moment. They rode with a blatant arrogance, staring contemptuously at the people around them, seven sets of lips curled in seven sneers.

"Who are they?" Kane asked the stranger.

"You must be new in town to be asking that. That's some of Flanagan's murdering trash," the man said in little more than a loud whisper, as if fearing the gunmen would hear. "Best thing to do when you see them scoundrels is to stand back, stand still, and keep your mouth shut and your eyes looking the other way."

"Are they really murderers?"

"Let's put it this way: I ain't one prone to using figures of speech. There's been some folks to disappear, never found, and I lay the blame at the feet of Flanagan's hired bastards."

Kane watched the riders go by, hoping fiercely that none of them was his father.

He was under no illusions that Bill Porterfell was a likely candidate for canonization. He'd abandoned more than one wife, and he allowed his own son to grow up believing him dead. In Wichita, Kane had learned from an old partner of Porterfell's that the man had a history of failure in almost every enterprise he'd undertaken.

But a member of a gang of hired toughs, maybe murderers? Kane didn't want to believe his father could be so low as that.

"What kind of man is Flanagan?" Kane asked the stranger.

"Not the kind you'd want moving in next door, that much I'll say."

"Is he behind the murders you talked about?"

"Well behind them. Hid in the shadows. But ultimately he's the one, yes."

"You're a miner, I suppose."

"No. Storekeeper. But I know right from wrong, and I know the miners are in the right and Flanagan is nothing but wrong."

Kane watched the armed riders moving on down the street and was about to address another question when a most unexpected thing happened. A stone, launched from somewhere in the midst of a clump of young men gathered on a boardwalk, flew through the air and struck one of the riders on the shoulder.

Kane noticed that the young men wore red bands around the biceps of their left arms.

"Damned Flanagan murderers!" The voice, like the stone, came from among the group, but the exact source couldn't be picked out.

"Oh, Lord," muttered the storekeeper. "You see the one that rock hit? That's Freddy Snowden. Little brother of the lead rider there, Ves Snowden."

The riders stopped. "Who threw that?" demanded Freddy Snowden.

No reply from the gathered young men, whom Kane figured were striking miners.

"I asked who threw that!"

Still no reply.

Freddy Snowden dismounted and walked toward the clump of miners. He was speaking, but he was far enough away that Kane couldn't understand his words.

"I'm going back inside," the storekeeper said. "I don't want to witness any murder." He turned and was gone.

Kane, however, couldn't pull himself away. He watched as the younger Snowden, his rifle leveled on the group, swore and demanded, generally acting like a man ready to kill somebody on the spot if he did not get an answer.

It might have come to that but for a movement of men from the opposite side of the street. Though not as heavily armed as the riders, they outnumbered them two to one and spread themselves out in a manner that suggested they were ready to use their advantage if it came to a fight.

Kane thought about putting some distance between

himself and the would-be combatants. Yet something—perhaps the possibility that one of the riders was William Porterfell—actually pulled him closer.

Words were being exchanged, more hotly by the moment. Kane came within hearing range and blended in with a rapidly growing crowd of nervous observers.

Just when it appeared that bloodshed was moments away, and the crowd was beginning to back away in the realization that not every shot might go where it was intended, three newcomers arrived. The crowd divided to let them through. Kane noted a badge glimmering on the coat of each of the three.

"That's enough, all of you," said the apparent leader, a brown-haired, lean young man with a scar on his chin. "Break this up and clear out. Now."

Ves Snowden addressed the man, whom Kane assumed was the town marshal. "A member of that band there threw a large stone and struck my brother Freddy while he was doing no more than riding harmlessly down the street, Mr. Dungooden."

"Riding down the street . . . with arms displayed, I note," Dungooden replied. "It's against town ordinance to openly display weaponry in a public place and in a threatening manner, and you well know that, Mr. Snowden."

Ves Snowden smiled. "I beg your pardon, sir. We didn't realize we were offending the law."

"Hell!" Freddy Snowden said, snorting with contempt. He'd come back to join his brother once the marshal appeared. "Them badges there ain't the law in Three Mile. The law in Three Mile lives in that big house yonder on the hill. And you know it." Freddy Snowden looked around at the watching people and grinned. "Hell, he knows it *real* good the days that Flanagan sends him his little payments to keep him good and obedient! Of course, he can't own up to that. No, no. Wouldn't look good. So he's got to come out and make a little show like this one every now and then to show he ain't afraid of no Flanagan men."

"Shut up, Freddy," Snowden snapped. "You keep yapping and you'll find yourself answering to Flanagan."

Dungooden said, "Mr. Flanagan is an important man in this town, no doubt about it. But, number one, sir, he ain't the law. Number two, he ain't bought the law in this town, whatever you might say. And number three, you'll not make such a parade of arms as this in the future, any of you . . . you understand?"

Snowden, smiling slightly and exuding an air of contempt, touched his hat in salute and said nothing. But he turned to his brother and said, "Mount up, Freddy." Then to all his band: "Boot the rifles, gentlemen. We don't want to make the good marshal nervous. Might give him a case of the running bowels and offend that pretty new bride of his."

A disdainful, forced laugh ran down the line of riders. Dungooden, backed by his two deputies, didn't react to the derision. "I appreciate your cooperation, Mr. Snowden," he said, holding Snowden's gaze without even a blink.

Snowden and his riders moved on down the street as before, soon winding around a bend and up in the direction of Flanagan's mansion.

Kane, who had grown tense as a stretched wire during the confrontation, let out a slow breath and relaxed.

The sensation he had experienced earlier, the realization of what was odd about this town, came to mind again.

It was simple: This town had about it an ambience excessively rich in tension. On every face were lines of worry, in every movement of almost every person was edginess far beyond the norm. The atmosphere in this high mountain town was polluted by something more than smelter discharge and chimney smoke.

The crowd dispersed. Kane stepped off the boardwalk, waited for a clearing in the traffic, and crossed to the cafe.

The flapjacks were as good as promised, but Kane hardly tasted, much less enjoyed, them. The high-strung atmosphere of this overgrown mining camp had gotten to him.

He'd read in that reprinted newspaper story about the miners' complaints. Most seemed legitimate: lower-than-average wages at the Flanagan Hill Mine, poor safety, overly long hours, lack of medical insurance in a dangerous job.

The story had hinted at other complaints, too, though it had cautiously avoided going any farther than hinting. The impression was strong that some miners believed that some of the earliest agitators for the strike had come to a bad end in a mining accident that wasn't really an accident at all. They also believed that Yancey

Tobin, who had emerged as the strike's true leader, had survived at least three attempts on his life.

Kane remembered the man he'd seen coming out of the newspaper office. Guarded. Yancey Tobin? It could be.

He finished his meal and decided to head back to his rented bed and retire early. He was weary and eager to get this anxious day behind him.

He hoped he could find his father quickly and easily, that the meeting would go well, and that soon he could leave this place—if he was lucky, in the company of William Porterfell.

Chapter 12

When Kane rose the next morning, he gathered his possessions from his rented locker and exited the big dormitory flophouse—where he'd spent a surprisingly restful night despite the unending chorus of snores that had shaken the ceiling of the place all night long. He was struck in the face by a cold wind as soon as he reached the street.

He looked skyward, watching gray clouds slide across the big sky, and realized that the relatively agreeable weather of late was soon to be a memory. That was a winter sky if ever he had seen one. Snow had fallen in the night, not much of it considering how high in the mountains Three Mile was, but enough to remind him that winter was sweeping in. And as a young man on the move, he didn't welcome it.

He was quite hungry and thinking again of flapjacks, so he headed directly to the nearest cafe and ordered a big plateful, along with cold water. There was no proper syrup to be had here, but there was excellent molasses. He soaked down the slightly overbrowned flapjacks and had a good breakfast indeed. When he was through, he ordered a second plateful, this time with a side order of thick-cut bacon.

He left the cafe strengthened and energetic and with a mind toward finding a more permanent place to stay. Just what he would do after that he wasn't sure. He had to find his father somehow, but he was still determined to stay away from Eiler Flanagan and his men.

He happened to look beyond the upper line of the opposite row of buildings, and when he did, he saw something he hadn't noticed the day before. High on the mountainside, looming in the gray atmosphere and quite visible because of the fresh snow, was a gathering of buildings, surrounded by heaps of rock and rubble. A mine, and a very big one. This was the Flanagan Hill Mine itself, the huge and successful silver producer that was the heartbeat of Three Mile. But it was a stilled heartbeat at present. Except for a crowd of men milling about the outer edges of the grounds, he saw no movement, no sign of work. The men, he figured, were miners, picketing around the perimeters to show their solidarity. He watched them for a few moments, then turned his attention back to his more immediate surroundings.

For an hour Kane simply walked around, getting his bearings in this unplanned, haphazard town, learning which alley led to which street, where the best-looking cafes and shops could be found, and watching all the while for signs advertising rooms for rent. There were quite a lot of them, and Kane called on a few . . . only to have the odd experience of discovering that none of them, despite their advertisements outside, had rooms to rent to him.

His good mood suffered a fast, intense illness and died. He glanced at his handsome but Indian-looking reflection in a storefront window and knew why he was being rebuffed.

It wasn't fair, being denied lodging just because he had too much Cherokee blood in him to suit this landlord or that. And as he dwelled on it, a thought came that was shameful but that would not leave him: *I wish both my mother and father had been white. I wish I had no Indian blood at all, so that people would treat me like a man instead of an unwanted human cur. I'm sorry, Toko, but that's how I feel right now.*

This bitter thought was still running through his mind when he heard a loud, oratorical voice, reflected off the false front of a miners' goods store directly across from him. He listened, trying to understand the words. All he could make out was the name of Eiler Flanagan, repeated several times through an otherwise unintelligible but angry-sounding discourse.

Kane wandered around the corner and saw a tall, bearded man standing on a crate, speaking to a clump of other men around him. They looked like miners, and Kane noted that each wore a red armband, just like the rowdy group of young men who had faced off with Flanagan's riders the day before. This group was reacting quite vocally and favorably to the venomous-sounding words of the speaker.

Kane wondered if the red armbands served as badges for the strikers. He hadn't noticed any such band on the arm of the man he thought might be Yancey Tobin.

Kane went to the back of the crowd and listened to the speaker.

The man was lambasting the name of Eiler Flanagan, calling him a tyrant, a murderer, an arrogant waster of human lives. It sounded much like the diatribe Kane had heard from Pete Rampling. The more the man went on and the more the crowd indicated its support, the more angry he seemed to grow, the more virulent in his invective. Kane began to feel alarmed as he realized that this fellow was advocating outright armed rebellion of every miner in Three Mile, even the small independents and those affiliated with some of the lesser, nonstriking mines. When the man, apparently quite serious, then put forth the idea of attacking Flanagan's very house and burning the place to the ground, the men with the red armbands cheered and threw their hats to the sky.

Now Kane understood even better why the term "war" was being so widely used in referring to this strike.

The speaker stopped suddenly in the midst of a new tirade and gazed over the heads of his listeners. Kane looked in the same direction and saw another, smaller group of men approaching. For a moment he feared it was some of Flanagan's private gunmen, because those on the outer edges of the group were heavily armed. In the midst of them, however, was the same mustached man he'd seen leaving the newspaper office. Judging from the way he was guarded and the sudden silence his presence brought to the men in the armbands, Kane figured he must be someone of importance. The mustached man wore no armband, nor did his guards.

A tense conversation ensued between the speaker and the auburn-haired newcomer, who spoke with a musical Irish brogue. As the exchange progressed, it grew more spirited, but only on the part of the already worked-up man on the crate. The other fellow kept much more calm, which seemed only to further rile the original speaker.

At last the speaker threw up his arms, shook his head, and said, "Very well, then! If you think what I've been saying is so unreasonable, then you take my place and see what kind of case you can make, Tobin!"

Kane took another look at the auburn-haired man. So it *was* Yancey Tobin himself, leader of the strike against the Flanagan Hill Mine.

Tobin agreed to the speaking invitation, though some of his guards were distressed by this. "Don't get up on that crate, Yancey," one said. "You'd make an easier target."

But Tobin got onto the crate anyway and began to speak directly to the faction in the armbands. Meanwhile, his guards kept their eyes in constant motion, studying every person on the street around them, even scanning rooftops and windows.

They honestly fear he's going to be shot down by some sniper, Kane thought.

Tobin, however, seemed unworried, his words flowing easily and without strain, obviously the product of an intelligent mind. He talked of restraint, of waiting, of avoiding violence, of not playing into the hands of Eiler Flanagan by taking an extremist approach to what should be a civilized, ordered negotiation between two sides of a troublesome issue.

His words, which struck Kane as well reasoned, did not get a good reaction from the men in the armbands. Some disagreed quite vocally, but with a certain deferential tone that revealed that Tobin was respected even when his views weren't.

Other men, however, who had joined the group after Tobin showed up—men without armbands—clapped and shouted their support of Tobin's moderate words.

Tobin was interrupted less by the armbanded miners than by his own persistent cough. Several times he was forced to cut off a sentence to hack, and each hack brought a look of pain to his face that he tried without success to hide. Kane realized he was looking at a very ill man who was doing his best not to show it.

Despite the distraction of Tobin's cough, Kane grew caught up in his words. The man had a charisma that could not be denied; it was not surprising that he had risen to leadership.

From Tobin's words Kane put together a picture of the situation. Tobin was the heart and soul of the strike, the man who symbolized the miners' effort and who—judging from the bodyguards—was most personally endangered by it. But he was also a temperate man, seeking peace over strife and a negotiated resolution to the affair. Others, clearly, were less peaceably minded; a more radical faction of strikers had developed, advocating violence against Flanagan and his hooligans. And this group, obviously, identified itself by means of red armbands.

Kane stood listening for a few minutes longer but decided at last to move on. Interesting as the affair was, it wasn't his. His immediate business was to find a place to lodge that was better than the human warehouse he'd stayed in the previous night. After that, he had to figure out how best to go about finding his father, short of presenting himself at Flanagan's door.

Turning away from the now sizable crowd of listeners, Kane gave out a few coughs of his own, lingering symptoms of his lung-searing experience in the Dodge City fire, and began walking down the street, swinging his carpetbag and looking for other signs advertising lodging. Surely someone in this town was willing to rent a room to a tenant regardless of his complexion and heritage!

Kane had gone only a block before he realized that he hadn't left the impromptu rally alone.

Someone was following him, and closing in on him by the moment.

"All right. Let's have it."

The words were Kane's, spoken in the face of the man who'd trailed him. Kane had timed out the man's pace, stepped into a recessed doorway, and at just the right moment stepped out again to cut him off.

The follower, surprised, gasped and stepped back a couple of yards, eyes wide.

Kane looked at the fellow, who was about his own age . . . and very familiar.

"Tsani? Is it you?"

The other nodded and sighed. "Kanati, you scared the life out of me, stepping out that way!"

"You had me a bit worried myself!" Kane replied. "I couldn't figure out why you were following me. Tsani, I can hardly believe it! You're the last person I'd have expected to see!"

"I live here now, Kane. Me and Aganstati both." He lowered his voice a little. "But we're not Tsani and Aganstati now. I go by John, and Aganstati is Stanton. We use the last name of Ridge, and as far as anyone here knows, we're nothing but white men."

Kane examined this man, whom last he had seen when they were youths together, along with Tsani's older brother, Aganstati, in the Cherokee section of the Indian Nations. It wasn't surprising that the pair could pass themselves off as white men. There was obviously a substantial white bloodline in both of them, and both were sufficiently white of skin and Caucasian of features to be perceived by any unknowledgeable soul as white.

Tsani, or John Ridge, went on. "I saw you standing in the crowd. It took me a while to persuade myself that it was really you. But it is! I'm amazed to see you here."

"What are you and Aganstati . . . Stanton . . . doing in Three Mile?"

"We're miners. We have a little claim of our own, that way." He pointed southwest. "A cabin there, not much, but we've got enough of a strike to get by, and better yet that we'll still find. I feel sure of it."

Kane noticed, but did not comment on, the tremendous strides that Tsani had made in speaking English since he'd last seen him. "So you're not part of the strike."

"No, not directly. We're independents. But I support the strikers. Very much. But I'm not a Yancey Tobin man. He's too soft. I support the Red Bands. But tell me what *you're* doing here. Are you planning to be a miner?"

"No. Not me. I'm looking for someone. It's a long story." And one, Kane thought, that he wasn't sure it would be prudent to tell in full.

"Where are you living?"

"Nowhere, really. I was looking for a room."

"You don't need to look farther. Come with me, Kane. I've got a wagon parked over there, with some supplies. You can stay with Stanton and me."

Kane didn't have to think long about that invitation. He grinned. "Thank you, Tsani—John, I mean. You'll have to pardon me. It'll take me some time to get used to calling you and Aganstati by different names."

"Just as long as you don't let it slip in front of the population here. We want nothing known about what we really are."

"Are you ashamed to be Cherokee?"

John Ridge's gaze broke with Kane's. He looked across the street. "I don't like to think of it that way. I think of it as facing the world the way it is. And there's no good place for an Indian in a white man's country."

Kane thought about the rebuffs he'd just received from half a dozen potential landlords. "You're right, I suppose. I've been turned away just now from several different rooms. And I know why."

"You may be only half Cherokee, but in the eyes of whites, that's the only half that matters," John Ridge said. His bitterness, though veiled, still came through.

"Come on. Let's get on. Stanton will be as happy to see you as I am."

"It won't hurt your reputation, having an Indian staying with you?"

"Do I detect a cutting edge in those words, Kane?"

"I don't know. Maybe."

"Well, I'll overlook it. We do what we have to do to survive. Come on. There's the wagon."

Chapter 13

"We got our grubstake the hard way," John Ridge said. Candlelight from the table bearing the remnants of a simple but much enjoyed meal flickered its glow against his face. Outside, a bitterly cold wind howled, and new snow was falling. "We worked for it, raising and selling cattle. When we finally had enough, we came here—on horseback, not even wanting to spend money for a train—and made a little more getting-started money by selling the horses, our saddles, pretty much everything we had. Stanton took a job at the smelter for a time, while I started exploring for a spot to claim.

"I finally found one, and we posted our claim. We used the money that we had left, plus what Stanton earned at the smelter, to buy two donkeys and some tools. We started digging. Four dry holes before we finally made contact! But it was a good contact, assaying out at a decent enough level, so Stanton quit his smelter job and we went to work on our claim full time. We began running drifts in two directions about a hundred feet down.

"We worked the simplest way at first, using the donkeys and a gallows over the mine—the old rope-and-pulley method. As we began to make some money, we put in a whim so we could get better use of the donkeys. And we put in this cabin. To begin with, we lived in a tent. Next thing we'll do is shelter the entrance of the shaft, which, frankly, is something we should probably have done before now."

"Did you ever think of working for one of the big mines, like Flanagan Hill?"

"We considered it when we first came here but decided against it. Our idea had always been to have a mine of our own, not to labor ourselves to death just to line the pockets of someone like Eiler Flanagan."

"And we've been grateful a thousand times over that we decided what we did," Stanton threw in. "The Flanagan Hill Mine has claimed more lives than a plague."

"That's one of the complaints of the strikers, isn't it? Poor safety?"

"Yes. And too low wages, and a tendency for those who die in Flanagan Hill to just happen to be the same ones who complain a little too much, or say something bad about Eiler Flanagan. It's just amazing! Keep your mouth shut, ignore the risks, act like some deaf, dumb, and mute little underling who'll do what he's told with no questions asked, and you can make it at Flanagan Hill. Otherwise, you can wind up gone . . . one way or another."

"Are you telling me that Eiler Flanagan is a killer?"

"Directly or indirectly, he is. He may not be the one who makes the decision—sometimes it may be the mine boss who has a grudge against somebody, and that somebody winds up down a hole or crushed under timber or stone—but in the end, it's Flanagan."

"Don't forget about Sally Josephs," Stanton said to his brother.

"Oh, yes. There's a good case for you, one that shows you just what this strike is really all about. There was a miner, a friend of Stanton and me, just a simple fellow named Jack Josephs, who had a pretty wife. Eiler Flanagan made no secret of wanting her for himself. So Jack Josephs winds up killed at the base of a shaft by a falling bucket, and who shows up to 'comfort' the widow but Eiler Flanagan himself. He all but tried to take her home with him from the burying! It was a sickening thing to see."

"What happened?"

Stanton answered that one. "She spat on him. Right in front of everyone gathered for the burial. And she said that her husband was dead because of Eiler Flanagan's mine. Then she packed her bags and left town."

"That's right," John said. "And then the report came back that she was caught by some 'ruffians' at a train station in western Kansas and beaten, robbed. And worse."

"Flanagan was behind it?"

"You don't make Eiler Flanagan look a fool and not pay for it. That's why Yancey Tobin has to have bodyguards."

"What about the man talking on the crate today? He was implying that Flanagan ought to have his house burned down around him. That's a lot more severe than anything I heard Yancey Tobin say."

Stanton said, "That was Caleb Creede. He's the one behind the Red Bands—the ones with the red armbands. He's bold, and I admire that—but he'll not survive, I'm afraid. The Red Bands are a new group, a smaller clan within the overall group of strikers, and I don't think Flanagan really understands yet what they're advocating. When he does, wait and see if Caleb Creede doesn't wind up mysteriously missing. Or maybe has an 'accident' that no one happens to see. That kind of thing is Flanagan's style."

"That's right," John said. "Just take Pat Tobin. Yancey's older brother. He was the first to start talking up the strike idea. He died alone, outside of town, in a wagon accident. No one to witness it. The odd thing was, it wasn't his wagon. It was Flanagan's."

"And then Yancey took over?"

"That's right."

Kane puzzled it over. "After his own brother being killed, you'd think that he would have been out for blood."

"Any sensible man would," John replied bitterly. "But Tobin isn't sensible."

"I wouldn't say that," Stanton cut in. "Yancey Tobin is a religious man. A Roman Catholic, like most of the Irish-born miners, but much more devoted than most. It was him who wrote the letters and made the pleas that finally brought a Catholic priest to Three Mile. Tobin is loyal to his beliefs and principles. He believes in forgiveness and patience and the gentle approach. Which is why the hotter-headed strikers get impatient with him." He glanced at John. "Not to mention my revenge-minded brother."

"Tobin struck me as a reasonable man," Kane commented.

"Reasonable men wind up dead when it's Eiler Flanagan they're dealing with," John said.

"And unreasonable ones, too. You wait until Flanagan gets Caleb Creede assassinated," Stanton said. "That will either end the Red Bands or bolster them. I'd wager the latter. I think a lot of Yancey's moderate strikers will go over to the Red Band side if Flanagan begins to kill off the strike leaders."

"But how could Flanagan think he could do such a thing and not end up being brought down by it in the end?"

John Ridge aimed a finger at Kane. "Eiler Flanagan believes he's invincible. He believes he's his own law, his own God, his own judge, jury, and executioner. And it *will* bring him down in the end. He just has too much arrogance to understand that."

"But there's law in Three Mile. That marshal named Dungooden . . ."

John Ridge gave a loud, disdainful grunt. "Dungooden is no threat to Flanagan, believe me."

"Why not?

"Because the law here has been bought," Stanton said. "Eiler Flanagan has Dungooden on a string, and everybody knows it. Dungooden tries to cover it by putting on little shows of authority when Flanagan's men get too unruly, but it's all false. A joke. Flanagan's men have taken to mocking him in public—they don't even try to hide the fact that their boss has bought Dungooden out."

Kane was ready to leave this topic. The idea of his father being affiliated with such a beast as Flanagan was making him very uncomfortable.

He slapped on a grin and changed the subject. "I've got to tell both of you," he said, "that I'm amazed at how well you speak English now. You sound like any white man."

John smiled. "Well, perhaps we should tell you that you're the inspiration for us on that score."

"Me?"

"That's right," Stanton said. "It was watching you through the years, seeing how your mother made sure you spoke English well, knew how to read, that made us begin to think we should stop being Cherokee and become more like the white men . . . like you."

Kane felt something twist inside. "What do you mean, like me, Tsani?"

"I'm John! John! Not Tsani. I don't use my Cherokee name anymore, even in private."

"I'm sorry. John, don't take this the wrong way, but I'm not sure I like hearing that you've used me as a model of how not to be what you were born to be. Toko always used to say, 'A man should not deny the blood the Great Creator put in his veins.' " But Kane's own words stung him even as he spoke them, because he abruptly recalled his own recent thoughts about the undesirability of a Cherokee heritage in a world run by white men.

John Ridge shook his head solemnly. "When it's Cherokee blood that the Great Creator has put in your veins, there's little to be thankful for, Kane. Not in a land where a man with skin colored anything but white has ten obstacles thrown in his way every time he tries to take a step forward."

"But surely it's not right, throwing away everything you are."

"Not everything we *are*," Stanton said, with surprising force. "Everything we *used* to be. And never will be again. I'm a white man now. So is John. We have a *chance* as white men."

"But a lot of Indians, of all kinds, have done well for themselves, and as what and who they really are, not as some kind of imitation white men."

"And many more haven't done well," John said.

"Yes," Stanton cut in. "And even those who have succeeded on their own terms are never seen as men who have done well. No, they're always *Indians* who have done well. Always different. Always set apart. Always, in the end, rejected and left out."

Kane didn't know what to say. He stood and said, "I'm tired. I think I'll go to bed now."

"I was hoping you'd tell us exactly what's brought you to Three Mile," John said.

"Maybe tomorrow." Kane pushed his chair back in place and headed for the pallet that had already been laid for him in the light of the hearth.

That night Kane dreamed he was a child and old Toko was searching for him, looking none too happy. In the dream Kane tried to hide, but everyplace he went, Toko was there, finding him in the end and frowning at him.

Kane awakened to bustling sounds going on around him. He opened his eyes and saw Stanton Ridge leaning over in an uncomfortable position, trying to cook something at the fire and hardly able to do it because Kane was in the way. Kane sat up.

"Here, Aganstati . . . I mean, Stanton. Let me get out of the way."

"No need, Kane. You go ahead and sleep. John and I start early, but since you're not mining, there's no reason you should have to."

But Kane did get up, and Stanton clearly was happy to have better access to the fire. Kane folded his pallet and put it in the corner, then looked out the window at the snow-blanketed landscape. From the Ridge cabin the town was visible, and with snow covering its worst warts, it was actually a pretty sight. Kane watched the smoke of hundreds of chimneys belching skyward, then let the curtain fall.

Bacon sizzled enticingly on the fire. Kane washed himself in a common bucket in the far corner and put on some of the new clothing that Ben Flanagan had given him. Out of the corner of his eye he noticed the Ridge brothers eyeing his clothes and wondered how they would react if they learned that those garments had come to him courtesy of the brother of the hated Eiler Flanagan. Perhaps they would learn it. He'd already decided to tell at least some of his story to the Ridges. Just how much was something he would determine as he went along.

Breakfast was a wonderful experience, as always on a cold and wintry day. When the last crumb was gone, Kane looked at the brothers and announced, "I'm in Three Mile to find William Porterfell, my father."

Two confused frowns met his words. "Kane," said Stanton, "your father is dead . . . isn't he?"

"So I thought all my life, until lately. He's not dead. And as best I know, he's in this town."

"But if he's alive, why did you not know it, growing up? We all grew up believing he was dead."

"I didn't know because, I suppose, he didn't want me to know."

"Does your mother know?"

"My mother's dead."

"What? When?"

"Recently. And no, I don't think she knew. I never was able to ask her. She died before I could."

"I'm sorry she's dead. I always loved your mother. Illness?"

Kane looked them in the eye. "Murder."

A stunned silence. Then Stanton asked, "Who?"

"Some men. White men."

"But why?"

Kane was finding this harder than he'd anticipated. He looked away, blinking, thinking that this wasn't really the best way to have started off a day. "Maybe we'll talk about it more later."

"Do you know exactly where to find your father?"

Kane debated. Should he go ahead and tell them that his father, as best he knew, was a hired gun for the most wicked man in Three Mile? Knowing what these two thought of Eiler Flanagan, he simply couldn't. "I don't know exactly, no. So I suppose I'll just do some general searching, you know. Asking questions, looking around. Somebody is sure to know him."

"I can't quite picture your father being alive," John said. "Will you know him when you see him?"

"No," Kane admitted.

"Will he know you?"

"How could he know me? He's never seen me in all my life." Kane was surprised by the bitterness in his own voice.

"Then . . . how will you know when you find him?"

Kane shrugged.

"Is there anyone in town who could help you?"

There was, and he lived in a mansion, embroiled in a strike against his mine, and from all Kane was hearing, he was the devil himself and a man Kane still had no ambition to meet—not yet, anyway. "I'll find someone," he said. "I'll begin looking tomorrow. Somebody is bound to know William Porterfell."

The next day, after three hours of idly wandering through the town and having no luck at all, Kane was about to head back to the Ridge cabin in disgust when trouble suddenly found him.

"You!" a voice called. "Hold up there!"

Kane turned. Two armed men from the same little gaggle of Flanagan riders he'd seen before were striding toward him. Instinctively he began to back off from them.

"What do you want?" Kane asked.

"Is your name Porterfell?"

"Why would you want to know my name?"

"It *is* him!" one man said to the other. "Grab him!"

Kane, though piqued with curiosity about why Flanagan's men would be looking for him and wondering if this had something to do with his father, wasn't in the mood to be grabbed. He ran back through the alley, turned left at the end, and circled the rear of a building, dodging garbage, almost tripping over a pile of discarded lumber. A fence rose before him. He leaped for the top of it and was about to swing over when the weak structure gave way beneath his weight and collapsed. He fell amid splinters and shards. He looked back and saw one of the men round the corner.

"Hey! You, there, redskin! Stop!"

Kane got up and ran on, across the opposite side of the fence, which did not, he was thankful, collapse like the first one. He reached a hillock, rugged and rocky, covered with scraggly growth. He scrambled into the thick of it, hoping to break through quickly while his pursuers struggled with the fence.

It didn't work out that way. One of the Flanagan men, the smaller and more athletic of the pair, had pulled far ahead of his companion. He came over the fence with ease. As for Kane, he was snatched and caught by branches and briars, so that when he at last emerged on the other side of the hillock, his pursuer was already making his way through, and doing a better job of it than Kane had. And the slower one was beginning to catch up.

Kane ran into a cluster of sheds and tents and tried to

lose himself. He saw a row of buildings ahead, their backs facing him. He headed for an alley.

His pursuers broke through the thicket and paused, looking around.

"Where'd he go?"

"Hell, I don't know. You got through first—didn't you see him?"

"No."

The other looked around. "Well, we've lost him. He could have run in any direction from here."

"Too bad. Flanagan might have rewarded us if we'd been the ones to catch him."

"I still can't figure what Flanagan wants with a sorry half-breed."

"Same thing he wanted with his daddy, I suppose, whatever that was. I reckon it's Flanagan's business, not mine. All I do is my job."

The pair looked around for a few minutes more, then turned and walked back the way they'd come. This time they rounded the thicketed hillock rather than taking the shorter but more difficult route straight through it.

Kane waited a full five minutes before he came out of his hiding place. He climbed slowly down the same gutter pipe he'd used as a ladder to the nearest flat roof, where he'd lain on his belly and watched his pursuers trying to find him.

And he'd listened. He'd heard everything they said, and though it mystified and troubled him, it also allowed him to surmise certain things. First, it was clear that Pete Rampling had spilled the truth when he was questioned in the Flanagan house, so Flanagan knew that

Kane really was in Three Mile. Second, it showed that Flanagan had some interest of his own in Kane and Bill Porterfell. What was at work here was not some kind-hearted desire to unite a long-separated father and son.

Kane headed for one of the nearby sheds and went inside. Seated in the cold semidarkness atop a stack of firewood, he thought hard about this strange situation. He'd escaped from Robert Blessed—for good, if he was lucky—but now someone else was after him. Someone far more powerful than Blessed.

With Blessed he'd at least understood why he was being pursued. Not so with Eiler Flanagan.

When he was sure he was safe, Kane rose and left the shed. Carefully he walked up an alley to the street. He pulled his collar up and kept his face down as he headed back out of town. He would stay clear of Three Mile for a day or two. Maybe longer. With Flanagan's men on the lookout for him, it was simply too unsafe to show himself.

John and Stanton Ridge didn't know it yet, but they were about to gain a new mining assistant, free of charge.

Chapter 14

In all his life, Kane had never done harder labor.

The monotony of it was the worst part. All of it became a steady, unending rhythm, from the slow, relentless jolting of picks against rock and dirt, to the persistent creak of the pulley as the big bucket of earth and ore went up and down, again and again.

After only a day of labor, Kane knew that the last thing he ever wanted to be was a miner.

The second day, to his surprise, was better, though his muscles were incredibly sore. He found in the very mundaneness of the work a certain comfort. A man could labor in this way and let the hours roll past unnoticed, his mind concentrating on the immediate goal, problems and fears ceasing to matter.

But it was never fully so for Kane. He knew he was wasting time, avoiding rather than dealing with the situation that faced him. Though he didn't discuss with the Ridge brothers what had happened in town, every moment, in the back of his mind, he puzzled over his confusing situation.

At the heart of his puzzlement was the mystery of Eiler Flanagan's obvious interest in him. He couldn't make sense of it.

It should have been simple: Eiler Flanagan, who happens to have in his hire William Porterfell, receives a wire from his brother saying that Porterfell's son wishes to come see his father, unannounced. Eiler Flanagan replies that this is all quite fine, and as a gesture of kindness to his brother agrees to have someone meet the visiting son at the station. This is done, but the visiting son doesn't show up, sending instead a message that he will not be coming after all. At this point, it seemed to Kane, the expected response would be for Flanagan to simply say well and good, and the entire matter be forgotten.

But it hadn't worked out that way. The delegates who had been sent to meet Kane at the station hadn't been mere servants, but hard-eyed hired gunmen. The message Kane had sent to them via Rampling hadn't generated the expected shrug, but a capture and interrogation for Rampling. And now, Flanagan's hired guns had obviously been told to be on the lookout for a young Indian-looking man in Three Mile. And they'd come awfully close to catching him.

It terrified Kane. So he hid here in this mine and labored, and tried to lose himself in work and the conversations of the Ridge brothers.

He didn't like this hiding out but didn't know what else to do. And making it harder to endure was an entirely unrelated matter, one he tried to ignore as irrelevant but that increasingly galled him as time went by.

That was the thorough, almost eager way the Ridge brothers hid and denied, even to themselves, the fact that they were Cherokee. In one way, Kane had to admire the skill they exhibited in this exercise. Physically, they'd always been light-skinned enough to potentially pass for white men, but until now they'd never tried to do it. They'd always talked, acted, and thought like the other young Cherokees among whom Kane had grown up.

No more. They'd worked hard to drive any Cherokee dialect out of their speech. No use of the Cherokee language took place in their cabin or about their mine. They refused to talk with Kane of their common past except in the most minimal way, and then with eyes shifting and voices lowered, as if they feared there were spies all about, ready to reveal the terrible secret that they were *Indians*! Even their thought patterns seemed altered; the Ridge brothers were trying their best not only to pose as white men, but to actually *be* white men.

Three days after he'd begun working with the Ridges, Kane found opportunity to discuss this matter. It was the end of a long, difficult day that had been devoted to starting a new drift at the base of the shaft. They'd encountered some very hard stone and had made much less progress than they'd hoped, leading Stanton to make an unexpected comment about packing up and heading back to the Nations and forgetting this business of trying to gouge a living out of the reluctant earth.

As the three walked through the dusk, stretching

their cramped and overworked muscles, Kane asked Stanton about what he'd said.

"Would you really ever go back to the Nations? And to being . . . what you were?" He was shamed to realize he'd just found himself unwilling to use the word "Cherokee."

Stanton frowned. "No. No, I wouldn't."

"Why?"

"Because an Indian is an Indian. A white man is a . . . a man. I'm sorry to say that, but it's true."

"Aren't Indians men?"

"Not the same kind of men as whites. You have to face the truth, Kane. For generations the white men and the Indians fought over this land, and the whites have won. It's their land now, and they intend to keep the best of it for themselves. You can rage and rant against it and declare yourself proud of who you are, like your old friend Toko loved to do, but the fact is that as long as you keep yourself an Indian, that's all you'll ever be—an Indian. A piece of half-human refuse to be hidden away like an animal on some reservation, despised and left out of the best of life. An Indian has little hope in this nation, Kane. That's why you should be grateful for the white blood that's in you. And why John and I are grateful for the lightness of our skins."

Kane frowned, hating these words and hating even more that he couldn't bring himself to fully disagree with them.

"You don't think I'm right, I can see."

"I don't like what you say."

"That's old Toko talking in you. You spent too much time listening to his old-man ideas."

"Toko wasn't what you think. He understood that a man has to live in the world as it is. He believed that my mother was right to make sure I could read and write in the English tongue and that when I spoke English, I could speak it like the white men do. But he also believed a man should admit who and what he is and be proud of it."

"And what became of him? He died an old Indian who was no more than an Indian, owning just a little house, a few trinkets."

"He had his pride."

"A man can starve on his pride. A man can live like an animal on his pride."

Kane felt a rush of anger—the memory and legacy of Toko were precious to him, and he didn't like the deprecation in Stanton's words—but the conversation was suddenly cut short when John Ridge frowned, pointed to the southeast, and said, "What is that?"

The others, too, had seen what he had: a small group of men were moving through the woods at a fast pace, three on horseback, and in the midst of them, one on foot, struggling to keep pace.

"It looks to me like—"

"Quiet!" Kane demanded in a sharp whisper. "Quiet . . . and back away, behind those trees."

John, whispering, said, "Who are they, Kane?"

"Some of Eiler Flanagan's riders. I recognize them

from town. And the man with them has a flour sack over his head and his hands tied behind him."

Kane always had possessed better eyes than his peers. His description was already complete, and the others were only just now making out the details he'd reported. Kane was right. These were Flanagan men, and their treatment of the man with them did not bode well for his future.

Stanton Ridge declared, "They're going to kill that man!"

Kane shook his head. "No, they're not. We're not going to let them."

"What do you have in mind, Kane?"

Before Kane could answer, John Ridge tensed and said, "They've just seen us."

The riders had come to a stop and were staring up through the trees at them. The impression was that they hadn't realized they were in a mined and inhabited area. What they'd come for was surely not intended for observing eyes.

"They're stuck now," John Ridge said softly. "We've seen the blindfolded man and they know that we know what they're up to—and they're wondering what to do about it."

The riders talked among themselves, just as the Ridges and Kane were doing, and two of them began moving up the slope toward the miners. They were armed.

"Aganstati, where are the rifles?" John Ridge asked—in *Cherokee*, Kane noted with surprise, and using Stanton's real name. The tension of the moment, Kane figured. At such a time as this, a man revealed himself as what he was, not what he pretended to be.

"Right there, leaned against the shed," Stanton replied, in English.

"Let's fetch them," John said, making off in that direction as he spoke.

Kane still had the pistol and under-coat holster he'd bought in Dodge. Though for comfort's sake he'd not worn the pistol while working in the mine, he always strapped it back on after they decided to call it quits for the day.

Kane reached under his coat for his pistol just as the closer of the two oncoming riders hollered at the Ridge brothers to halt, and the second dropped the reins of his horse and raised the Winchester repeater he carried.

Kane let out a yell, warning the Ridge brothers. John turned his head and saw the rider about to shoot, reached out, and pushed Stanton aside as the rifle blasted. The bullet sailed by harmlessly.

The rider came closer, working the lever.

The other rider, meanwhile, yelled again for the Ridges to halt and reached for his sidearm.

Kane had his pistol out and cocked by now, and he fired it in the general direction of the first rider. As he did so he realized this was the first time, other than two test-shot firings on a small, enclosed range behind the store where he'd bought the pistol, that he'd shot the weapon.

The rider grunted and grabbed at his forearm, dropping the pistol he'd drawn. Kane gaped, unable to believe his barely aimed shot had been so well placed.

The rider with the rifle fired again, this time at Kane. The bullet spanked into the trunk of a tree beside Kane, who reflexively pulled away, turned, and sank to the ground. He cocked his pistol again and fired at the rifleman. The bullet went wide, but it did cause the rider to pull to a halt, dismount, and take to hiding in a clump of trees.

Kane moved behind the nearest ample tree himself, trying to shake off a mounting sense of unreality. Was he really in the midst of a gun battle? How could this be? He'd just spent a day laboring in a mine, hiding away from danger and troubles—and yet here he was.

And down the slope, there *they* were, the lone rider who had remained below to guard the blinded prisoner and the prisoner himself—no longer blindfolded. Kane was stunned to see that the man had somehow shrugged free of his bonds—though the loose ropes still encircled his wrists and arms—had pulled away the flour-sack blindfold, and was now struggling for all he was worth with the man who was to have guarded him. The man had lost his weapon and was about to lose his seat in the saddle because of the prisoner's fierce struggles. His body hung at an odd angle, his horse moving beneath him and nickering.

The man whose face had been unveiled when the flour sack came off was Yancey Tobin.

The dismounted rider hiding in the trees took a shot at Kane, but the Ridge brothers, now armed and behind cover, fired back. The gunman lost his spirit for battle very fast, especially when all the gunfire caused his riderless horse to bolt down the slope. Kane watched the man make off through the woods, keeping as much cover between himself and his enemies as he could. In moments he was out of range and off looking for his horse, leaving his two companions to deal with these troublesome, intrusive, bullet-slinging miners on their own.

Yancey Tobin finally succeeded in getting his foe out of the saddle. Once down, however, the man was free to struggle a bit more effectively, and Tobin suddenly had his hands full. An unfortunately timed fit of coughing also struck the Irishman, and in moments his former guard had the advantage and was laying some painful blows on Tobin's supine body.

Stanton Ridge raised his rifle and fired. The bullet caught Tobin's antagonist in the calf and drove him down. Tobin got up and scrambled away, still coughing terribly.

The wounded man down the slope came up and began hopping, stumbling, limping away. He went over a little rise and was gone.

Only one Flanagan rider remained now, and as he realized his situation, he turned his horse and headed back down the slope. The Ridge brothers fired at him, but not really, Kane realized. Their shots were going high, ripping the evergreen treetops, intended not to strike the man, but to frighten him off.

Tobin, still coughing, was suddenly caught in the fleeing rider's path. Kane anticipated that the man would pass Tobin by in his eagerness to get away, but that didn't happen. The fellow guided his horse right at Tobin, knocking him down and trampling him.

Kane jerked as Stanton Ridge's rifle barked to his left.

The rider yelled, let go of his reins as his arms spread spasmodically, and fell from the saddle.

Stanton Ridge's shot had struck him right in the spine, halfway down his back.

The horse, now unencumbered, ran on and was gone.

Kane came out from behind the tree, holstering his pistol as he ran down the slope. Tobin was trying to rise, coughing and groaning and not quite making it.

Kane reached Tobin and knelt beside him. "Are you hurt, sir?"

Between coughs, and with dribbles of blood on his lips, Tobin managed to say he was fine.

The Ridge brothers, meanwhile, reached the fallen rider, who lay moaning, breathing raggedly. Kane left Tobin and joined his friends.

The man lay on his back in a puddle of blood that slowly spread beneath him, being absorbed into the layer of old brown evergreen needles that covered the ground. His chest was also bloody. The bullet had passed clean through him.

The man's eyes shifted from side to side, studying their faces. "I'm dying!" he said. Blood came up as the words came out. He choked and spat and groaned.

John Ridge knelt on the man's opposite side. "Want us to fetch you a doctor, mister?"

The man tried to reply but couldn't. He was fumbling under his coat. Trying to find his wound, Kane assumed.

Stanton Ridge went to John's side and also knelt. "I'm sorry I shot you so bad, mister."

The man didn't reply. He was looking at Stanton, glaring strangely, his eyes very red and foamy, his moist lips even more so. "You killed me, redskin!"

Stanton was stunned to have been recognized as an Indian when he'd been so confident of his ability to pass himself off as a white man. "I'm not a redskin, I'm a white man," he mumbled in a small, thin voice that wasn't really his own. Kane thought it sounded incredibly pitiful.

The wounded man pulled his hand from beneath his coat and shoved it up, fast. There was an odd kind of thudding noise, and Stanton grunted strangely. The man grinned, relaxed, and died on the spot, his hand falling back.

Stanton rose and looked down at his belly. A knife was sticking out of him. Kane gazed at it, watched blood trickle out and down from the place where the blade had entered flesh. He had not even noticed that the dying man had a knife sheathed at his belt. Even if he had noticed, he never would have supposed that in his last moments of fading strength, the man would be able to use it.

"Look at that!" Stanton said, sounding surprised but otherwise unemotional. "He stabbed me!"

John, now risen, stared aghast at the knife in his brother's midsection. Stanton chuckled strangely, terribly, and pointed at it. "He stuck it right in me! And John, he knew I was an Indian. After all we've done to change ourselves, he still was able to tell!"

Stanton went weak and pitched forward into his

brother's arms. He died as John Ridge lowered him to the ground.

Kane stood slowly and stared at the dead bodies at his feet.

Chapter 15

Kane sat by the fire, silently watching John Ridge, who sat slumped beside his brother's bed. On that bed lay the corpse of Stanton Ridge, formerly Aganstati of the Indian Nations.

John Ridge hadn't spoken since he and Kane had laid the body there. He just sat and stared, with Kane off by the fire, watching him.

"I'm so sorry. All this happened because of me," Yancey Tobin said. He was on the opposite side of the fire from Kane, his cough now quieted.

"It wasn't your fault," Kane said quietly.

"But I feel it was," Tobin replied. "If not for the courage and kindness of all of you, intervening on my behalf, this tragedy wouldn't have occurred."

Kane looked at Tobin. "Those gunmen . . . Flanagan's men."

"Yes."

"They were going to kill you."

"Aye, that they were."

"At Flanagan's orders?"

"I have no doubt. The man hates me. I should have

175

been more careful, I suppose. I'd left the company of my protectors, though only for a few minutes. They caught me. I should have realized how closely they were watching." Tobin glanced over at John Ridge. "God forgive me. God forgive me for the loss I've unwittingly brought to this house."

Kane stared into the fire. "I know how you're feeling. There've been people lately who've helped me, and they've paid the same kind of price."

"May I ask your name?"

"Kanati Porterfell. I'm usually called Kane."

"Porterfell? There was a man among Flanagan's riders named Porterfell."

Kane was at full attention. "One of those out there today?"

"No, no. This fellow is no longer with Flanagan. That's why I happen to know his name; he's somewhat famous among my strikers as the one Flanagan hireling who wasn't willing to do the wicked things Flanagan demanded. So he left."

"Was his name William Porterfell?"

"Indeed. You know him?"

"He's my father."

"No!"

"It's true. I came to Three Mile to find him. I'd been told he was still with Flanagan."

"You were told wrong. He was too good a man to continue in such a vile kind of work."

Kane couldn't hold back a smile. The idea that his father could be the kind of man who would maim and threaten and murder for a man such as Eiler Flanagan had bothered him deeply. To know William Porterfell had turned away from it all filled him with an unexpected burst of family pride—a brand-new experience for him.

"I gather you haven't found your father." Tobin coughed again, and winced.

"No . . . do you know where he is?"

"I'm sorry, but no." Another cough, wracking the man's entire body.

"You're sick," Kane said.

"No," replied Tobin. "Nothing to be worried about."

Over beside his brother's bed, John Ridge lowered his head and cried. For ten minutes he wept quietly, with Kane and Tobin sitting uncomfortably, guiltily, and listening.

A little while later, they realized that the weeping had ceased. Kane found that John Ridge, weary with grief, had fallen asleep in his chair, his head hanging and one hand resting on the bed of his slain brother.

John Ridge was the only one who slept that night in the Ridge Cabin. There was potential for danger here. The surviving Flanagan riders might return, bringing with them others. The cabin might be besieged.

Kane and Tobin sat up with rifles, watching and listening. No attack came. At times Tobin coughed terribly, but when Kane asked him about it, he vehemently denied that anything significant was wrong.

John Ridge slept through the night in his chair. When morning came he awakened and stared at the body of his brother, still silent.

Tobin approached him. "I'm very sorry, my friend, for this terrible murder of your brother."

No reply.

"I lost a brother of my own . . . I know the pain."

John Ridge stared at his sibling's unmoving, graying countenance.

"I'll pray for you, and for his soul."

It was as if John Ridge was in another place, cut off and unhearing.

Kane wasn't sure John would hear him either, but he spoke nonetheless. "I'm going to go with Mr. Tobin into town. I'll see him reunited with his guards, and then I'll come back and we'll see to Stanton's burial."

John looked up at Kane and said something, in a whisper and with a trembling chin, that struck Kane as very strange, considering the things the Ridge brothers had said before.

John Ridge spoke in Cherokee: "His name wasn't Stanton. His name was Aganstati."

The morning was misty and peaceful, incongruous with the anxiety Kane felt. He and Tobin paused only a moment beside the dead body of the gunman, who lay where he had fallen. Kane felt his boot toe nudge something and looked down to see the crusted knife that had stabbed away the life of Aganstati. He shuddered.

Tobin knelt at the dead man's side, lowered his head, and whispered words. Kane was stunned to realize he was praying for the fellow. Who would pray for an enemy who had been ready to kill him?

Tobin rose and they moved on, heading down a long,

twisted trail toward the dirty, jumbled town. Neither spoke. Tobin coughed a bit but kept it under control. Kane had the impression that the man had grown skilled at managing that cough, from much practice.

At the edge of town they saw riders coming their way. For a moment there was fear, then relief came when Tobin said, "It's my guards, my own people. Thank God."

Kane and Tobin were swarmed, Tobin receiving emotional greetings, handshakes, embraces, Kane receiving mostly wary, uncertain glances, until Tobin revealed Kane's part in driving away the Flanagan men who had been ready to kill him. After that, Kane enjoyed a reception almost as hearty as Tobin's.

Kane was swept along with the crowd to a house on the other side of Three Mile. It was bigger than many of the town's typical hovels but far smaller than the ominous-looking Flanagan mansion that loomed within view on the hillside, and certainly too small for the number of people who swarmed toward it, Tobin and Kane at their head and center.

Before Kane knew it, he was inside the house and seated at a table on which was spread food and drink. Ruddy, sturdy men, cheerful in their relief at having found Tobin, their beloved leader, spilled out a story of having searched the town and the surrounding countryside all night by torchlight, facing tense moments with Flanagan's riders, seeing, for a few moments, Flanagan himself on his porch with a spyglass as he watched the milling, searching strikers scouring the town. Many a follower of Tobin's moderate strike policy had been ready to turn Red Band and attack the Flanagan house in force, believing that Flanagan's riders had at last killed Tobin. Fortunately the night had passed with no such attack coming, and now, God be praised, Tobin was found again.

Tobin told his own story, and the joyful, relieved mood inside the crowded house changed to one of anger. Tobin described how he'd been taken, tied, blindfolded, and led out of town for a certain execution. Only the intervention of Kane and two other miners had saved his life, though, sadly, at the cost of the life of one of his benefactors.

For Kane's sake, Tobin asked those around him if any knew what had become of William Porterfell, the Flanagan hireling who had turned his back on his employer and since vanished. No one did.

The topic shifted to the strike in general and the conditions that had led to it. Kane listened, ever more enthralled and outraged, to accounts of terrible mine accidents, some of which might not have been accidents at all. He heard stories of terrible safety conditions, of threats against those who dared to protest. He heard of the attractive wives of miners approached by men in Flanagan's hire, who told them clearly that favors shown to Flanagan would result in better working conditions for their husbands but that refusal might generate unspecified "problems." He heard how the husbands of women who did refuse tended to be among those sent to the most dangerous areas of the Flanagan Hill Mine. Several had died.

And last of all, Kane heard Tobin tell of his own late wife, who had died on the porch of this very house. A stray bullet, fired from no one knew where and by no one knew whom. Fired after Tobin had first begun to emerge, in the black bowels of Flanagan Hill, as a man who might be a problem for Eiler Flanagan. A man who spoke for the working men of the mines and dared to breathe the threat of a strike.

When Tobin had finished his story, Kane was looking at the man with awe.

"Your own wife was killed by Flanagan . . . yet you talk of avoiding violence? I would think, sir, that you would be among the Red Bands, ready to burn Flanagan's house to the ground."

"I could never prove that Flanagan was behind my wife's death," Tobin replied. "In my heart I believe he was, but I don't know. There were drunken men firing off their pistols all over town that day, shooting into the air. And the bullet that killed my wife on the porch struck from a high angle. It could have been an accident."

"It was an assassin," muttered one of the others in the room, eliciting a supportive mumble among the rest.

"Assassin or accident, I still believe strongly in the principles of peace. 'Inasmuch as it is in you, live peaceably with all men.' The inspired words of the apostle himself."

"But Flanagan has since then hired an army of gunmen . . . men who murder, who would have murdered *you* yesterday, if by chance you hadn't been brought to where you were."

"There is no such thing as this 'chance' you mention, Mr. Porterfell," Tobin said. "I believe that fully. We live out our lives in a world permeated with design and purpose, including that which seems to us meaningless and random. That is my conviction. And because of that conviction I seek to follow the peaceful and orderly ways. Because there is an order, you see, that underlies all that there is."

Tobin was a philosophical soul, that was obvious, though his words struck Kane as esoteric.

Kane spoke privately to Tobin before he left. "There's two things I want to ask of you," he said. "One is a favor, the other is information."

"You need only ask."

"The favor is for a couple of your men to go back with me to the Ridge cabin and to help me lay my friend to his rest."

"Consider it done. And the information?"

"I want to know if you have any idea why Eiler Flanagan would want to get his hands on me." He briefly described his escape from Flanagan's men on the street a few days before. "Might it have to do with my father?"

"Perhaps," Tobin replied. "Eiler Flanagan is a hateful and vengeful man. It may be that through you he wants to somehow punish your father for deserting him. But I don't know. To have his men chasing you through alleys and thickets seems to me to require a stronger motivation than simple anger at some deserting employee."

Kane shook Tobin's hand and prepared to depart. "I advise you not to remain out in that cabin," Tobin urged him. "If Flanagan is already after you, it will only grow worse now that you've given help to me. Go and get your friend buried, then bring his brother back here.

You can stay in my house, under my guards' protection, both of you."

"Thank you," Kane said. "I'll do that." He wondered, though, if he could ever convince John Ridge to leave his cabin and the mine that was, after all, his source of livelihood.

Kane came out of the cabin and spoke to the two burly guards Tobin had sent to accompany him.

"Stanton Ridge's body is still there, laid out, dressed for burial. But his brother John is gone," Kane announced.

"Do you want us to look for him?"

Kane thought about it, then shook his head. "No. No . . . I suspect he's gone because he wants to be. I suspect he has his reasons."

They buried Aganstati near the cabin and marked the grave with a stone. Kane kept an eye out for John Ridge, hoping he would return, but he did not.

They rode back into Three Mile together and returned to the house of Yancey Tobin.

Kane was given a cot in a room that was so tiny it hardly seemed more than a storage closet, but he was glad for it. Here in Tobin's house, where there were guards all around, he felt protected. But his spirits were low nevertheless. A pervasive sense of hopelessness had descended upon him with the abrupt death of Aganstati.

That night he went to sleep thinking first about John Ridge and where he might have gone, then about his father, wondering where he was right now.

One thing seemed more sure the longer he thought about it: Bill Porterfell probably was not in Three Mile any longer. If there had been trouble and danger for him here, he probably had simply fled. It would fit with his character. Kane knew from his own life experience as a boy who had never laid eyes on his own father, that Bill Porterfell was a man who was expert at running away.

Chapter 16

For two days Kane did not leave Tobin's house. He struggled against depression and fear. He listened to the conversation in the house, heard reports on the status of the strike, of the latest radical assertions of the Red Bands, of Eiler Flanagan's continuing rebuff of every negotiating offer sent to him. He grieved for Aganstati and worried about what had become of John Ridge.

Meanwhile, he found the household unusual and interesting. Living in this moderately sized house was Tobin and a small band of his most loyal assistants and bodyguards, the most vigilant and devoted men Kane had ever seen. And every one of them bulky, strong, and ready to take on all of Flanagan's private army on their own if need be. Kane was glad Tobin had such stalwart protectors, chief among them a hulk of a man named Ed Trumbling, who stood five inches above six feet and packed nearly three hundred pounds of muscle onto his frame.

There was no longer any question about Yancey Tobin's state of health. The coughs seemed to be getting worse, and often a look in Tobin's eyes hinted at pain that was felt every moment and fought against in vain. The time or two that Kane broached a cautious inquiry about Tobin's health, however, brought only terse denials. Kane let the matter drop, not wanting to offend a man he was beginning to see not only as a host but also as a protector and friend. He and Tobin conversed often, and as different as they were, they had discovered a mutual compatibility that effortlessly drew them together.

The third day, Kane quietly left the Tobin house and returned to the streets of Three Mile. He visited one of the banks there and deposited the bulk of the money that Ben Flanagan had given him, having decided it was foolish to keep such an amount on his person in a town with more than its share of footpads and confidence men, where he was apparently a target of Eiler Flanagan.

After Kane left the bank, he turned up his collar against the wind-driven snow and headed out to the Ridge mine, hoping he'd find John back there again.

John was not there, but someone obviously had been. The cabin was a mess, the door standing open . . . and oddly, there was writing on the wall. A mad scrawl, words hard to read because they were so poorly shaped. Whoever had written them had been either very drunk or very distraught. Maybe both.

And whoever had written them had written them in the alphabet of the Cherokees.

Kane ciphered out the writing slowly and was stunned. He recognized these words: they were an ancient Cherokee war chant.

He left the cabin puzzled and disturbed. Had John Ridge himself written the words? Was it he who had rampaged through the cabin, all but destroying it? Had his grief over his brother's death been so great as that?

The snow was coming down harder now, and the air was growing colder. Kane hurried back into town, keeping his eye open for any sign of Flanagan's riders. He saw none, though he did spot a group of Red Bands talking around a fire built in the middle of the street. He recognized Caleb Creede among them; he seemed to be doing most of the talking, and as before, his words were full of bitterness and threats against Eiler Flanagan.

Kane wondered how long it would be before the Red Bands quit talking and started acting.

He lifted his eyes and studied the distant Flanagan Hill Mine, barely visible through the driving snow. It loomed like an ominous, hungry beast above the town, and Kane felt a shudder that was not caused by the icy wind.

He was nearly back to Tobin's house when he heard his name called. The voice was familiar but not welcome.

"Kane Porterfell! The very man I've been hoping to see!"

He stopped and turned. Pete Rampling was stalking across the street toward him, fists balled and face red, and Kane wasn't at all sure it was because of the cold weather.

"Pete, listen, I'm glad to see you . . . I want to tell you that—"

Rampling reached him and shoved a finger almost against his nose. "No, you don't tell me nothing! I'm

187

doing the telling here! What the hell kind of situation did you send me into? Just give them the message and they'll go away, he says! They got no reason to bother you, he says! Hell, they drug me off with them, up to this big house where Eiler Flanagan himself spat a bunch of questions at me, and I swear I thought they were going to kill me!"

"I'm sorry. I had no idea they'd do such a thing. There was no reason for it that I could see, and I still don't know why."

"Well, I can tell you why! It's because Eiler Flanagan wants to get his hands on you, that's why! Why the hell didn't you tell me them gunmen were Flanagan's men?"

"I'm sorry. I really am."

"I swear, I thought the man was going to have his roughnecks slice my throat right there in his sitting room! He got right in my face, threw questions at me right and left, wanted to know who I was, where you were, why you hadn't come, who'd sent me . . ."

"What did you tell him?"

"What do you think? I told him the truth! I wasn't about to keep telling your little lying message with my neck on the chop block! I told him I'd rode into town with you on the train, that you got spooked when you saw his men on the station platform, and that you sent me to lie to them while you scurried off like a rat for cover!"

"I figured you'd told them. Some of those same men have tried to capture me since."

Now that Rampling had vented some steam, he

spoke a little more calmly, though he was still seething. "What does Flanagan want you for, anyhow?"

"I was hoping you could tell me, based on the questions they asked you."

"Sorry. They didn't give no information, just demanded it. And I reckon they must have finally believed I didn't know nothing, because they let me go. I scampered out of there with my tail between my legs, swearing to myself that if ever I seen you again, I'd peel the hide off you."

"Are you going to do that?"

Rampling shoved his hands into the pockets of his coat. "Hell, I should . . . but it's too cussed cold to fool with it. All I can tell you is watch your back. Flanagan wants you bad. And your pappy, too."

"He said something about my father?"

"Yep. Asked me if I knew Bill Porterfell, if I could find him, if you'd already found him. All kinds of things. I told him I knew nothing about Bill Porterfell, that I'd never heard of the man until you named him to me."

"But you do know him. You're a friend of his."

"Hell, you think I was going to admit that? They'd probably have held me prisoner just to try to get him!"

Those words gave Kane a chill, reminding him of his own brief captivity in the house of Robert Blessed, where he'd been held for that very reason: as bait to attract William Porterfell.

"By the way, Kane, don't come to me for no more favors."

"I won't."

"You just watch your back, Kane Porterfell. This town ain't a safe place for you."

Rampling turned and walked off into the swirling white.

Kane went the rest of the way to the Tobin house at a fast trot, keeping his head low.

That night, he and Yancey Tobin sat before the fireplace of Tobin's house, staring into the flames and talking.

"Is there any chance this strike will ever end by negotiation?" Kane asked him.

"I don't know. I hope and pray so. Flanagan has cut off every attempt we've made lately. I've sent a couple of capable men a few times to try to reason with him, but they're not allowed even to come close. Twice they've been driven off by some of Flanagan's men on pain of death. Now I'm afraid to send any emissaries to Flanagan. He's a stubborn man. Negotiations don't fit his personality. He doesn't like to give way to anyone. Just likes to give orders."

"I know this might be something I shouldn't bring up, but I heard not only that your wife might have been killed by a Flanagan man, but that Flanagan had your brother killed."

"My brother died in an accident. Whether it was engineered by Flanagan I can't say."

"Other people have a stronger opinion. The Ridge brothers told me Flanagan killed your brother because he was the first to bring up the idea of a strike."

"It's a common belief around Three Mile. No one really knows."

"But the wagon that crashed with him was Flanagan's wagon."

"That's a tale that's spread so far I can't stop it. But it's not true. Pat had bought that wagon himself, two days earlier, from a man who had bought it from Eiler Flanagan a month before that. So it wasn't Flanagan's wagon at the time Pat was killed."

"Do you hate Flanagan?"

"I do my best to hate no one, Kane."

"You're a religious man."

"I take seriously the teachings of one who was far greater than you, me, Eiler Flanagan, or anyone else in this town will ever be. If that makes me religious, then I suppose I'm religious." He coughed and grimaced, dug into his pocket and produced a handkerchief with which he wiped his lips. He quickly refolded it, but not before Kane caught a glimpse of dark blood specks on the cloth.

Kane said, "I met Eiler Flanagan's brother. Did I tell you that? In Dodge City."

"They say he's a good man."

"He is. What about Eiler? Is he as bad as people say?"

Tobin did not answer at once. "It's God who judges, not man . . . but I believe that in the day He judges Eiler Flanagan, He will have to judge him . . . sternly."

"I've never known anyone so slow as you are to speak ill of another," Kane said.

"Some people think me foolish and naive—not so much for what I believe, for among the Irish miners in this town there are many Catholics—but because I try so hard to actually live by what I think is true."

"What do you believe?"

"Among my most fundamental beliefs is that all the world around us, all of reality, is ordered by the Creator. Than an underlying part of that order is that we were all made to give ourselves for others, *all* others, including the undeserving. Perhaps *especially* the undeserving. Isn't that the example of Christ, to give oneself for the good of those who on their own possess no merit?"

Kane knew relatively little about Christianity and so had nothing to reply.

"You've told me you are part Cherokee—there's a story I've heard from out of the history of the Cherokee that puts me in mind of what I'm trying to express. A North Carolina man named Tsali . . ."

"Yes," Kane replied. "A Cherokee man who was killed, and because of him a remnant of the Cherokees was allowed to remain in North Carolina and not go on the Trail of Tears."

"Aye, yes. A wonderful and sad . . . and *stirring* tale, that one is. To give oneself for the welfare of others—that's the fundamental principle of all reality, Kane. I believe that. And that's what I want to do. What Tsali did. To give myself for my people."

"You *want* to die?"

Kane expected a quick negative reply, but to his surprise Tobin thought the question over for a little while before answering. "I believe that all men must die, and therefore, when they do, they may as well make that death worthwhile."

"Isn't it better, though, to live?"

Tobin coughed again, harder and longer. The handkerchief came out once more. "Yes, it is. But no one lives forever. The end comes for all . . . and sometimes a man is privileged to see it coming and to pray for ways to make his death worthwhile."

Kane was finding this conversation increasingly strange. What could he make of Yancey Tobin? The man was obviously an idealist of the most extreme sort, seemingly obsessed with the idea of death, yet eschewing violence.

It was easy to see how the average miner, hardworking, straightforward, simple-thinking, would find it difficult to follow such a philosophical sort as Yancey Tobin, especially with straight-out fire-breathers like Caleb Creede around.

The conversation became less obscure when Tobin, prompted by Kane, told what he knew of the personal character and habits of Eiler Flanagan.

"As best I can understand him, he's a man very obsessed with the wealth of this world. You've seen his house, a virtual mansion in the midst of a town mostly of shacks and tents. And power . . . he thrives on it. This army of ruffians he's assembled is as much for the satisfaction of his own need to be Napoleon as for any 'protection' of his mine. There's been little violence against his mine, whatever he may claim, and what vandals have struck have all come from among the Red Bands, who are a minority of the strikers. A misguided minority, I fear."

"Do you know Flanagan personally?"

"Not well. I don't know that anyone knows him particularly well."

"Is he married?"

"He was. He says his wife died. Others say he forced her to leave after she sold something he valued more than he valued her."

"What was that?"

"A jewel, I'm told. Eiler Flanagan is a collector of jewels. He's involved in the diamond brokerage business as a sideline, but mostly it's a hobby for him. No, more than a hobby . . . it's his greatest passion. His joy. His god."

After Kane retired to his bed, he lay awake a long time, thinking very hard about what Tobin had said about Eiler Flanagan, thinking about himself and his own quest, putting together intriguing but unprovable possibilities that kept his mind spinning and speculating.

When he finally fell asleep, Tobin was still seated beside the fire, coughing.

Chapter 17

Kane awakened slowly, stirred back to life by a general hubbub elsewhere in the house. He sat up, rubbing his face, frowning, trying to make sense of what he heard. Morning light streamed through the frosted, snow-flecked little window above his cot, and cold air seeped in around the panes.

Tobin was coughing again in the other room, but worse than before, uncontrollably this time. And there were voices, all but shouting back and forth, sounding worried. Trumbling's was loudest of all. Kane rose quickly and dressed, finger-combed his hair, and went in to investigate.

Several of Tobin's guards were gathered around him as he sat slumped over in the same chair he'd sat in the night before when he and Kane talked by the fireside. Apparently he'd spent the entire night there—something Kane would later be told was not uncommon for him. That chronic cough of his fared better, Tobin believed, when he sat up rather than lay down, and the fireplace drove the dampness out of the air around the hearth.

Michael Tatum, one of the guards who had gone with Kane to bury the body of Aganstati, turned as Kane entered the room.

"Come here, Kane, see if you can talk some reason into him," Tatum said. "He's very ill, but we can't get him to agree to go to a doctor."

Kane moved around until he could see Tobin and was shocked at the look of the man. He seemed drawn and pale, and his lips were unusually red. Red, Kane knew, from coughed-up blood.

Whatever Tobin might say, he was very sick, probably consumptive, and Kane knew it. He suspected that Tobin knew it, too.

"I don't think he needs to go to a doctor," Kane said.

"What? Can't you see the shape he's in?"

"That's what I mean. He doesn't need to go out into the cold and snow in that condition. Tell me where I can find a doctor, and I'll go bring one here."

Ed Trumbling stepped forward and gave Kane a doctor's name and directions to his dwelling. Tobin tried to say something—Kane knew he was going to protest his going out into the town, since Flanagan was looking for him—but his coughing kept the words from coming. Kane was glad; he wanted to fetch the doctor, wanted to do something practical to help the man who'd given him protection and shelter and friendship.

He bundled himself up and left the house. The snow had piled about a foot high in the street, but the wind had blown it severely, causing much higher drifts here and there but keeping the main part of the street relatively clear.

Despite the weather, Three Mile was almost as bustling as usual. Kane kept a sharp eye out for anyone who might be a Flanagan man.

He found the doctor at his breakfast. Kane's description of Tobin's symptoms and condition roused the man to fast action. He threw on his coat and hat, hoisted a heavy black medical bag, and stepped out into the street, trudging along very fast. Kane had been prepared to lead the doctor to Tobin's house, but it was obvious that he already knew where it was. Probably he'd treated the ailing strike leader before.

Kane followed, but jerked to a quick halt when he caught a glimpse of a face in the doorway of a cafe—a face that was almost but not quite turned his way—looking past him at a dog romping in the snow with its pups.

Kane felt sick. The face was that of a man whose last contact with him had been broken when the late Lewis Washington unceremoniously yanked him off a boxcar on a moving train: Wilson, the former Pinkerton detective turned hired agent of Robert Blessed.

Wilson was not only alive, Wilson was *here*! It had to mean that Blessed was alive, too, for he doubted Wilson would have continued the pursuit if his employer was dead. And it also meant that somehow, probably in Dodge, the pair of them had discovered that Kane had come here and had followed him.

Kane had dared to hope the pursuit was over. Not so. Nothing had changed. They were still after him.

Kane realized too late that he was doing precisely the wrong thing, standing there in the middle of the street, staring at Wilson's image through the glass. He'd been so stunned to see the man that it had paralyzed him. And now, just as he realized it and began to turn so that Wilson would not see his face, Wilson's eyes drifted toward him and their gazes meshed.

For a terrible moment Kane and Wilson stared at one another across the width of half a snowy street, a boardwalk, and cafe window. Through the dimming glass Kane watched recognition sweep over Wilson, and then the man vanished from the window.

Kane turned and ran, angling across to the far side of the street. He reached the mouth of an alleyway just as Wilson emerged from the cafe door and looked wildly up and down the street. Kane almost made it into the alley without being spotted . . . but not quite. A glance back revealed Wilson coming after him, pulling on his coat as he ran.

Kane thought of Tobin's warm house, those thick walls, the guards there, vigilant and protective . . . but he decided it would not do to go there with Wilson following. If Wilson learned where Kane was staying, he would not be safe there, guards or no guards. Wilson and Blessed would wait him out, somehow find their chance to get him.

Best to lose Wilson before heading back to Tobin's. And Kane was reasonably sure that he could manage to do it in this maze of a town.

He went out the other end of the alley, turned right, circled a building, cut through a backyard, across a fence, through another alley, out onto a different street . . . and ducked behind a water barrel, from there to take a good look around and assess his situation. No sign of Wilson. He waited for Wilson to emerge from the alley, but he didn't. Kane was relieved. He'd thrown him off.

He remained cautious, however, as he came out of his hiding place. Walking down the street, he tried to figure out just where he was in relation to Tobin's house. In losing Wilson, he'd managed to lose himself, too.

Using the imposing Flanagan house as a landmark, Kane figured out which direction he needed to take to find Tobin's place again. He'd just set out that way when he looked over his shoulder and saw Wilson come racing around the corner of a building. Wilson stopped, his breath coming in white gusts, and looked frantically around.

Kane slipped closer to the wall, moved into the shadows beneath the overhanging porch roof of a store, and ducked into the nearest recessed doorway. He peered out of the nook and saw Wilson still looking around but wandering toward him. Kane put his hand to the knob of the door behind him, opened the door, and slipped inside.

He found himself inside a simple but nicely outfitted small shop. At first he was confused, for he couldn't tell what was sold here. Several glass cases were set up, but they contained nothing but closed and locked metal boxes.

A door at the shop's rear rattled, and a white-haired, keen-eyed little man with an apron around his lean middle and a magnifying eyepiece sashed to his forehead came up to the front. He was carrying another locked box similar to those in the cases, and he stopped and frowned as soon as he saw Kane.

Kane said hello and tried to look casual, masking the near panic he was feeling because of Wilson, who was even now passing the store on the street and still looking around furtively. Kane saw him and reflexively stepped farther into the shop, which drew him closer to the shopkeeper.

"What are you doing?" the man demanded, stepping backward.

"Nothing . . . nothing. I'm sorry." Kane watched as Wilson walked by and out of view, then focused his eyes in a little closer and read the reversed letters painted on the shop window: CAVENDISH DIAMOND BROKERAGE

A jewel store! Of course! Now Kane knew what was in the locked metal cases. And also why the shopkeeper reacted so strongly to Kane's unexpected movement toward him. Keeping shop with such valuable merchandise would make anyone nervous.

"Look, you, why did you come in here like this?" demanded the man, whom Kane assumed was Cavendish.

"I was just trying to get out of the cold for a few minutes," he said rather feebly.

"Well, this isn't a hotel lobby. If that's all you're after, I suggest you go rent a room or nestle down by the fire in some cafe. This is a diamond brokerage."

Kane, trying to be as casual about it as possible, worked his way around to allow himself a view out the window in the direction Wilson had gone. To his regret, Wilson was still on the street, much farther up now, almost to the corner, but still searching, still seeming to suspect that Kane might be somewhere in the immediate vicinity.

"Well, then," Kane said, "I want to look at a diamond."

The man was instantly skeptical. "*You?* You want to buy a diamond?"

"Maybe. I just want to look right now." He glanced out the window again. Wilson was headed back up the street, peering into windows now.

"How old are you?"

"Old enough to want a diamond. Can we go in the back and look at some?"

"Oh, no, you'll not be going into the back! You want to look, you can look right here!"

Wilson was getting closer, looking now into the window of a shop across the street. Next would be this one, Kane guessed.

"Listen . . . do you have a back way out of here?"

"I told you, you're not going into the back!"

"Look, sir, I've got a man after me. He's a strong-arm robber who stole an entire wagonload of good-quality silver ore from my father. He's on the street now, looking for me."

"What are you, some kind of Indian? You look it."

"Please, sir, he's headed this way!"

"Then go out and meet him. He's not my problem."

"Listen to me! My name is Kane Porterfell, and that man out there is a danger to me, and if you let him find me in here he'll tear this place to pieces trying to get at me!"

The man looked at Kane differently all at once. His

eyes shifted to the street outside the window. Wilson was trudging through the snow toward the door.

"Back here," Cavendish said, motioning Kane behind one of the display cases. Though the front of the case was glass, the back was made of metal. He ducked behind it just as Wilson pushed open the door.

"Hello, sir!" Cavendish said brightly. "How's the snow suit you?"

"I'm looking for somebody, old fellow. Young, Indian-looking man. Important I find him. You see him pass by here?"

"Why, yes . . . I think I saw him head into that alley across the street there not ten minutes ago."

Wilson looked back over his shoulder, grunted, and nodded. "Thanks. Obliged." He closed the door and was gone.

Kane rose. "Thank you, sir. You don't know what a great favor you just did for me."

"Kane Porterfell, you say."

"That's right."

The man grinned. "Remarkable."

"What are you talking about?"

"Remarkable that you should come in here."

Something was amiss. Kane eyed the door. When he looked back, Cavendish had a small revolver in hand and was grinning even more broadly. "A diamond broker always keeps a small arm on hand—never knows when he might have to protect himself or his inventory." He chuckled. "Our owner is going to be so pleased to see you!"

Kane stared at the pistol. "You're not the owner?"

"No, no. It's still my name on the door and I'm still the jeweler and manager, but I sold the entire business to Mr. Eiler Flanagan two years ago."

Kane stared at the man for a couple of moments while what he'd just heard sank in. Then he acted, out of instinct, not even knowing until he made his move what that move would be.

His right foot shot up and caught Cavendish's pistol hand full force. The little man yelped as the weapon went flying and Kane shoved him back against the wall. The metal case the broker had been carrying fell to the floor, snapping open and spilling red stones everywhere. Rubies, advertised on the front glass as one of the secondary specialties of the brokerage.

Kane ran for the door, yanked it open, and barreled out onto the street. He was in such a hurry that he didn't notice the handful of mounted men proceeding down the street through the snow. He ran directly in front of one of them, making the man swear loudly and yank back on his horse's reins.

Kane looked up and saw Ves Snowden glaring down at him. "I'll be damned!" Snowden said. "Look who we got, boys!"

Cavendish appeared in the doorway of his shop, rubbing the back of his head, which had soundly smacked the wall when Kane pushed him.

"It's Porterfell! It's the one Mr. Flanagan wants!" Cavendish yelled at the riders.

"We know that already!" Snowden yelled back. He reached for his pistol, ready to seal Kane's captivity.

Kane would have none of it. He yelled loudly and

leaped in the face of Snowden's skittish horse, which backed and reared slightly, just enough to divert Snowden's attention from his pistol to his perch. As he struggled to keep his seat, Kane ran for the nearest alley, which happened to be the same one Wilson had traversed minutes before.

But Wilson was no longer there, and Kane ran on. He heard Snowden cursing, then ordering a general dismount and pursuit. Kane pushed himself harder, knowing what it was to be a mouse in a town full of cats. Everywhere he turned, danger lurked. Everywhere he showed his face, he was met with threats and pursuit.

It was enough to make him mad, and the anger spurred him.

The riders, now pedestrians, pursued hard. Kane went back to his old ploy of zigzagging through this alley and that yard, trying to lose the men chasing him. But he sensed that they were dividing, spreading out to cut off potential routes of escape. And he realized that these men knew the town much better than he did.

His lungs stinging from gasping the frigid air, his breath clouding and trailing behind him as he ran, Kane headed for a nearby barn, hoping he could hide there. But just as he reached it, a man stepped out from behind a shed and cut him off.

"Got you this time, you red dog!" Wilson said as he brought back his pistol and swung it forward.

Kane took the blow on the side of the head and fell. It hadn't been enough to knock him completely out, but he was stunned. As Wilson grabbed him, picked him up, slung him across his shoulder like a sack of feed, Kane found himself unable to react or resist.

"Come on, redskin," Wilson said. "Let's go get you reintroduced to Mr. Blessed."

Kane never recalled much about his strange journey through the back alleys of Three Mile, draped like a corpse over the shoulder of Wilson. He would later remember that not all the journey was made in that way— he was dragged some of the distance—but all in all the trip was a blur experienced in a half-conscious state.

He began to come out of it when a jolt of cold water splashed in his face. He jerked, focused his eyes, and had the most unpleasant experience of looking into the faces of Wilson and Robert Blessed, side by side. Kane was seated in a straight-backed wooden chair, his hands tied behind him.

"Well! Mr. Porterfell! Back together after all these days of separation!" Blessed said. "I'm sure you're as happy about it as we are. No doubt you worried quite a lot that you wouldn't see us again." He laughed.

Kane groaned and closed his eyes. His head hurt where Wilson had pistol-whipped him, but when he touched the place he detected no broken skin. He'd taken the flat of the pistol, a blunt blow, and that had saved him a laceration.

Blessed slapped him. "Open those eyes! I'm talking to you, half-breed!"

Kane did open his eyes and enjoyed seeing Blessed jump back as he spat at him. Blessed cursed and hit Kane again.

"You spit at me again and I'll cut your tongue out," he said. "You've cost me a lot, you worthless savage! Because of you my partner is blind, two of my hired men are dead, and I'm damned lucky to be alive myself. Same for Wilson here."

"I'd hoped you were dead, both of you," Kane said. No reason to mince words with these villains.

"A little bit rude, ain't he, Mr. Blessed?" Wilson said. "Imagine saying a thing like that!"

Blessed stared at Kane a few moments, then slapped him again. "Ah! Yes! That felt good . . . that one was for me, Kane. For all the hell you've put me through."

"Hit him again, Mr. Blessed. Hit him one for poor McGrath."

Blessed did. Kane struggled to retain consciousness.

Blessed dropped to one knee to look Kane in the face at eye level. "Thought you'd shaken us off, didn't you! You were wrong. Very wrong. And you know where you made your mistake that enabled us to track you here? By playing the hero in Dodge City. Dragging poor unfortunates out of the fire! Very wonderful of you, of course. But it made your name famous. Believe me, it was easy enough to find out where such a popular figure as yourself had gone."

"So you've got me. What now?"

"What now? What do you think? You're going to take pen in hand, Mr. Porterfell, and write out those letters you destroyed. Every word! You do still remember them, don't you?"

Kane could have lied and said he didn't, but he feared that doing so might make them decide he was useless to them. And expendable. He remembered the letters quite well, in fact. He'd made a daily practice of reciting them to himself ever since he'd memorized them. "I remember them. But what good will they do you? You still don't have my father, and he's the only one who knows what was in the one letter I don't have memorized."

"We're quite aware of the situation. We're also quite aware that your father came to this town from Dodge, which is the only reason you did the same. That means we can lure him just as we originally planned to lure him . . . with you, his only son, as bait. Have you found your father, boy?"

"No. My father's long gone. I've given up even trying to find him. And without the letter he has, the ones I've got memorized are worthless to you. So you might as well let me go."

"Let you go? If you become worthless, boy, we'll 'let you go' with a bullet through your brain. Now get ready to cooperate with us. I don't believe for a moment that your father's gone from this town. If he was, you'd be gone yourself."

"All right," Kane said. "You want your letters, you'll have them. I don't see I have any other choice."

"Damn right you don't. Wilson, get that paper over there. And a pen and ink. Mr. Porterfell is about to demonstrate that excellent memory of his to us."

"I can't very well write the letters with my hands tied," Kane said.

Blessed produced a folding knife and cut the cords

binding Kane's wrists. Kane wriggled his fingers to get the blood flowing again.

Out somewhere beyond the walls, he heard the blast of a steam whistle. A train was rolling into Three Mile. Kane wished it were going out of Three Mile instead with him aboard it.

"Get up from there. Go over to yonder table and get started," Blessed said.

Kane had just come to his feet when the door burst in. Blessed and Wilson both roared in surprise and scrambled for their weapons, but it was too late.

Ves Snowden pushed his way in, shotgun lifted, with several other Flanagan men following, including his grinning younger brother.

"Good day to you folks," he said. Then to Blessed: "Don't know who you are, Mister, but that Injun you've got is of great interest to the man who employs us. We'll be taking him with us now." He looked at Wilson. "You're damned easy to follow, you know that?"

Blessed gaped and blubbered, and Wilson looked like he might swell up and explode.

One of the other Flanagan men asked, "We just going to leave them?" He gestured at Wilson and Blessed.

Snowden thought about that one, and asked Blessed, "Why'd you snatch Mr. Porterfell there, anyhow?"

"That's my affair and none of yours."

"Tell you what. You and your friend there, you come along with us, too. Just to be on the safe side. We'll let Mr. Flanagan sort you out."

Blessed bellowed, "I don't know who the hell you are, but I have no intention of going anywhere with—"

The shotgun jammed into his face made Blessed shut up fast. He stared down the twin black eyes of its muzzle, then looked helplessly at Wilson.

"Let's go," Snowden said. "And waste no time about it. Mr. Flanagan's waited long enough to catch his little Indian boy here."

Chapter 18

The train rounded the final bend and began to slow as it approached the station house at Three Mile. Newcomers to the town craned their necks and peered out windows at the destination they had finally reached, most of them with ambitions of quick silver strikes and wealth that would last a lifetime. These types scarcely noticed the fenced graveyard they'd passed just before reaching the town, where every day men with identical ambitions to their own were laid away, victims of the trials, dangers, and deprivations that were the life of a silver miner.

One passenger did notice the graveyard, where even at that moment three black men were busy digging a fresh grave in the snowy and cold earth. She watched them in silence, thinking it a bad omen to see such a thing upon arrival in a new place, then turned her eyes toward the smoking, ugly town.

She carried no baggage except one new, spacious valise of leather and an equally new umbrella. Her dress, fashionable without being ostentatious, was also new, purchased hurriedly in Kansas shortly before her departure, specifically for this journey and the meeting she intended for it to lead to. She wore a heavy woolen cloak to shield her against the cold.

She joined the queue of passengers disembarking the train. The wind stung her face as she stepped out onto the platform, and she followed the general rush into the station house, where multiple stoves belched a wonderful heat. She stood close to one of these for several minutes, letting the chill gradually wear off.

Meanwhile, she looked out the windows on the side of the station house that faced the main part of town. She was quite wary of this place, having read, during her journey, newspaper stories about the terrible strike under way here at the Flanagan Hill Mine—owned, ironically, by the very man she planned to call upon before this day was through.

The stories had talked much of vandalism and random violence associated with the strike and had hinted that expectations were for the violence to increase. Specifically mentioned was a faction of striking miners who wore red armbands and advocated insurgent activities against the mine and its owner. The story, from a Denver newspaper and written by an editor with obvious leanings in favor of management over labor, made the so-called Red Bands out to be quite a dangerous bunch, so she looked particularly for the infamous symbol on the arms of the men she saw moving about in the town.

It wasn't long before she spotted an entire group of them. The cluster of Red Bands, bearing weapons and flaunting their red armbands like badges of pride, walked across a street within view of the station and, as she watched, engaged in an argument with several mounted armed men. Her eyes grew large as the confrontation grew in intensity and people nearby on the street began to hurry away. More people in the station house noticed the encounter and began crowding to the windows, blocking her view.

As she angled for a new position, a shot rang out, and a collective outcry filled the station house. Startled people backed away from the windows, then drew near them again. She found a place that allowed her a new view and saw that one of the Red Bands had fired a shotgun, which was still smoking. As she watched, he shoved it skyward and emptied the second barrel even as he was yelling something at one of the mounted riders.

So the shooting was aimed at nothing but the sky and was no more than noisy punctuation for an argument. Still, it was quite disturbing. She clutched her bag and backed away from the window, feeling very nervous indeed about being in this town.

"Miss . . . your dress!"

The speaker was a man to her left. She turned, surprised to have been spoken to, then saw him rather frantically gesturing toward one of the nearer stoves. Her dress was perilously close to the heater and actually beginning to smoke at the hem. She quickly danced away from the stove, while the man, for good measure, knelt and slapped at the hot fabric with his hand, just to make sure it didn't catch.

"Thank you, sir. You may have saved me from a tragedy."

He rose and touched his hat politely. "Glad to have been of service."

"Sir . . . do you live in Three Mile?"

"Yes, ma'am."

"Then perhaps you can give me directions. I need to find the house of Mr. Eiler Flanagan."

The man looked startled. "Eiler Flanagan?"

"Yes."

"Uh, you're a relative, perhaps?"

"No. It's just that I have an urgent message to deliver to someone I believe may be his guest, or at the very least, someone whose whereabouts I expect Mr. Flanagan could tell me."

"I see." The man was looking at her with far more concern than she could account for. "Well, if that's the case, I'll be glad to show you the way. If you'd step outside onto the porch yonder, I'll point out his house to you. It's quite visible from almost anywhere in town."

She looked out a window. "Are those men who were arguing gone?"

He took a glance of his own. "Yes. As usual, they've yelled some words, fired off a shot or two, and moved on. Thank God they're still mostly shooting at the clouds and not at each other."

"I saw the red armbands. They were strikers?"

"One faction of them. The men on horseback were some of the soldiers of fortune hired by . . . well, never mind. Come now, let me show you the house you're looking for, Miss . . ."

"Railey. Carolina Railey."

* * *

Kane, along with Blessed and Wilson, had been stepping along quite speedily, walking in the midst of the band of Flanagan men who had taken them. Kane thought it the strangest kind of feeling, having gone in one moment from being a prisoner of Blessed and Wilson to now being their fellow captive. He had ludicrous thoughts of the three of them slicing their palms, shaking hands, becoming blood brothers, and planning daring escapes together. He wondered if he would be better off in Eiler Flanagan's clutches than in Blessed's.

The sound of the two shotgun blasts from a nearby street brought the entire band to a stop and led to sharp debate among Flanagan's riders along the lines of "What do you reckon?" and "Think we should go see about it?"

Blessed took advantage of the pause to declare, "I don't know what the hell this is about, but I refuse to be treated like a common—"

One of Flanagan's mounted men shut him up quickly with a boot to the side of the face that just about knocked him down. Kane almost wanted to congratulate the fellow.

Ves Snowden said, "Hell, the most important thing right now is getting this red coon to Mr. Flanagan. I don't hear no more shooting. Maybe just some kid firing shotgun blanks for fun."

The forced march resumed. Blessed was quiet as churchtime now, Kane noticed, and working his jaw from side to side. Kane hoped it would bruise dark as midnight.

As for Wilson, he looked downright terrified. *Quite*

different, isn't it, Mr. Wilson, to be the terrorized instead of the terrorizer! Kane thought with some satisfaction.

The group had reached the final corner beyond which they would turn up the avenue to Flanagan's house when an unexpected opportunity presented itself to Kane.

The Red Band group that had just been involved in the shotgun incident near the train station came down the street from the opposite direction and saw Snowden and the other riders with their prisoners. Already worked up from the previous showy, though insubstantial, encounter with the other gaggle of Flanagan men, they were quick to challenge this new group, particularly since the hated Ves Snowden led it and since Snowden, who was no more an officer of the law than he was the pope, had prisoners.

"Snowden! Damn your black soul, who's that you got there?" This came from a burly man who seemed to be leading this bunch of Red Bands.

"Move on!" Snowden yelled back. "This is none of your affair, and we'll shoot you dead, damn you, if you try to interfere with us!"

Kane chose that moment to seize his opportunity. "Murder!" he yelled at the Red Bands. "Help us! They're going to murder us!"

That was all it took. The Red Bands were suddenly bristling with weaponry, pulled out from underneath their coats. This, of course, fully distracted Flanagan's riders, and Kane took advantage of it. He let out a howl as if he'd been stabbed or brutally struck and rammed his shoulder hard into the flank of a horse beside him,

screaming again and again. The horse, Freddy Snowden's, nickered and moved, then reared. Kane rammed
into a second horse, getting even faster results.

The Red Bands ran in close during the confusion, and
someone fired a shot. Freddy Snowden groped for Kane,
but Kane dropped and rolled right under a horse. It was
risky, and indeed he was almost trampled, but he made
it without being hurt or caught. He came out on the
other side, running.

He was free! As the Red Bands surrounded Snowden
and his cohorts, and as Blessed and Wilson cringed in
the midst of rearing horses, cursing men, and dodging,
furious Red Bands, Kane heard a pistol crack, loudly,
and a scream. It sounded like Wilson. Looking back, he
saw Wilson crumple to the ground, hand to his side.

Kane ran as hard as he could for the nearest corner.
He didn't care where he wound up, as long as it was far
from this place and out of reach of the many grasping
hands that seemed to want him. He would ultimately
take his refuge back at the Tobin house—but for now,
any port in this endlessly confusing storm would suit.

Carolina Railey was striding nervously toward the
Flanagan house when the Red Bands came by, and she
was just coming around a corner when the altercation
broke out. She heard a voice—was it familiar? It seemed
so—giving the shocking outcry of "Murder," then she
heard yells and curses and the whinnying of scared
horses.

She saw only a few moments of it—a confusing, roiling muddle of men and horses—and that was all she

needed. Her nerves had been taut enough at the outset of this unexpected journey; since arriving here less than an hour ago, what peace of mind she'd had left had already been shaken by explosive violence, twice. It was just too much.

Carolina ran back the way she'd come, then turned into the first convenient doorway, a cafe, and shoved past people who were coming out of the cafe to investigate all the hubbub.

She took a seat in a far corner, closed her eyes, and breathed slowly, trying to relax. Meanwhile, the sound of fighting outside still reached her all the way from down the street and around a corner.

She'd been in Three Mile not even an hour yet, and already she was developing a bitter hatred of this town.

She never knew how the fight came out or, for that matter, what it was about to begin with. All she knew was that it ended with the Red Bands breaking away and leaving and Flanagan's riders, with none seriously hurt, going on up to Flanagan's house, with two men on foot and apparently captive. There had been three prisoners to begin with, so one had gotten away. One of the two still captive had a fresh bullet hole in him. All this information Carolina picked up from a man at the doorway who had kept an eye on it all.

The captives had been taken to the Flanagan house! The very place she had been about to go! She was grateful that the timing had worked out as it had. She would not have wanted to be at Flanagan's dwelling when those riders came back in with prisoners. And what was a mine owner doing, taking prisoners in the first place? What was going on in this town—a labor strike or a war?

Carolina ordered a meal and ate it as slowly as possible, then a dessert she did not really want, also consumed at a snail's pace, followed by coffee slowly drunk, cup after cup.

She was in no hurry to leave this cafe, and she wasn't sure anymore that she could really do what she'd come to do.

It had seemed simple enough: come to Three Mile, find Eiler Flanagan, through him find Kane, and give Kane the message she bore. She supposed it still was simple . . . it just wasn't appealing to think of going to the house of a man who hired armed riders to do battle in the streets of his own town and to haul prisoners to him like he was some feudal lord.

After a while, though, Carolina began to feel ashamed of herself. It wasn't like her to be this way. She'd faced down a hundred—no, a thousand—varied dangers in her unusual, traveling life and had never sat and pined as she was doing here in this cafe.

Whatever Flanagan and his men were involved in, it was not her affair. She needed to talk to Eiler Flanagan only to establish contact with Kane, and no more. There was no reason for her to be afraid.

She finished her last cup of coffee, paid her bill, and left the cafe. On the street she let the invigorating cold air sweep over her. A man passed and tipped his hat to her. She gave the briefest of polite smiles in return, threw back her head, and began walking in the direction of Flanagan's house with such obvious determination that she looked haughty. The man who'd greeted her watched her go, muttered something to himself about feminine pomposity, and continued on his way.

When the Flanagan mansion was in full view before her, she paused, giving herself one last chance to change her mind. But she had to find Kane somehow and reminded herself that Eiler Flanagan was the only conduit to Kane that she knew of in this town. It seemed quite likely that Kane himself was residing somewhere in Flanagan's house at this very moment, probably by now united with his father—happily, she hoped.

With a steady stride and erect posture, she began climbing the low hill toward Flanagan's imposing, towered edifice of a house.

The door was large and black and bore on its varnished face a huge brass knocker. Carolina reached up, took it, paused only a moment, then pounded brass against brass firmly, three times. The knock echoed back through the big house beyond the door.

A few moments later she saw something move on the door—a little slide at the base of the knocker, previously unnoticed, had shifted to one side, then back into place. Another moment or two, and the door slowly opened.

Before Carolina stood a sad-faced, middle-aged black man with a headful of very thick, graying hair. He wore an old but nicely cleaned and pressed suit of the kind a doorman at a big-city hotel might wear. His brown eyes studied her a little while before he spoke in a rather tired-sounding voice.

"May I be of service to you, ma'am?"

She had mentally rehearsed what she would say. "Yes, I hope so. My name is Miss Carolina Railey. I've come from Dodge City, Kansas, to meet Mr. Eiler Flanagan in hopes that he can direct me to a friend of mine, Mr. Kanati Porterfell, who I believe was to have met Mr. Flanagan at this house several days ago." She got it all out without taking a breath.

The man stared at her a little longer. His expression hadn't changed, but it seemed to Carolina that his eyes had, at precisely the moment she had called the name of Kanati Porterfell. They looked . . . more sad, maybe. Or scared? It was odd, and vaguely distressing.

"So you wish to see Mr. Flanagan?"

"That's correct."

The servant looked over his shoulder, back into the house, then at her again. "I think Mr. Flanagan might be busy."

"Would it be asking too much if you called on him to see?"

"Ma'am . . . are you sure you want to . . ." He cut off, then after a brief silence said, "Are you sure you want to see Mr. Flanagan?" She wondered what he'd initially been about to ask.

"Is there some reason I shouldn't?"

No answer at once, and that silence was as strong a "yes" as he could have spoken. Carolina felt her heart began to pound a little harder. It was quite obvious that he didn't want her to enter, and she couldn't get over the feeling that he was trying to protect her. She could easily imagine that those expressive, sad eyes were saying to her silently something that his servant's position would not allow him to voice in words: *Get away from here! Run!*

She almost did run. The only thing that stopped her was the necessity of getting the message she bore to Kane as quickly as possible.

"I'll see if he can see you, ma'am," the man said, resigned. "Please do step inside."

Carolina did. The door closed behind her. The servant looked at her one more time and walked slowly across the well-appointed room toward another door almost as big, and even blacker than the one she'd just entered. He knocked, paused, and went inside. The closure of the door echoed in the big room.

She drew in a slow breath. Wise or foolish, she was here. And she hoped Kane was, too, and that all was fine with him, and that all her fear was nothing but a meaningless case of nerves.

Carolina studied the carpet, the paintings on the wall, the gilding of the mirror frame . . . then turned her head quickly when the servant reappeared.

"Miss Railey, Mr. Flanagan is in, and he's very eager to meet you. If you could step this way, I'll see you in."

Chapter 19

High on a mountainside, Freddy Snowden paced back and forth in the snow, smoking, muttering the occasional curse beneath his breath, and staring with hatred at the band of orderly miners gathered, with signs and bonfires, just past the property line of the Flanagan Hill Mine.

"Look at them, Paul!" Freddy declared, waving the latest of a series of hand-rolled cigarettes in the direction of the miners. He'd been sent by his brother to help guard the mine, a duty he hated, and he was in quite a terrible humor because of it. "Bunch of unappreciative bastards! The only thing keeping them from destroying this mine right now is us being here." The "us" referred to a delegation of Flanagan gunmen, who outnumbered the strikers two to one, meandering about the mine property with arms brandished. Most of the gunmen, except for a small, elite guard unit headed by Ves Snowden, lived on the mine property in big dormitories made of rough-cut lumber, assembled specifically for them at great expense by Eiler Flanagan. This, combined with the fact that several of the gunmen actually received better wages from Flanagan than Flanagan was willing to pay his miners, was continually irksome to the strikers, indicating to them a lack of good faith on Flanagan's part.

The gunman with Freddy Snowden looked closely at the miners and said, "I don't know about that, Fred. Them ain't Red Bands, just your plain strikers. You know, Tobin's group."

Freddy spat into the snow. "Hell! Beyond a piece of red cloth about the arm, there ain't no difference amongst them that I can see. All of them come out of the same cesspool as far as I'm concerned. As for Tobin, don't you believe all that bilge about him being peaceful and religious and all that, while Creede and his Red Bands are the radicals. I guaran-damn-tee you that Tobin's the one *really* behind the Red Bands. He just puts on that peace-loving front to make himself look good to the public."

"Reckon?"

"Hey! Look there!" Freddy Snowden pointed. "See him? That's Creede! Old Mister Red Band hisself!"

"I don't think that's Creede, Freddy."

"The hell it ain't! Looks like him to me. See what I told you? The Red Bands and Tobin's bunch are really one and the same. And there's Creede moving among Tobin's men to prove it."

"I still don't think that's Creede."

"Yeah, well, them spectacles you're wearing are so cussed thick you can't see through 'em, then. That's Creede. Damn, I hate that man!" He paused, then looked up at a snowy crag overlooking the scene, then at the foot of the trail that led up from the mine clearing to that bluff, a favorite spot of picnickers, in warmer weather and peaceful times. "I'll be damned! From up there, a man could—"

"Freddy, don't you do it! The time will come for somebody to snipe down Creede and Tobin, too, but that's for Flanagan to decide, not me and you."

"Hell, he don't have to know who done it! Just that it was done. You wouldn't say nothing, would you?"

"Freddy, don't."

"You'll keep that mouth shut, right?"

"Well, yes, but—"

"That's all I need to hear."

"I still don't think that's Creede."

Freddy Snowden wasn't listening. He went to his horse and unbooted his Winchester. Grinning, he winked at his partner, glanced around to make sure no one else was watching, and trotted over to the base of the trail.

Ten minutes later, Freddy Snowden was sighting down the long barrel of his rifle and wishing he had a scope. From this range he might miss his target altogether. Further, he was beginning to wonder if he'd been wrong and that really wasn't Caleb Creede down there.

So he hesitated, not quite willing to squeeze the trigger. Once he fired, he'd have to get out of there quickly to avoid being caught. It was important that the one or maybe two shots he'd have time to get off found their target.

It was also important that the target be the right man.

"Hell!" he muttered to himself, lowering the rifle and

squinting through a new fall of snow just now getting started and making the shot even harder to line up.

He heard something behind him. Frowning, he turned his head. "Paul? Is that you?"

His eyes went wide. He opened his mouth to yell, but there was no time. It was over as swiftly as the *swoosh* of a descending axe and the thud of tempered metal into skull bone.

Below, Freddy's partner waited for his promised shot. He'd anticipated it for five minutes now, and it hadn't come. He wondered if Freddy had changed his mind. He hoped so.

Ten minutes passed. Paul began to worry about Freddy Snowden. He should have been back by now. Maybe something happened to him up there.

Another five minutes, and he decided to go look. He climbed the trail and circled around toward the overlook where Freddy would be. A popular, pleasant spot in summer months, it was a desolate locale at this time of year. Paul shivered as he made his way toward the edge.

The snow was falling harder now, sticking heavily to the rocky soil, but not yet to the still-warm body of Freddy Snowden. Paul gaped at it and advanced slowly, knowing and yet unable to fully believe that Freddy was dead. And whoever had killed him hadn't stopped at merely taking his life. He'd also tried to cut away his—

The blow crashed in the back of Paul's skull and dropped him to the snowy ground, where he lay un-moving, slowly settling, his final breath seeping slowly out of him like air from a deflating bellows. His killer knelt and touched a blade to Paul's hairline, but the work went no more cleanly than it had with Freddy Snowden. After a few moments of effort that did little more than mangle the skin, the killer rose and vanished into the snowy, barren wilderness.

The eyes of Eiler Flanagan were the coldest and most probing ones Carolina Railey had ever seen. She sat in a plush chair across from Flanagan, who was seated on the other side of his desk, looking at her in a way that she believed was intended to be disarmingly friendly. If so, the effort was failing. Eiler Flanagan was far more interested in her and what she had to say than he wanted her to know. Every sweep of the man's eyes over her made her feel menaced, and she wondered if she'd been wrong to come here after all.

She couldn't tear her attention away from those dark but sparkling eyes. Those icy cold eyes . . . cold as jewels. That was the most apt analogy she could come up with, perhaps because of what she had noticed the moment she entered this strange museum of a room: case after heavy glass case of displayed jewelry, gems of all kinds. And around the wall, heavy oak shelves laden with volumes, most of them on the subject of gemstones, if her sweeping glance had given her an accurate picture.

Carolina had been talking for several minutes now, Flanagan listening and trying his best to hide an inner agitation she couldn't account for, but to which she felt sure she was contributing.

"Now, let me be sure I understand you, Miss Railey,"

Flanagan said. "You wish to see Kane Porterfell in order to deliver him a message . . . a warning, as it were."

"That's right, sir."

"And this warning involves your sighting, in Dodge City, of a Mr. Robert Blessed and some cohort of his . . . and these two are enemies of young Mr. Porterfell."

Carolina wondered why she was having to go through this so many times. Either Eiler Flanagan was a dense man, or he was enjoying hearing what she was saying. She spoke precisely, trying to be as clear as possible without betraying anything that Kane might consider private. "That's right again, Mr. Flanagan. They've been in pursuit of Kane for some weeks and are quite dangerous men. When Kane left Dodge to come here, he didn't know if he was still being pursued. The fact that I saw Robert Blessed and Wilson, the latter being a hired agent of Mr. Blessed, proves that Kane is still being chased, and therefore is still in danger. Thus, I left Dodge City to come here and tell him, in person, that I'd seen Blessed and Wilson and to make sure that he is still well. Kane made his name well known in Dodge, you see, by saving the lives of your nephews in the fire that destroyed the Excelsior and the hotel. It wouldn't be hard for Blessed and Wilson to discover that Kane has come here and follow him. Many people in Dodge know that Kane went on to Three Mile."

"Ah, yes. Now I understand it all! Kane is quite fortunate to have such a fine friend as yourself, Miss Railey. Of course, such a fine and pleasant young man deserves good friendships."

"So Kane *is* here . . ."

"Why, of course! It was all set up in advance by my brother and myself. Did you meet my brother, Ben, in Dodge?"

"No, not personally, but I knew he and Kane had become friends and that he'd wired you to arrange for Kane to come here and meet his father. Did that happen, by the way?"

"Indeed. Kane and his father have had a very happy meeting and are growing closer to one another by the day."

Carolina smiled. "I'm so glad."

"No more so than I. Right now, in fact, they're out together in town, doing one thing or another. It's hard to keep them apart. I've given William Porterfell several days of freedom from his hired duties for me, just so he could spend time with his son." Then abruptly: "One question for you, Miss Railey. Why did you go to such trouble to come all the way to Colorado to give a message to Kane when you could easily have wired the same information?"

Carolina reddened. "It's because ... well ... sir, I have a great affection for Kane. I found that when I was away from him, I missed him very badly. And like I told you, I wanted to see with my own eyes that he was well and safe."

Flanagan smiled. "And so you will, as soon as he and his father come back. Kane's staying here in this house, you know."

"I thought perhaps he might be. It's one reason I came to you."

"And you, of course, will stay here, too. I have several unused bedrooms, the nicest being in the tower you may have noticed when you approached my house. A bit of a castlelike feature, I suppose, but I like the visual effect it gives this place. You'll stay in that room. I reserve it solely for visiting ladies of distinction." He smiled even more broadly, and Carolina relaxed. She'd misjudged this man. Whatever coldness there was in his eyes, it didn't seem reflected in his treatment of her. He was cordial, polite, and seemingly truly pleased to make her his guest.

"I thank you, Mr. Flanagan."

"Your visit here is a delight, Miss. The only part I find distressing is your mention of these men pursuing Kane. A terrible thing! Do you have any idea why they would do such a thing?"

She knew from that question that Kane hadn't told Flanagan his full situation, and she'd certainly not do so without Kane's approval. "That's a question probably best answered by Kane himself . . . a private matter to him. I'm sorry."

"You are indeed a jewel, young lady. Discretion is the better part not only of valor, but also of friendship— even romance, eh?" He chuckled. "Rest assured that if any untoward characters come nosing about here for young Mr. Porterfell, I'll not stand for it! He's a dear friend of mine now, and I'll see him protected at any cost." He drummed his fingers on the desktop as if to punctuate his point. "Now, let me have you shown to your room." He jingled a small bell on his desk, signaling his servant. Then he said, "By the way, Miss Railey, there are several people living in this house at the moment, all of them men and some of them perhaps not, shall we say, *refined* men. They're employees of mine, rather rough sorts, but just the kind I need at present. We have a miners' strike going on in Three Mile just now, you see, and I happen to be very deeply involved in it. But rest assured you'll have every privacy and not be bothered. I'll see to it."

She rose as the sad-eyed servant reappeared and received his orders from Flanagan to take her to the "tower room" upstairs.

"Mr. Flanagan?" she said as she turned to go. "Is there a place here where I can wait for Kane to get back?"

"Oh, let's have some fun with it and surprise him," Flanagan said. He'd stood when she did. "You can rest in your room, enjoy some of the books you'll find shelved there—all of them decent and creditable volumes, by the way—and when Kane returns, I'll have you brought down to surprise him. Fair enough?"

"Quite fair, sir."

"Miss, may I ask you a question I hope you'll not find impertinent?"

"Certainly."

"Have you about you a trace of some Mediterranean ancestry?"

She rather dreaded answering; one never knew what attitude one might encounter concerning Indian ancestry. "Sir, my mother was a Cherokee, just as Kane's was. My father is a white man."

"Oh! I see!" Flanagan smiled but failed to fully hide a certain little twitch in his left cheek. "Interesting! I've always held the red race to be the highest of the lower races, quite capable of elevation to intellectual and moral heights when placed in the proper society. And in your case, other aspects of your breeding elevate you quite naturally as well." He beamed at her, and what progress the man had made in gaining her favor he lost all at once. But she could say nothing under the circumstances.

"Thank you for your help to me, and to Kane, sir," she said.

"Certainly."

With the servant showing her the way and taking her bag, she departed and climbed the stairs toward the tower room.

Eiler Flanagan paced back and forth, his eyes gleaming, his mind racing. How marvelously things were coming together, just as he had feared opportunity was evading him! First he'd lost William Porterfell, then Kane Porterfell had failed to appear, been caught by his men this very day, only to escape . . . but now Flanagan had none other than Robert Blessed himself, a man with a name and background very familiar to him, and Kane's lady friend besides! Further, he now knew for certain that Kane was living in the house of the cursed Yancey Tobin.

He'd not be there long. When he learned that the lovely Miss Railey was locked away in Flanagan's tower, he would come running, all but begging to cooperate as long as his beloved lady could be kept safe.

Flanagan chuckled to himself. He felt as light-footed as a schoolboy.

Crossing the lush room, he pulled an old, worn volume from a shelf and let it fall open. He knew what page would be revealed, because he'd stared at it so often that the book always opened naturally to that spot.

As it did now. He looked at the richly engraved picture of a large, fabulous diamond, the likeness based on an original depiction drawn in the early years of the century when the diamond was displayed for two months in London, shortly before it disappeared.

Flanagan stared unblinking at the engraving for a full minute, then turned the page. Several sheets of loose paper fell into his hand. On one of them was a list of names, written in his own hand many years ago, under the heading "Patrick's Raiders—Crosslin's Station, Kentucky." His eye scanned the list, stopping at certain names—Robert Blessed, Jason Wyrick, William Porterfell.

The door opened abruptly. Startled, Flanagan turned, dropping his book. It thumped loudly against the floor, a couple of pages tearing, the loose papers fluttering down like falling leaves.

Flanagan knelt and scooped up the book and papers, swearing at the man who had entered so rudely. It was Ves Snowden.

Snowden, his face pale, didn't even seem to hear his employer's castigations. He even interrupted, "Mr. Flanagan . . . Freddy has been killed. And Paul Green with him."

"Freddy? Your brother Freddy?"

"That's right . . . killed on the overlook above Flanagan Hill . . . their heads caved in, like with a hatchet,

and their bodies cut on, both of them. And the fore-
heads, sliced on—big, ugly cuts right across the upper
part. God! Why would anybody do that?"

"Are you lying to me about all this, Mr. Snowden?"

"I'm not lying, sir. I swear. They just brought the bodies in. I seen them myself and came straight to tell you."

"Where are the dead men now?"

"Back in the stables. God, my brother is *dead*!" He
sounded as if he might cry, though it was doubtful that
such a hardened, heartless man retained the memory of
how to shed tears.

Flanagan rubbed his chin. "The damned Red Bands,
I'd wager. I knew it would come to this at some point.
This may be the time for us to take a firmer hand with
these damned strikers." He was silent for a spell, thinking, still rubbing his chin. "Ah, well. I'll think about it
later. Other and bigger things to deal with right now."

"Bigger things? They killed my own *brother*, Mr.
Flanagan!"

"Your brother knew the risks of his position. I'm sorry
he's dead, but it's not my chief concern just now, and I'll
not throw a lot of false sympathy your way."

Snowden stared, too stunned to be angry.

"Right now, Mr. Snowden, go over to my personal
bar there, take a bottle, go to your room, and have
yourself a drink. Have several. Get yourself pissing
drunk if you want. I give you leave, considering what's
happened. I promise your brother's death will not go
unavenged."

Snowden was already eyeing the bar.

"Tell me something—the man you brought in today, how is he?"

"Blessed, you mean? He's fine."

"No, not Blessed, the other one! The wounded one."

"Him? He's hurt right bad. I don't know he'll live."

"I see. Well, it doesn't much matter in his case. Blessed's the important one. On with you now, Mr. Snowden. Get your bottle and go. I've got a lot to think about and notes to write for my upcoming interrogation of Mr. Blessed. I truly am sorry about your brother."

Snowden knew he wasn't, of course, but it didn't matter. Flanagan had made up for his callousness with that offer of a free bottle. Snowden picked the best bottle of whiskey Flanagan had under his bar, tucked it close to himself like a beloved baby, and left the room, slamming the big black door shut behind him.

Chapter 20

Kane's port in the storm, randomly chosen, had been a smokehouse redolent with the smell of old ashes and smoked meats. But it was safe and kept the wind and occasional spits of snowfall off him, and he'd remained inside for many long hours.

Too cautious perhaps. But hidden in the shed, he couldn't know what the end of the fight had been. Maybe Flanagan's riders had prevailed and were still scouring the town for him. Maybe Blessed and Wilson had gotten away in the confusion and were still on his trail. Or maybe the Red Bands had lost all semblance of restraint, taken the advantage, and wiped out Snowden and his scoundrels, staining the snow red with their blood.

When he finally opened the shed door and stepped out, it was dusk. More snow had fallen and the wind was even colder. He saw and heard nothing to make him think he was in danger.

His stomach grumbled; he was half starved, having eaten nothing all day. He wondered how Tobin was doing and marveled that a day that had begun with no more than a quick run across town to find a doctor had detoured so unexpectedly into fight, flight, and hours of hiding.

He would have quite a story to tell, and probably one or two to hear, once he was back with Tobin again.

Now he headed for Tobin's, watching his back and keeping to the darkest places all the way.

News of the death of Freddy Snowden and Paul Green spread wildly through the ranks of Flanagan's mercenaries. There was no doubt in any mind that the fault lay at the foot of one or more of the radical strikers, probably one of the Red Bands. It was infuriating to the ruffians that tactics they might themselves employ had been turned against them.

The Flanagan guards would admit the anger to one another. What they didn't admit was the fear.

The two slain men hadn't been merely killed . . . they'd been *mutilated*. And that wasn't something that normally happened. It was one thing to shoot a man, another to hack on him. And why those odd cuts around the forehead? What was *that* all about?

Playing the tough in the midst of a strike wasn't unusual when the other side was responding with no more than noise and the occasional thrown brick. Murder and mutilation cast a different light on the matter.

The guards promised one another that they'd get to the bottom of this. And if it happened again, the Red Bands, Caleb Creede, Yancey Tobin, and the strikers in general would be far from ready for the sheer hell that would descend upon them in retaliation.

That night it did happen again, though it would be a

month before the bodies were found. Two Flanagan guards, unhappy with their situations, deserted and rode out of Three Mile, planning to descend the mountain to warmer climes for the winter. They made it only a mile out of town before two quick, well-placed bullets knocked them out of their saddles.

One died at once. The other was merely paralyzed, his body numb from the neck down. But he could still feel from the neck up, and when the knife touched his forehead, he felt the pain and tried to cry out. His diaphragm was paralyzed and useless, however, and would not draw air into his lungs, so his cry was feeble indeed.

He died of suffocation even as he pondered the mystery of why the man who had shot him and was now cutting on his brow, had painted his face so savagely.

Carolina awakened and looked around her room, trying to remember where she was. She sat up in almost total darkness. Now she remembered: Eiler Flanagan's house, the tower room, a bed that had looked too inviting to be ignored when she'd been led up here earlier in the day. She'd intended only to close her eyes for a few moments, not to fall asleep.

Now it was night. She rose and fumbled around the room until she found a lamp and matches. By lamplight she found a couple of other lamps and fired those up as well. The glow of the flames was cheery. She went to the little fireplace, and with some of the wood and tender stacked there, got a small, warming blaze going.

She examined the pocket watch she carried in her handbag and discovered it was even later than she'd thought. No wonder she was so hungry! It rather surprised her that no one had come up to awaken her for dinner. Surely Eiler Flanagan, who seemed quite debonair and congenial, fed his guests!

Carolina opened her bag and dug out a hairbrush. In an oval wall-mounted mirror, she watched her reflection as she brushed out her still-too-short hair, missing badly the long locks that had been singed in the Dodge City fire. It was hard indeed to make herself look presentable with such short tresses.

As she was putting her brush back into the bag, she paused, then began to search through the bag's contents, ever more rapidly and with a growing frown. At last she emptied the bag on the bed and examined every item, until she knew at last that what she was looking for wasn't there.

Before she'd left Dodge, her father had given her his small derringer for protection. She'd kept it in her bag ever since, had noticed it this very morning, in fact . . . but it wasn't there now.

Sometime since she came to this house, someone had removed it from her bag. But when? The bag had remained at her side even while she talked to Eiler Flanagan.

It could only have been rifled after that, while she slept.

Someone had come into this room and gone through her things while she lay there, sleeping unknowingly.

Carolina let that sink in, shuddered with a cold horror, and wondered who it had been. And why.

That question, once mentally posed, made her angry. She would just find out why!

Carolina marched to the door, put her hand on the knob, turned it.

The knob did not respond.

She was locked in.

Kane was more chagrined that he was willing to admit to discover that his all-day absence from Tobin's house hadn't been much noticed. There had been plenty of other matters to occupy the attention of Tobin's entourage—namely, the near death of Tobin himself.

The man had almost choked. That cough of his, combined with a severe lung inflammation and congestion, had almost taken his life. But the doctor Kane had fetched had done his work well, and Tobin had come through.

He was resting now, and Kane was with him.

"Remarkable!" Tobin said in a weak voice, having just listened to Kane recount his adventure of the day. "It's a puzzling situation for you now, I suppose: an old set of enemies falling in the clutches of a new set . . . kind of like one shark swallowing another. But I don't understand why this Blessed fellow is after you. What do you have that he wants?"

Kane thought it over quickly and decided there was no reason for Tobin not to know the truth. "They want me not for what I have but for what I can lead them to. A treasure."

"A treasure? What kind?"

"The Punjab Star, or so I believe. Have you heard of it?"

"Of course I have. But surely you don't mean *the* Punjab Star? The missing diamond?"

"That's right. Last believed to have been brought to a rural location in Kentucky called Crosslin's Station and there somehow lost in the midst of a wartime bank robbery involving members of the Confederate guerrilla band called Patrick's Raiders—a group that counted among its members both my father and Robert Blessed."

"Ah, so there's the connection! But how does that make it somehow possible for you to lead anyone to the Punjab Star?"

"I can't, not by myself. But I have information, up here"—he tapped his forehead—"and my father has a bit more information, and when you put what I know together with what he knows, you find at the end of it all the Punjab Star. Assuming, of course, that you can break the code."

"The code? What code?"

"My story is a little complicated, but I'm willing to tell it if you're interested in hearing it. At the very least, maybe it can give you some distraction at the end of a long and difficult day."

"Please, tell me."

Kane did. He began at the very start, with his previously simple if impoverished life in the Indian Nations, living with his mother, believing, as did she, that his father was long dead. Then came Robert Blessed and Jason Wyrick, wartime companions of the late William Porterfell, saying they had come for the sake of his memory to take Kane to St. Louis to become part of a successful mercantile business. And so Kane had gone with them, with his mother's blessing.

It had soon proved to be all lies. There was no intention for Kane to be trained in any business. He'd been taken for use as bait, the plan being to hold him hostage until William Porterfell turned himself over to them, along with certain knowledge that he possessed, that being the contents of one missing coded letter that Blessed and Wyrick needed to ferret out the mystery of the lost Punjab Star diamond. All the other letters and the rest of the information, Blessed and Wyrick already possessed.

But Kane hadn't cooperated. He'd escaped, snatching the letters and at the first opportunity, using skills taught him by his old Cherokee mentor to commit them to memory. Then he destroyed them.

More than a handful of coded letters had been destroyed along the way. His mother had been murdered, and he'd lost friends and helpers, such as Cypress and Lewis Washington. He'd done some killing himself in self-defense, but this he didn't mention to Tobin. He told how Robert Blessed had pressed a hard pursuit of him. But Kane continued to run, looking for his father, wanting both to know him and also to warn him of the danger that shadowed both of them.

He told it all, right up through his arrival in Three Mile and his first introduction to Tobin. Tobin listened with gleaming eyes and a face burnished by the flickering light of the fireplace. When Kane was finished with his narrative, Tobin stared at the flames for many moments, thinking it all over, piecing it together in his mind.

"Kane, how certain are you that the missing treasure is the Punjab Star?"

"Relatively sure. I found some historical literature along the way here that linked Patrick's Raiders and the Crosslin's Station robbery very firmly to the Punjab Star legend. An old friend of my father's told me that my father had mentioned the Punjab Star. And Blessed all but directly confirmed for me that the diamond was what he was after."

"Tell me this: Does a roster, however complete or incomplete, of the membership of Patrick's Raiders exist?"

"Of course. You can find the names in any number of historical books."

"Then it all makes a certain sense."

"What are you talking about?"

"About the question of why Eiler Flanagan was so eager to get his hands on William Porterfell, and you."

"Can you explain what you mean?"

"Yes, but keep in mind that it's my speculation— though a likely one, I think."

"I want to hear it, if you're up to telling."

Yancey Tobin, pallid and weak, coughed and said, "I'm up to it."

When some minutes later he was finished, Kane had much to consider. One by one he followed the threads of Tobin's speculations and found them reasonable.

It was a remarkable picture, but a coherent one, and it made Kane very glad he'd been able to give Flanagan's men the slip.

The last place he needed to be, given what Tobin had just told him, was in the house of Eiler Flanagan.

* * *

A new round of snow began a little later in the evening. A lone Flanagan gunman, having given in to the temptation of one of the casinos, came staggering out, broke and drunk, and cursed the weather. He'd lost every cent he owned; to be snowed upon out of a bleak, wintery sky was nothing but a further insult.

He staggered along, cold and still swearing, toward the stable to claim his horse. It would be a cold ride up to the big dormitory at the Flanagan Hill Mine, and he dreaded it.

He never made the ride. A painted shadow descended upon him as he neared the stable, and a blade made quick work of it. He was dead, his throat slashed, even as he slid slowly to the ground, still held by the man who had attacked him.

This time things worked better. The scalp came off cleanly as intended, unlike the others.

But once the killer had the scalp, he had no idea what to do with it. So he merely tossed it into the snow and dragged the dead man over to a nearby dry well. With a heave, the body was up, then gone.

He stood alone a moment, enjoying the dark pleasure that came with revenge, then vanished into the snowy mountains.

He would be back later, for more of them. They would know that a warrior was among them.

In the earlier days of their performing careers, when Carolina was quite a young girl, she and her father had worked for a couple of years with two other traveling actors, performing not only magic tricks, mentalist feats, escapes, and the like, but also brief melodramas, done in full costume and with visual effects that were really no more than conjuring tricks wrapped up and presented in a new fashion.

In one of the melodramas, Carolina had portrayed a child caught in a violent wolf attack in backwoods Kentucky and rescued at the last moment by the intervention of the legendary Daniel Boone, portrayed by her father.

That melodrama had stuck with her long after they ceased to perform it, because it represented to her something she had come to detest more as she had matured: the idea of finding oneself in a dangerous situation and doing nothing more than wailing and moaning about it while waiting for some other person to come along, play the hero, and set things right.

Carolina had decided years ago that she would never in real life act like that child character in the melodrama. When she found herself in trouble, she would extricate herself from it by her own efforts and not wait even one moment for some idealized hero to come along and do it for her.

So it was that she was already hard at work on getting herself out of this locked room. And really, it wasn't a difficult escape at all, because Eiler Flanagan had underestimated her, probably simply because she was a female.

Above the door was a single-paned transom window, hinged at the top and latched at the bottom, which could be opened or shut according to the ventilation needs of the moment. For a lean and healthy young woman such as Carolina, who all her life had been escaping from boxes and tied bags and such in stage performances, climbing up and out of that window wasn't the slightest challenge.

Flanagan had probably assumed that by putting her in a tower room and locking the door, he'd taken all the precautions needed to keep a simple female imprisoned.

The only problem was timing. She had to make her escape when there was no chance that anyone might see her and recapture her. And she had to do it silently.

She'd waited for an hour, her ear pressed to the door, and had occasionally heard voices from below. For a long time, however, she'd heard nothing. And now it was late, after eleven o'clock.

This was the time.

Carolina moved a chair over to the door. Climbing atop it, she hooked her hands on the lower edge of the open transom, clambered up by using hands and feet, and pulled her body into the space.

With the skill of many years of practice in wriggling through small spaces, she squeezed through the window, gripped the edge just right, and swung down.

In the hall now, and no one had seen her. But it was dark, the only light coming through the transom window she'd just passed through. She waited for her eyes to adjust to the darkness, then went to the staircase.

It was good they hadn't guarded her, but also a little insulting. Did Flanagan really believe her to be such a shrinking violet that she didn't even merit a guard at her door? She supposed he imagined her cringing and weeping, too frightened even to try to conquer her situation. Not that she understood what her situation was. It made no sense at all that Flanagan had locked her up. She couldn't fathom what his motive could be.

She descended the staircase quietly. Near the bottom she saw a window that looked into the house's central area. Carefully she approached it, dropping down and crawling beneath it to avoid being seen, for there was light in the room beyond that window and the sound of male voices.

One of them she recognized, the other one . . . maybe she recognized it, too.

She rose just enough to look into the room, and she couldn't stifle a little gasp at what she saw.

Eiler Flanagan was in there, seated in a chair, leaning forward and talking very intently to an equally intent second man.

It was Robert Blessed.

Chapter 21

Robert Blessed sat in a straight-backed chair, with several of Flanagan's guards close to him. Now Flanagan was pacing back and forth before him, still talking, though Carolina was not able to hear him well enough to understand what he was saying.

Wilson, meanwhile, was also seated, but off to the side. He had an ugly, bloody bandage tied around his middle, and his expression was ghastly, his face pallid. He was a man obviously in pain, maybe in danger of his life. Carolina could only suppose he'd been shot. She remembered the battle on the street today between Flanagan's men and the Red Bands and what the man in the cafe had said about one of the apparent prisoners of the Flanagan men being wounded. Perhaps it had been Wilson.

Why did Flanagan have the pair here? Why was he interrogating them? What did he want from them . . . or who?

She watched a while longer, unable to pull herself away, but soon realized she dare not remain here. There would be no escape this way. The only window was this one, opening into Flanagan's big office, and the only door led into that same room.

Carolina knew she shouldn't linger, but should return at once to her room upstairs. She was intrigued and troubled by the sight of Blessed and Wilson, however. She was particularly caught up with Wilson. Would they let the man slowly die?

The main door of the big room opened and the black servant who had admitted her to the house entered, bearing a covered tray and followed by another of Flanagan's gunmen, a young, smiling, cocky fellow whom Carolina disliked on sight. The servant, seeing what was under way, looked aghast, then quickly hid his reaction. The gunman watched it all, still grinning.

She suddenly understood: A tray . . . food! That tray was intended for her!

She darted back up the stairs, wondering if it would even be possible to climb back into her room before they reached it. She stumbled, making noise . . . had they heard her? They mustn't learn she'd gotten out!

She got up and ran the rest of the distance, though now she was limping.

The window seemed higher this time. She put her foot to the knob, tried to climb.

She could hear them mounting the stairs now. She shoved up, trying, failing . . .

They were coming up fast, feet clumping loudly, and she still was not inside. She breathed a quick prayer and tried again.

* * *

His name was Edgar, and he'd been a servant of Eiler Flanagan's since young manhood. In that capacity he had watched the man age and change, had seen the decline of all that had initially been likable and good in him and the rise of all that was bad. This Eiler Flanagan was not the same person Edgar had once served happily, and any affection that servant had held for employer had died years before. Now another, quite different emotion grew where that affection once had prevailed. The moment Flanagan had begun bringing in his army of mercenaries, turning a labor dispute into a war, Edgar had begun to hate him.

With the young gunman at his heels, Edgar reached the doorway of the tower bedroom. He shifted the tray to one arm and reached out to knock, then found his eye caught by a fragment of color above him. He glanced up and saw a shred of cloth hanging on a loose nail on the frame of the window. He looked down again, without calling his younger companion's attention to the cloth, and knocked.

"Miss Railey? It's Edgar. Mr. Flanagan's servant. I've brought you food."

They heard weeping on the other side of the door.

"Miss Railey?"

Her answer sounded petulant and upset. "You want me to open the door for you? How can I, when I'm locked in?"

"No, ma'am, we know you can't open it. We only want to make sure it's proper for us to open the door just now."

"Open it! And let me out of here! Why was I locked in?"

Edgar produced a key and unlocked the door as he expertly continued to balance the tray with his other hand. It swung open to reveal a crying, red-faced Carolina, looking both scared and furious.

"Where is Mr. Flanagan? Why has this outrage happened? How *dare* you lock me in this room! Mr. Flanagan will be furious with you!"

The gunman, grinning, his eyes playing all over Carolina, said, "Flanagan's the one who had it done, gal."

"And who are you?"

"I'm the fellow sent up here to make sure you don't try to run past Edgar here and get away." His eyes flicked up and down, head to toe, one more time.

"Your meal, ma'am?" Edgar said.

"I insist on seeing Mr. Flanagan!"

"I'm sure you will, ma'am, later on. Now, your meal?"

"Bring it in!" She stepped aside, looking cross.

The young gunman continued his lustful staring and smiling. She glared at him fiercely.

"Miss," Edgar said.

"What?" she replied haughtily.

"Let me show you something here, the food . . ."

"I'm entirely capable of dealing with food without your help."

"Please, miss."

Making quite a show of her exasperation, Carolina walked over to Edgar and put her hands on her hips. "Very well."

He lifted the cover of the tray, revealing fried chicken, potatoes, beans, biscuits. "The chicken is overly greasy, I'm afraid. You can see for yourself."

"This is what you wanted to show me?"

"Yes, ma'am. And please look again."

She glanced down and saw him slip a small piece of folded paper beneath the edge of the plate. Her eyes met his, and quickly, silently, she barely nodded.

When they were gone, she waited a few moments, then unfolded the paper and read, "You are in danger. Do nothing for now. I'll return later."

She read the note again, twice, crumpled it, and tossed it into the fire.

She ate the meal, though her nervousness had affected her stomach and it rebelled at the intrusion of food. Then she waited, and waited, and grew tired of waiting.

She glanced up and with a jolt saw the strip of cloth she'd torn from her dress when she'd climbed back into the room at the last moment before Edgar and that grinning young gun had come up the stairs. She retrieved it and tossed it into the fire. Thank God they hadn't seen it!

When would Edgar return? Maybe not even this night. Maybe he'd be kept from it forever. He hadn't even fetched the emptied plates.

She would wait no longer. There was another way out of here, not as easy or direct as passage through a doorway and down stairs, but just as effective, even if a bit theatrical and clichéd, stolen from the pages of a hundred cheap melodramas.

Carolina pulled the cover back from her bed and stripped away the bottom sheet. Sitting on the edge of the bed, she worked a small tear into one edge of the sheet and slowly ripped off a long strand of cloth, all the way down. She repeated the process, then twisted the two pieces of cloth together, tying knots every several inches. She studied it with concern. Would it be strong enough to hold her? She decided to tie in a third strip as well. She hoped she would have enough cloth to reach all the way from her window to the ground, three floors down.

Concentration on her work carried her away, so she was startled when she heard a soft rap on the door.

"Miss?" Edgar's voice, a whisper through the door.

She quickly stuffed her handiwork beneath the bed and let the cover hang down to cover it. "One moment!" she said, just loud enough for him to hear.

"Please hurry, miss."

"Yes . . . yes, you can come in now."

The key rattled, the door opened. Edgar slipped in and closed the door behind him. Carolina was standing in the middle of the room. He locked the door and turned to her.

"Miss, you must not let Mr. Flanagan know I've come to you."

"I won't. Why have you come?"

"To warn you, miss. And to tell you that I'm going to find help for you."

"What's happening here? Why am I locked up?"

"I don't know all the story, miss, just what I've been able to piece together from what I hear. But I've heard a lot. Mr. Flanagan doesn't know that I pay much attention. Or that there are places in this house where a man can hear almost all that goes on in his big office downstairs."

"Is he down there now?"

"Yes, miss. But he's dozing. He sleeps down there often, in his big chair. Sometimes he spends the entire night that way."

"You came up here with him there?"

"Yes, miss."

"Can you help me escape?"

"No, miss, I wouldn't want you to try that. It's far too dangerous. Let me bring help to you. By the way, miss, I think you've already escaped this room once. Am I right?"

"You saw the cloth above the door."

"Yes. But don't worry. That stupid young fellow with me didn't see it."

"Why am I being held prisoner?"

"Mr. Flanagan wants to use you to bring Kane Porterfell to him."

"But I thought Kane *was* here."

"No, miss. He never came. And Mr. Flanagan was furious."

"Why didn't he come?"

"I don't know. Maybe he was warned in some way."

"Why does Mr. Flanagan want Kane?"

"He believes that with Kane he can lure Mr. William Porterfell to him."

"But I don't understand. William Porterfell *was* with him. He worked for him, did he not?"

"Yes, ma'am. But the real reason Mr. Flanagan hired him was that he knew William Porterfell had been one of Patrick's Raiders back in the war days. And with Patrick's Raiders lies the secret of the Punjab Star. And

Mr. Flanagan is obsessed with the Punjab Star. He always has been."

"How did William Porterfell get away from Mr. Flanagan?"

"Mr. Flanagan made an error, miss. He tried to hide the true nature of his interest in Mr. Porterfell, thinking that he was best off slowly gaining Mr. Porterfell's trust and favor, not letting him know at once what his real interest in him was. What he didn't count on was that Mr. Porterfell is a good man. Too good to do the kind of things he was expected to do working as one of Mr. Flanagan's hired guns. So he left. Ran away."

"So he's not in Three Mile?"

"Yes, he is. Or was. He was spotted twice after he left, but no one was able to track him. He's out there somewhere, hiding. I don't know why he didn't leave town."

"And Flanagan believes that with Kane in hand, he can lure William Porterfell back . . ."

"Yes, ma'am . . . and you're the means to get Kane."

"There were men downstairs, being questioned."

"Yes, one named Blessed. I heard a lot of what was said. Blessed and Mr. Flanagan are both after the Punjab Star. They've agreed to help one another. The other man, though, Wilson, I'm afraid bad things will come to him."

"What?"

"He's wounded already. And Blessed told Mr. Flanagan that Wilson was 'unessential.' They'll let him die, I'm afraid. Or maybe even speed it along."

Carolina was horrified to think she was in the hands of a man so ruthless—and she was further horrified to think that he and Blessed were now affiliated. Thank God Kane had not come into Flanagan's hands, as planned! "Does Flanagan know where Kane is now?"

Edgar turned and stared at the door. "Did you hear something on the stairs?"

"No, no. Tell me, quickly! Where is Kane?"

But Edgar didn't answer the question. "I heard something . . ." He dug out his key, trembling, and went to the door. Fumbling, he hurriedly opened the door, looked out, then slipped into the hallway. Before he closed the door, he said to her, "Don't try anything. Don't anger Mr. Flanagan. I'll be back, with help. Somehow. I promise."

"But tell me where—"

It was too late. The door closed, the key turned, and Edgar was gone, leaving Carolina alone, with many vital questions still unanswered.

Chapter 22

As badly as he hurt, as much blood as he'd lost, Wilson knew he could yet live if only they'd let him see a doctor. And that made what was happening all the harder to bear. They were leading him out for a fate no one had spoken to him, but that he realized nonetheless, but if only they'd let him go and find treatment, he would gladly turn away from it all and forget everything he knew about Robert Blessed and his quest for the Punjab Star.

They didn't have to kill him.

He was jolting along on horseback, every impact making him hurt. His hands were tied together before him and also to the horn of his saddle. His horse was being led by the two riders who had custody of him. They were bound for the mountains outside town, moving swiftly through the darkness toward a fate that he was smart enough to know he would never talk himself out of. They'd probably like it if he begged for his life; it would make it more fun to kill him. He would not give them that satisfaction. They'd kill him, but he would die with his dignity intact.

He cursed Robert Blessed. After all he'd gone through for the man, he was now betrayed and cast out, to be conveniently eliminated. Blessed had found himself a rich and powerful partner in Eiler Flanagan. Wilson, wounded and weak, was worthless now. Expendable.

Only one thing gave him any compensatory cheer, and that was the knowledge that much the same fate would surely come to Blessed in the end. Did the man really believe that Eiler Flanagan would share such a prize as the Punjab Star? Once Kane and William Porterfell were in hand and the contents of those letters were re-created and decoded, Blessed would become useless to Flanagan, just another piece of worthless baggage to be cast off, as Wilson was being cast off now.

They rode far out of town, into the cold and snowy mountains. All was quiet and oddly beautiful. Wilson, shivering and suffering, looked at the dark wilderness surrounding him and thought how grand the world was and how bitterly he hated the thought of leaving it.

One of the riders stopped his horse, turned, and looked behind him.

"What is it?" his partner asked.

"Don't know . . . I heard somebody back there. I been hearing it for the last half a mile."

"I don't hear nothing."

The other listened hard, then shook his head. "Maybe I'm wrong."

They rode on, but did not make it a hundred yards before the same thing happened again.

"Did you hear that? I know I heard something that time!"

"There warn't nothing. What's wrong with you? You getting too nervous for this line of work?"

They moved on until they reached a narrow draw, where the horses were halted and the Flanagan hooligans dismounted. They untied Wilson's hands from the saddle horn and forced him to dismount.

"I ask only one thing of you," he said. "Make it swift. Shoot me through the head, not the body."

"Shut up. Get over yonder and kneel, back toward me."

Despite his sorrow and suffering, Wilson managed a burst of pride and defiance. "No. No, I'll kneel, but I'll face you. I'll not be killed by some coward who skulks behind me, afraid to show his face."

"Suit yourself, then. You're just as dead either way it goes."

"You going to do it, Jess, or me?" the other asked.

"I don't care, Maynard. We can flip for it."

"All righty."

Jess dug out a silver dollar. "Heads or tails?"

"Heads."

The coin spun in the air. *They're flipping for the chance to kill me*, Wilson thought. *Flipping a coin to see who gets to put a bullet through my brain.*

"It's tails. I won it."

"How can you tell heads from tails in the dark?"

"I can feel it. Here, feel it for yourself. It's tails."

"Feels like heads to me."

"Hell, I'll light a match then . . . damn! You made me drop my dollar!"

"Strike a match and we'll find it. And flip it one more time."

"Aw, forget about it. You want to shoot him, you shoot him."

"Hssst!"

"What?"

"Something out there."

"Where?"

Wilson had heard it, too, and seen a flash of movement. Out there, close by. *And*, he thought, *human*.

He'd never been a praying man. He was now. He prayed that whoever was out there was there for him.

"Yonder. Did you see it?" Maynard asked.

"No."

"I did."

"It's just your eyes playing tricks on you."

"The hell! I seen something."

Jess drew his pistol. "I'll go take a look, then. I'll show you you're wrong."

In silence, Maynard and Wilson watched Jess recede into the night. In silence they saw the glint of metal rising and falling. The crunch of bone broke the silence, and the sound of Jess collapsing.

Maynard backed toward Wilson, reaching for his pistol. Wilson watched, past him, as a strange, painted figure appeared faintly in the night, approaching them. The pistol went up; Wilson, though weak and faint and losing more blood from his wound, found the strength to lunge against the pistoleer and knock him down. The strange figure drew nearer; a bloodied hatchet rose and fell, once and then again.

Wilson watched as the painted man took the scalp of

the man he'd just killed, then tossed it aside. Wilson fainted then, pitching to the side.

When he awakened, the bonds had been cut from his hands, and his wound had been bound up. He slowly got up, and though dizzy and unsure that he could go more than a few yards, wept with joy at being alive. He began walking across the snowy terrain, reaching the horse upon which they'd brought him out here. He struggled into the saddle and began to ride very slowly back toward Three Mile.

It had taken her very little time to decide not to take Edgar's advice. She would not wait here, would not co-operate with Flanagan. It had never been her way to wait for someone else to get her out of trouble.

She'd finished her makeshift rope and believed it would hold her. Her window was unsecured; this room, unlike the one in which Kane had been held in the house of Robert Blessed at the outset of his adventure, hadn't been refurbished to emulate a jail cell. Flanagan simply assumed that no young woman would dare try to creep like a fly down a sheer three-story wall.

She put out all lights but one, which she cranked down very low. She went to the window and threw it open. Snow had begun to fall again and the wind was icy. It sliced through her as she tied the fabric rope se-curely in place and threw the length of it out the window. It reached nearly to the ground.

Fetching her valise, Carolina tossed it out the window; it thudded softly to rest in the snow below. She put on her coat and pulled it tightly around her, breathed a prayer, took hold of the rope, and began her descent.

It was harder than she'd anticipated, largely because she was dressed so poorly for such an exercise. And the wall was slippery, sheened with ice. Her feet maintained only a tenuous hold on the wall as she eased slowly downward.

She was halfway down when her feet finally slipped. The lower half of her body jerked downward; her upper torso slammed into the wall, hard. The stretching fabric in her hands was thin and weak and she was unable to maintain her grip.

Carolina squelched the impulse to scream as she fell a story and a half straight down to the ground below. She struck hard, her face smothering in snow. Groaning, she rolled over, tried to rise, and collapsed again. There she lay, still, the falling snow drifting down onto her face. She stared up through it for half a minute, and then her eyes slowly closed.

Ves Snowden was very drunk, full of grief, and bitterly angry.

His brother was dead. Somewhere on the way to thorough intoxication, he'd finally gotten a grasp of that fact. Freddy was *dead*. And who could bear the blame except the damned strikers?

Ves didn't and probably never would know precisely who had murdered and mutilated his brother. So there was no one to blame but the two men who led the strike effort: Yancey Tobin and Caleb Creede.

So drunk that he could hardly keep his balance, he

stood now before a large oak gun cabinet, property of Eiler Flanagan, and now damaged by Ves Snowden, who had pried open the lock and removed a prize shotgun and a box of ammunition. Muttering murderous words to himself, his mind full of bloody visions of the soon-to-come deaths of both Tobin and Creede, Snowden loaded the shotgun, slammed it closed, and dumped extra shells into his coat pockets.

Wheeling dizzily, he got his bearings as best he could, fought back a strong impulse to fall down on the floor into a fast and deep sleep, and staggered to the door. He threw it open, squinted against the driving snow, and stumbled out into the whiteness.

His first destination would be the house of Yancey Tobin. Once done there, he would move on and find Caleb Creede.

Carolina felt warm, content. She did not want to get up.

But she knew she must. It would be death to lie here longer.

Her ankle . . . it hurt, it hurt so bad. She didn't want to have to put weight on that ankle. She wondered if it was broken. Just now she couldn't tell. She'd think about that, mull it over while she lay here, warm and comfortable in this soft, soft snow . . .

No. This was the end. She'd heard it came this way for those who froze to death. An ease of mind, a comfort of body, an overwhelming desire for sleep.

She opened her eyes, gritted her teeth, and pushed herself upward. The pain came now. Preparing herself, she squeezed her eyes closed and got to her feet. She kept her weight on her good foot, the left one, then slowly transferred it to the right one, until the pain was too much and she almost fell.

She'd not be able to bear full weight on her right foot, which would create quite a challenge in walking, especially in a thickening snowfall. She looked around for something to use as a crutch. Nothing was close by, but beneath a tree about ten feet away, she saw a fallen branch poking out from the snow.

Hopping over, she bent and picked it up. It was substantial, about the right length, but had no crotch in which to prop herself. It was the best she could do, though. Using it as a walking stick, she began moving across the yard, praying that no one in the house would find her before she could get away. She realized she had forgotten her valise. Biting her lip, she hobbled back to where it had landed, bent carefully, maintaining her balance, and picked it up.

She resumed her journey away from the house, thinking that this surely must have been what it was like for Kane to escape from the house of Robert Blessed back in St. Louis. Except that Kane didn't have a hurt foot, a biting wind, and rising heaps of fresh snow to contend with.

She fixed her eye on the road at the base of the long, sloping yard. *One step at a time*, she whispered to herself. *One step at a time.*

But the steps were slow, too slow, the distance too far. The harder she struggled, the more frustrated she became. And her ankle, despite the help of the walking stick, hurt worse.

A door opened and closed back at the house. Loudly. She heard the voice of a man.

Panic hit her. Someone was coming out. She'd been seen, or soon would be, and with her ankle injured she could not run.

Carolina tried to hurry, but it was too much. She put her weight on the stick and it snapped suddenly, like a great twig. She fell, her weight coming hard onto her ankle. She cried out before she could stop herself.

The snow cushioned her. She pushed herself up, tried to rise, but couldn't. Her ankle throbbed.

The man was getting closer. And talking. He sounded strange. Drunk, maybe. Twisting her head, she saw him coming toward her. He carried a shotgun, and now he was close enough for his slurred words to be understandable.

He was talking of death and revenge. She heard the name Yancey Tobin, a string of curses, then the name Caleb Creede. Full of terror, Carolina tried again to get up. She succeeded, balancing her weight entirely on her good foot. But what good was it? He could see her clearly now, and she could not run. Did she think she could escape him by hopping like a monopode down a snowy hillside?

She stood there. It was all she could do, just stand there, holding a broken tree branch in one hand, her valise lying cockeyed at her feet. With a twist of frustration she saw that she'd come farther than she'd thought. She was almost at the road.

Too late to reach it now. He would be upon her in moments. She could see that the man was indeed drunk, or so she let herself conclude, because the only other alternative—that he was insane—was too frightening to consider. For a moment she dared hope that he would simply pass by her, not seeing her because of the snow-fall and his intoxication.

He did see her, though, and was cursing at her. That was all she could make out of his words—curses, slurred and terrible.

"Go away from me!" she said to him forcefully. "I'm not the one you're after! Go away!"

He cursed and raised the shotgun. *God in heaven, would he shoot me right here?*

She swung the broken stick at him and hit him in the side of the head. The shotgun swung wild but did not discharge. She saw that he had failed to cock it. "Go away!" she yelled again.

He swore once more, then hit her in the forehead with the butt of the shotgun. She collapsed backward into the snow. He teetered above her, looking down at her, murmuring foul things. He wavered, like a tree about to fall, and pitched forward on top of her, where he passed out cold.

The snow continued to fall.

Chapter 23

Kane opened his eyes and sat up, listening. An odd noise, one he'd not heard before, roused him out of bed. He struck a match and read the face of his watch. Two in the morning. He shook out the match, heard that odd sound again, and stepped into the hallway.

Trumbling was there, slumped against the wall in the dimly lighted hallway, dabbing at his face with thick fingers. When he saw Kane he gave a loud *harumph!*, straightened, and wiped his eyes very fast.

"Is something wrong?" Kane asked.

Trumbling paused, then said in a tremulous voice, "I'm afraid we're going to lose him, Mr. Porterfell. He's not doing well, not at all."

Kane heard a wheezing cough from Tobin's room. A groan followed, barely stifled. After a moment he heard Tobin's voice, barely above a whisper, speaking.

"Might I see him?"

"In a few moments, I think that would be a good thing. He's got someone with him now."

"Mr. Trumbling . . . is he dying?"

"I don't know, I don't know. I hope not. But he called in the priest for confession."

"That's who's with him now?"

"Yes."

Kane leaned back against the wall beside Trumbling, who was struggling not to weep again. After several minutes, the door opened and a somber priest emerged.

"How is he?" Trumbling asked.

"At peace. Ready for whatever comes," the priest answered.

Kane entered the room. The light was a little brighter. Tobin was sitting up in bed, looking somewhat stronger than Kane had expected to find him, considering the dismal predictions of Trumbling.

"How are you?" Kane asked.

"Better, maybe. Earlier I didn't know. I feared my time had come."

"I'm sorry . . . I must have slept through it."

Tobin waved it off. "I've had many close calls, with these lungs of mine."

"When I first met you, Yancey, you denied you were sick."

"It's because I was denying it to myself. But the truth is, Kane, that I'll probably not live to see another winter after this one. Perhaps not even the coming spring."

"Consumption?"

"I think so. Yes. The lungs are the plague of miners, you know."

"I'm sorry."

"So am I, in some ways. I have no fear of dying . . .

but there are regrets. I'm afraid I may die without seeing this strike resolved." He paused, then chuckled ironically. "On the other hand, I fear I will live long enough to see it erupt into some truly dreadful violence."

"You don't look to me like a man about to die."

"My strength comes and goes. Within the span of a few hours I can feel strong one minute, close to the grave the next. Unfortunately, I seem to be visiting the grave's edge more frequently."

"You'll not die, Yancey. You'll shake this off."

"Like I said, Kane, I don't really mind the dying. But I wonder if my life has been what it could have been. What good have I done those around me?"

"Much good. You're respected. You've stood for justice, peace . . . Trumbling was shedding tears for you just now. That's the legacy you've made for yourself with those who know you."

"I'm glad to hear it, then. I've wanted my life to be worthwhile." He stared at the cranked-down lamp on the mantel across the room. "I hope my death can be worthwhile as well."

"What do you mean?"

The man smiled. "To be honest, I'm not quite sure. It's just a feeling I'm trying to understand, and express."

Trumbling appeared at the door. "Yancey, there's a man been found. Injured."

Tobin sat up straighter. "One of ours?"

"No. I don't know this fellow. But Joe Banks saw him slipping off his horse at the edge of town and has brought him in. Joe says this is one of two men who were took prisoner by some of Flanagan's riders in the street."

Kane said quickly, "Let me see him."

"Right this way."

The figure, laid out on a floor pallet beside the fire in the main room, was bloodied, pale, almost corpselike. Kane walked over to him and looked down into his face. The eyes slowly opened.

"Hello, Wilson," Kane said after a long moment's pause. "It looks like you've been shot."

He was fifteen years old, but bigger than many men twice his age and shaving every day. Size and early maturity ran in the family of young Rich Clancey, and it was a good thing, considering the kinds of difficulties life had always thrown in that family's path.

Nocturnal wanderings in the snow weren't common for Rich, but tonight he'd had reason, even if no more of one than a missing cat. His widowed, laundress mother, who worked harder than any three miners to keep herself, her son, and her three daughters fed, loved that cat dearly. When it had gone missing a day before, Rich Clancey had decided to search for it until he found it, no matter how long it took or how far he had to roam.

Despite his determination, the cat remained unfound . . . but he'd found something, just now, and he wasn't sure what it was.

Just a lump in the snow, down at the base of the yard of the big Flanagan house, almost at the edge of the road. A lump . . . a *moving* lump.

Rich Clancey walked slowly toward the mysterious

something, mouth open, eyes narrowed, trying to make out what he could in this blasted darkness. He thought he might have imagined the movement, but then it happened again. He stepped back, startled, then got hold of himself and moved forward again.

A drunk, probably, passed out in the snow. But if he was moving he was still alive and maybe could be saved.

Rich Clancey knelt and began sweeping away the snow with his hands. He uncovered fabric—the back of a man's coat. He brushed more desperately now, uncovering the man further, touching the skin on the back of his neck and feeling alarmed at how cold it was.

"Mister, can you hear me?"

The man did not reply. Rich leaned over and put his ear against the man's back. He heard no heartbeat or sound of respiration. Yet the man moved again, slightly.

"Hail, Mary, full of grace ..." Rich whispered his prayer fast, fighting unearthly panic. How could a dead man move?

Then he heard something. A voice. But too high to be a man's. Suddenly he understood. There was more than one person here. Beneath the dead man lay another human being, alive. Perhaps a child, or a woman.

He rolled the corpse off to the side, and indeed, there was another person under it. He looked as closely as the darkness would allow and felt the clothing. A woman, he believed, though he wasn't sure. But definitely alive. The man above her had frozen to death, but his remaining body heat, plus his protective physical bulk, had saved her from freezing.

Rich Clancey positioned himself beside her, slipped his arms beneath her, and with a grunt worthy of a strong man lifting weights in a traveling show, picked her up. Once he had her balanced, he began walking through the dark town toward his home.

The snow began to fall more heavily, bit by bit burying the corpse of Ves Snowden, until at last no sign of him remained at all.

Mere minutes after Rich Clancey stumped away, Carolina Railey limp and half frozen in his arms, a small door on the side of the Flanagan mansion opened, and Edgar emerged. He was clad in a heavy coat and hat and carried a bag laden with his few possessions. In his pocket was a sealed envelope with the name of Kane Porterfell written on the outside.

He'd waited until this darkest hour of the night to make his escape because he knew there would be only one chance. If he were caught, he'd probably not be able to explain to Flanagan's satisfaction what he was doing. He did not want to be caught.

Edgar worried about the snow. It would leave tracks. With any luck, more snowfall would obliterate them before it was discovered that he was gone. But he would need luck even beyond that to make it out of Three Mile.

One stop to make and then he'd go on to the train station. There he would buy a one-way ticket as soon as the station opened, hide nearby, and await the first train out of town.

Once he was gone, he would never return. He was finished with Eiler Flanagan forever.

Edgar did not leave the yard unseen. The painted man, back now from the mountains, watched his small, dark form pass across the snow and vanish into the darkness. Should he kill this one? Was this nocturnal escapee another of Flanagan's hired gunmen? He wasn't sure, and that uncertainty saved the life of Edgar.

When Edgar was out of sight, the painted man slipped like a shadow to the house, paused at the same door Edgar had exited, and quietly entered.

One more life and scalp would he take before he was through. One more life, and Aganstati would be avenged.

"How did it happen, Wilson?" Kane asked. He was seated on the floor beside his old foe and pursuer, a man obviously not long for the world. Too bad the priest was gone—a man such as Wilson probably had plenty of sins needing confession.

"It was . . . Flanagan, one of his men. Shot me when I tried to get away from them . . . on the street."

As pitiful as Wilson looked, Kane was having a hard time mustering much pity for him. He knew the kind of man he and his partners-in-hire, Blessed's underlings, had been. "Well, obviously you did get away. You're here."

"A . . . miracle. That's the only way it happened. They'd took me out in the mountains . . . to shoot me. But he got them. Killed them . . . took their scalps . . ."

Scalps? "Who killed who?"

"The Indian . . . painted face . . . he killed the two men who Flanagan had sent . . . into the mountains to kill me."

An Indian with a painted face, killing men in the mountains? Wilson was surely talking out of his head. "Why would Flanagan want you killed?"

"He and Blessed . . . partners now. Both of them after you . . . after your father. They want the diamond. Me . . . I was already wounded, not needed by them anymore . . . in the way. So they sent men out with me . . . to finish me. Get me out of the picture."

"The diamond—you're talking about the Punjab Star?"

"Yes . . . yes."

In a steadily weakening voice, Wilson began to talk. Kane wondered what compelled the man to speak at all. Guilt? The need to compensate for a life of wickedness by sheer volume of confessional words? Whatever drove Wilson, he seemed glad to have Kane, of all people, as his audience, and what he said was worth hearing.

"When they took us, Kane, they questioned us . . . Flanagan himself, pumping questions at us, mostly at Blessed. He *knew* Blessed, even before we were there . . . knew who he was, anyway. He asked Blessed why we had snatched you, what we were after. He talked about the Punjab Star . . . Flanagan is a jewel collector, Kane. And he's been after the Punjab Star for years . . . studied the legends surrounding it, and its disappearance . . . he has books, lists of names . . . he knows the name of every man in Patrick's Raiders, Kane. It's how he knew Blessed. And he knows your father . . ."

"And for a time, my father worked for him," Kane said.

"Yes . . . Flanagan told it all, to Blessed. But I heard it. Flanagan's brother, in Kansas, sent your father to him to serve in his ... private army, to be one of his gun-men ... and Eiler Flanagan planned to question him, to see if he might know how and where the Punjab Star ... disappeared ... but your father got away from him. Quit his work because ... he thought it was wrong, the things Flanagan's men were doing. And Flanagan was furious ... wanted to get him back. So then came another telegram ... from his brother, saying that William Porterfell's son was coming to Three Mile ... to find his father. Flanagan believed he could use you as a hostage ... to get your father back and find out what he knew about the diamond."

It made sense now. So *that* was Eiler Flanagan's personal interest in him! *That* was why he went to the trouble of sending gunmen to meet him at the train station and why he'd alerted his riders to find and capture Kane Porterfell.

Wilson asked for water, and Trumbling, standing by, fetched him some. When Wilson had drunk a few sips, he was able to talk again, though he was weakening rapidly.

"Flanagan wanted you ... but you didn't come. So he had his men looking out for you ... all through town. But Blessed and me got you first ... and you know the rest. They took me and Blessed to the house after you got away ... wanted to know all about us. And Flanagan, of course, he was all excited when he found out it was Robert Blessed he had captured ... for he knew Robert Blessed had been among Patrick's Raiders.

"Blessed ended up telling Flanagan everything ...

about the letters, how they were written in code, what they were supposed to lead to . . . and Flanagan got more and more excited . . . in the end, he and Blessed joined up. Partners. And for me, a bullet through the head out in the mountains . . ."

"But you got away."

"Yes. Because of the Indian."

"Who is this Indian you talk about?"

"I don't know . . . killed both of them. Scalped them . . ."

Kane was rocked by a sudden thought: *Tsani?* He remembered the Cherokee writing he'd found in the cabin of the Ridge brothers, and the way John Ridge had spoken at the last in the Cherokee language, calling Stanton by his old name of Aganstati. But would John Ridge have reversed his course so extremely as to paint his face and begin a war of vengeance against the mercenary band who had killed his brother?

It was possible, Kane supposed, but surely it was more likely that the "Indian" of whom Wilson spoke was no more than a fevered fantasy.

"Wilson, why are you telling me all this?"

"I'm dying, Kane . . . I want to set things right. I've been a wicked man, pursuing you like I have. I want to tell you . . . I'm sorry . . . and that you need to be . . . careful, so careful. With Flanagan and Blessed together . . . they'll be after you, like devils . . . and after your father, too."

"I'll be careful."

"Kane . . . forgive me, forgive me for all I done . . ."

Kane looked at the man, remembered how relentless he and his partners had been in pursuing him. No sign of human decency or kindness had they shown. Wilson did not deserve to be forgiven.

But seeing him lying there, closer to death each moment, seeking some solace and release of guilt in these his final minutes of life, Kane could not be a human being and not sympathize with the man's suffering. He swallowed hard, with great force of will mentally erased the wickedness this man had done, and said, "I forgive you."

Wilson closed his eyes and smiled, one time. He did not open his eyes again, or speak. As the sun rose over the mountains, his breathing became slower, more labored, and at last stopped.

Kane stared at the dead man before the fire, rose, and walked back to his room, saying nothing.

A few minutes later, Kane answered a knock on his door. It was Trumbling, with an envelope in hand.

"Found this outside, stuck in the door," he said. "It's got your name on it."

Kane, puzzled, took the envelope. "Thank you."

"Who do you reckon left it?"

"I don't know."

"You going to read it?"

"Yes." But Kane did not move to open the envelope at once. Trumbling cleared his throat self-consciously, getting the message. He turned and left the room.

Kane tore open the envelope and read the message inside. When he was done he stared at the words, his eyes skimming over with tears. He shook his head quickly, getting hold of himself. A moment later he struck a match and burned the paper.

He didn't know who this Edgar was, or why he'd bothered to inform him of what he had . . . or even if what the letter said was true. He had to act on the assumption that it was. If there was even a chance that Carolina was at risk, he didn't dare act otherwise.

According to the letter, Eiler Flanagan had her. She was locked away in a room at the top of that big tower fronting the Flanagan house. Why she might have come to Three Mile was something Kane could not guess.

He sat down, thinking hard, trying to figure out what to do. After twenty minutes, he got pen and paper of his own and began to write. He folded the completed document and put it back into the envelope that he'd received, marked out his own name, and wrote in that of Yancey Tobin.

Quietly he left his room. No one was in the hallway. He went silently to Yancey Tobin's room, knelt, and slipped the envelope under the door.

Then he put on his coat and hat and left the house, walking through the snow toward the Eiler Flanagan mansion.

Chapter 24

Though the room where Eiler Flanagan spent most of his time was the spacious, ornate office downstairs, a place elsewhere in the house was his true private sanctum: a simple, small office on the second floor, with nothing in it but a battered old rolltop desk, a couple of chairs, and a sturdy safe, inside which he kept his most important personal papers, various small possessions of sentimental value—and several prized jewels that were the crowns of his collection. At times he would lock himself away in that little room and spend hours with his beloved gemstones, holding them, looking at them in the light, and dreaming of the day when he would own the grandest jewel of them all: the lost Punjab Star.

That fabled diamond had long been his obsession. He'd collected every fact, legend, and speculation about the missing stone that he could find and had examined in the most minute detail the stories about the wartime bank robbery at Crosslin's Station, Kentucky, where, according to some, the Punjab Star was lost. Or had it been lost? Others suggested the diamond had been

stolen by one or more members of Patrick's Raiders, the
Rebel band behind the robbery. So Flanagan had absorbed the lore of the often romanticized guerrilla band,
which had rampaged right under the noses of the Yan-
kees, more than once very nearly invading the North.
He'd obtained a roster of almost every man who had
served in the sometimes loosely defined band and had
gone over every name until he could all but recite the
entire list.

He'd been more than intrigued when one of those
names, William Porterfell, had turned up attached to a
man sent to him by his brother, Ben. Sure enough, it
was the same William Porterfell who had served in
Patrick's Raiders—indeed, one of the handful directly
associated with the Crosslin's Station robbery. But Flanagan had been too cautious; afraid to let Porterfell know
too quickly of his obsessive interest in what he might
know of the lost diamond, he'd let the man slip through
his fingers. The cable from his brother notifying him
that Porterfell's son was coming had seemed a perfect
opportunity to rectify the problem, but for some reason
Kane Porterfell had not shown up at the train station as
scheduled.

Eiler Flanagan was in his little office, the safe door
ajar, when a knock came at the door. He glanced at his
pocket watch and wondered who would be calling at
this hour. He closed and locked the safe, then pulled the
door open. Buster Keller, one of his bodyguards, was
there, still bed-rumpled.

"Mr. Flanagan, sorry to disturb you, sir . . . but you've
got a visitor."

"In the middle of the night? Who?"

"Kane Porterfell, sir. He just . . . showed up. Nobody else answered the door, so I got up. He says he wants to see you."

Flanagan paused just long enough for the incredible news to sink in, then nodded. "Thank you. Take him into my office downstairs . . . and watch him like a hawk. I'll be right down."

Five minutes later, Flanagan was standing in his office, looking Kane in the eye, studying him with the same consuming interest he might give to one of his favorite stones. He nodded slowly.

"I can see your father's looks in your face, young man. Truly you are Porterfell's son. I'm glad you've chosen to come here at last, even at this hour. I often am up all night. But why did you not meet my men at the depot, as we'd arranged?"

"Maybe because I don't feel particularly trusting when I find myself greeted by a group of armed men who look like they'd kill a man for spitting."

"My men are not church deacons, that I'll grant you. But tell me why you've come now?"

"Because I was informed that someone I care about is in your custody."

"Ah, yes! The lovely Miss Railey. Indeed she is. But how did you know?"

Kane would not betray Edgar—whoever Edgar was—and said nothing.

"Never mind, then. It hardly matters. What matters is that you're here." Flanagan chuckled and licked his lips. "By the way, Mr. Porterfell, there's another old friend of yours here, too." He called over his shoulder. "Mr. Blessed! Do come in now!"

Robert Blessed walked through the door. Kane glared at him but refused to react beyond that. Blessed looked haughty, but he seemed disappointed that Kane remained so calm after seeing him.

"My new partner!" Flanagan announced. "I understand you and he already have some history together."

"He's a murderer. A devil."

"Tut, tut, Mr. Porterfell! Sometimes a touch of ruthlessness is required to get by in this world." Flanagan leaned forward, right in Kane's face. "But let's put all the foolish talk aside. Mr. Blessed has told me the entire story—the letters, your capture and escape, his efforts to apprehend you. Now it's time for us to settle all our accounts at once. The bargain is simple: You re-create the letters you've memorized, right now, on paper, right down to the last dot on the last *i* and the last cross on the final *t*, and you can then walk out of here, alive. With your beloved Miss Railey safely at your side."

"Wait!" Blessed said, suddenly concerned. "You can't let him go! We'll need to hold him to attract his father! His father is the only man who knows what's in the one missing letter."

"Indeed. Good point. Good point. Well, Mr. Porterfell, let me alter my offering that much. You re-create the letters, and Miss Railey goes free. You, I'm afraid, may have to wait a while longer. Until your father is found."

"You may never find him. He's probably long gone from this town."

"Then you may be our guest for a long, long time. At least until we decide you are no longer useful to us."

"And then you'll kill me? Like you killed Wilson?"

Flanagan and Blessed glanced at one another. "What do you know about Wilson?"

"Never mind. Suffice it to say that your effort didn't succeed nearly so quickly as you intended. Tell me, have the men you sent to do that job returned?"

"No . . ."

"They won't. Something to do with a painted Indian."

"What do you know? Tell me!"

"I've said all I intend to say."

Flanagan glowered at Kane, then said, "To hell with it! What matters is the letters. You'll write them out . . . *now.*"

Kane looked from face to face, despising both of his captors. But with Carolina their prisoner—if in fact she was—he could hardly deny them. He might demand to see her, but what good would that do? Whether or not they had her, they now had *him*. He would cooperate.

From time to time Kane had fantasized about finding his father, re-creating with him the full body of the encoded letters, and in the end finding the Punjab Star, if in fact it could be found . . . but now none of that mattered. He was weary of all this and cared nothing for any missing jewel, no matter how valuable. He would write out the letters, and they could choke on them. Just let Carolina be free and safe. As for himself, he'd become quite adept at escaping lately. If he had to, he would do it again.

"Bring me paper and pen," he said. "I'll write your cursed letters for you."

Blessed chortled and clapped. Flanagan was more restrained, but Kane could tell it took a lot of effort. As the white-haired man hurried to a shelf for foolscap and a pen, it seemed as if it was all he could do to restrain himself from breaking into a dance of joy.

He worried at first that his memory might fail him under such pressure, but as his pen scratched over the paper, he found he could recall them all. One by one he wrote out the letters, retracing in his mind the path of memorization as Toko had taught him. He wrote steadily for an hour, and when he was done, he handed the finished documents to Flanagan.

"There, sir. Those are the letters, complete and accurate. You can trust them. If you can break their code, then you will have the facts you want."

Flanagan clutched the papers with trembling hands. He tried hard to maintain his dignity, but a laugh of pure excitement bubbled out of him, and the jig he'd managed to suppress earlier finally found its outlet, and he skipped and hopped.

"Now," Kane said, "I've completed my part of the bargain. It's your turn. Let Carolina go."

Flanagan was studying the letters closely. "Hmmm? Oh, no, young man. Not yet. Not yet. There's still one more part of the bargain for you to fulfill."

"But you said—"

"What I said doesn't matter now, Mr. Porterfell. What I *say* matters, and what I say is that you are going to leave this house, go to the place where you've stayed these past days, that being the house of damned Yancey Tobin, and there you will take the life of said Mr. Tobin. Once you have done that, and once I have the proof of the act in my hand, then, and only then, will Carolina Railey go free."

Kane stood, outraged. "I'll do no such thing! And I don't even believe you have her!"

Flanagan walked to his desk, yanked open a drawer, and tossed something small and metallic on the floor. Kane knelt and picked it up. It was an unloaded derringer, marked with the initials "F.R." He knew this little weapon. It belonged to Frederick Railey.

Firmly, triumphantly, Flanagan said, "That was removed from the valise of your young lady before she was locked up. Oh, I do have her here, indeed I do, and don't you doubt it. And yes, you *will* kill Yancey Tobin if you ever wish to see her again."

Blessed, as stunned as Kane by this sudden new demand, said, "But this is an absurdity! What does this Tobin fellow have to do with our purpose here? The goal is the diamond, not the satisfaction of some sideline interest of yours!"

Flanagan wheeled to face Blessed. "You dare to lecture me, sir? Do you wish to dissolve our partnership?" He shook the letters. "It is I who possess these letters now!"

"Yes," Blessed said, speaking slowly, restraining his emotions, and choosing his words carefully, "but you do need me, sir, to break the code."

Flanagan lifted a brow. "A good point. Though I rather believe that I could find other code breakers with relative ease. The United States Army is quite adept with codes, you know, and a man of my wealth and influence can tap that resource if need be." He looked hard at Blessed. "Now . . . will you leave this matter under my direction, or will we seek another mutual arrangement?"

Blessed's nostrils flared once, twice, three times, and then he surrendered. "Do as you wish, sir."

"That's my usual approach . . . I've come to rather like it." He turned to Kane again. "Go. And within twelve hours bring me proof of the death of Yancey Tobin. Then your young lady will be free."

"But why me?" Kane asked. "You have gunmen in your hire."

"Yes, but is that not precisely the point? They are in my hire, and what they do would inevitably be linked to me. I don't need that. I need Yancey Tobin to die a quiet, seemingly natural death, which is much easier achieved by someone with access to his house. Oh, it need not be violent. I hear the man is very sick. A pillow across the face while he sleeps under the influence of some strong medicine, a long needle plunged, undetected, into his heart or up through his nose into his brain—any of these subtle methods, or any other that your vile Indian mind can conceive, will do the job. And of course, there'll be no connection to me.

You're certainly no employee of mine! So . . . have we an understanding?"

After a pause, Kane said, "We have an understanding."

"Then be off with you. And no tricks. Any tricks and she dies. And by the way, don't consider going to the law. The law in this town lives in my purse."

"So I've heard." Kane turned and walked toward the door, but he stopped there and spoke to Blessed. "Don't think you'll ever see that diamond, Blessed. He's not going to give up any share of wealth for you, and you know it. The moment you decode those letters for him, you'll become as useless as Wilson was. And just as expendable. Tell me, though—was the code . . . something used by Patrick's Raiders?"

"Something like that," Blessed said. He was trying to look as haughty as usual, but Kane's words had shaken him. "Or some new code based upon it. I've not yet had time to break it."

"Twelve hours, Kane," Flanagan said. "Twelve hours, and no more."

Kane left the house without another look back or another word spoken.

Flanagan turned to Blessed. "The time has come to make yourself useful, Mr. Blessed. I want you to break this code."

Blessed's throat was dry when he spoke. "It may take time. Possibly even days."

Flanagan said, "Then days it will be, if it comes to that. But we'll waste no time getting started."

"And when I'm finished?"

"Have we not struck a bargain? Do we not have an arrangement?"

"Wilson and I had an arrangement, too."

"Mr. Blessed, I don't believe you trust me."

"Should I?"

"The question is, Do you have any choice?"

Blessed thought about it. "I suppose I'd best get started," he said.

"Yes. You can work upstairs, in a private, smaller office that I have there. More peace and solitude for you. Before long I'll have Edgar bring us some food. Where is that blasted Edgar, anyway? He's usually up long before dawn."

Blessed took the letters; it was as if they burned in his hand. But they weren't fully his, as the long-ago-destroyed originals of these letters had been. Flanagan had his claim on them, a claim strengthened by his wealth and power. He had the upper hand, and Blessed saw no way around it.

Worse, he knew that Kane was right. When these letters were decoded, he would be of no more use to Flanagan. One simple order, and he'd be hauled off to the mountains and disposed of, just like Wilson.

The more he thought about it, the more sure he became that it was going to take a long, long time indeed to break the code of those letters. He would make sure of it.

He needed all the time he could get, just to think, to find a way out.

* * *

Tobin was awake, to Kane's surprise. When Kane looked into his room, he got up and embraced him. He seemed stronger now, even in his rumpled nightshirt.

"Thank God!" Tobin declared. "When I read your note, I didn't know whether I'd see you again. Tell me, why in the name of heaven would you go to Flanagan's house?"

"He has her, Yancey. Carolina Railey. I told you about her. I believe I love her, Yancey. And he has her, and he's going to kill her, unless . . ."

"What?"

"Unless within the next twelve hours I kill you and bring him proof of it."

Tobin's reaction to that announcement was far more muted than Kane had expected. "Hmmm," he said. "I'm not surprised. That sounds like Flanagan's style." Tobin rubbed his chin, and—surprising to Kane—it seemed that a touch of color returned to his face and a brightness to his eyes. "So he seeks to make you his agent . . . to have you kill me, leaving him free to avoid any blame and, if all goes as he hopes, to end the strike." He shook his head. "Not that my death would end the strike. It has moved well beyond me now . . . the Red Bands, I'm afraid, are gaining ground. But I suppose what matters to Flanagan is just to get me gone for his own satisfaction. The man, at heart, is a deluded fool who thinks he's above all law and shielded from retribution for anything he does."

"What can I do, Yancey? I can't assassinate you."

Yancey fell into a terrible fit of coughing. The color drained from his face, and he sat down on the edge of the bed. It took a very long time for him to find his voice again, and Kane noticed, though Yancey possibly did not, that there was now a thin line of blood around the edges of his lips. "You can't assassinate me. Why not?"

"What?"

"Maybe what we should give Flanagan is precisely what Flanagan wants. Me."

"What are you talking about? You want me to kill you?"

"I'd never make a murderer of you or anyone else, Kane. God forbid. But my desire to make my life . . . and my impending, undeniable, soon-to-come death . . . to make these meaningful and worthwhile in some way—maybe this is my opportunity."

"You're confusing me."

"It's difficult to explain. I'd thought that my leadership of this strike might be the gift I was to give to this world. Now I see that my leadership has gradually died away. Caleb Creede and his more radical ideas have gained the influence that I once had. So perhaps I can make my life worthwhile in another way."

"Why do I never understand you, Yancey?"

Tobin smiled. "Perhaps what's important isn't that you understand me, but that I understand myself . . . and His purposes." He pointed upward.

Kane shook his head, tired of Tobin's endless obscurity. "I'll not kill you, Yancey. Nor will I let Flanagan keep Carolina. I'll get her out of there, somehow."

"Do you know he really has her? The man is capable of vast lies."

"I saw a small pistol. Her father's. His initials on it. Yes, he has her."

"We still have nearly twelve hours to figure this one out, Kane. My advice to you is to do what I intend to do. Think, very hard. And pray harder."

Chapter 25

The room was cold, but Blessed was sweating, and hoping Flanagan wouldn't notice. Curse the man! Did he think he was helping, pacing around in the background while Blessed tried—though none too rigorously—to begin the process of breaking the code used in the letters?

He had actually begun back in St. Louis, after the first of the letters came into his hands. At first he'd not comprehended what it meant—gibberish, for the most part, but with certain sentences thrown in that tugged at something in his mind. At last he'd grasped it: The letters were in a code not identical to but clearly derivative from a code that he and other central members of Patrick's Raiders had used for written communication during the war. He'd started trying to decipher the code right away and had been making good progress when all this business with Kanati Porterfell came up and the letters were stolen, a few of them still uncopied at the time. By that point Blessed had gotten far enough along in his decoding to know that the letters concerned the lost Punjab Star, and as soon as that was known the whole affair became his full-time obsession.

But Flanagan was a fool if he thought this code would be broken in one night, especially with him hovering around like a vulture, distracting and nerve-racking. Not that Blessed would break the code that quickly even if it were possible. He was quite concerned about what would happen to him once Flanagan had the decoded letters in his possession.

Someone knocked on the door again. Flanagan cursed and yanked it open. Buster Keller again.

"What?"

"Mr. Flanagan, I just thought you'd want to know . . . there's trouble up at the mine. Mr. Smithers sent down a rider to tell us. Some Red Bands trying to set fire to some buildings. They caught them at it and drove them off, but they're still lingering around. There's a battle liable to bust out up there, and they're wondering if a few of us stationed here at the house could be spared to help out."

Flanagan's mind was on other things right now. He waved his hand in Keller's face. "Hell, go on! Take the whole damned lot of you and go up there. Just leave me alone!"

"Sir, you really want all your personal guards gone? I mean . . . is that a good idea?"

"I don't pay you to question my judgement, Keller. Where's Ves Snowden?"

"Nobody's seen him lately, sir."

"Damn! Oh, hell, I remember. I gave him whiskey so he could drink off his grief over his brother. The Red Bands killed him."

"Freddy Snowden's dead?"

"That's what Ves said. Now take the men and get out of here."

"You're *sure* you don't mind being left alone while the Red Bands are on a rampage?"

"Go! Leave! Just give me some peace! There's important work going on here!" He slammed the door in Keller's face, then turned. Blessed was watching him.

"What's this? Watching the show? Get back to what you were doing!"

Blessed quickly buried himself in his work again.

Ten minutes later, when the house had been emptied of all Flanagan's personal guards, Flanagan began wondering if he should have considered what Keller said. *Perhaps it hadn't been wise to send every guard away. Oh, well. Too late now.*

Just to be safe, he decided he'd best get a weapon. He told Blessed to keep at his work, and he went down to his bigger office, then out to the hallway and the gun cabinet where he kept his shotgun.

He found the cabinet damaged and empty. His shotgun had been stolen! He glared at the place where it should have been, cursed, and headed back upstairs. He'd deal harshly with whoever stole that shotgun! But for now he wouldn't worry much about it. Everything would be fine. No one would bother him tonight.

Just then he heard a rap on the front door. He wheeled, listening. Another rap.

Flanagan crept up the hall and into the front room. He stared at the door, then tiptoed up to it, sliding back the cover of the viewing hole and looking out.

He stared in amazement, unable to believe what he saw.

Standing on the other side of the door, pale-faced, sickly, and shivering, was none other than Yancey Tobin himself.

Flanagan unlatched and opened the door, then stood staring at the man he hated, the man for whose murder he had bargained with Kane.

"You!" Flanagan said, for he could think of nothing else to say.

"Yes, me. I'm sorry to call on you at such an hour, Mr. Flanagan, but my business is rather urgent. And I see by your clothing that you haven't retired tonight."

Flanagan couldn't believe that this conversation was taking place. He didn't answer, just stared as if not trusting his eyes.

Tobin coughed suddenly, his body contracting in pain. "Please," he said in a choking voice. "I'm very cold and very sick. May I come in?"

Flanagan stepped back and let Tobin enter.

"Why have you come here?"

Tobin struggled a few moments longer with his cough and finally got control of it. He turned and faced Flanagan. "I'm told that you have a young woman imprisoned here and the price of her freedom is my death. So I've come to you. Here I stand before you, a man already dying. If you want me dead, all you need do is wait. Or, if you are too impatient, you can kill me yourself. But I'll not let you make an assassin out of a good young man, Mr. Flanagan."

Flanagan chuckled. "So *that's* it, is it? The bold, great Tobin, king of labor, spokesman for the strikers, has come to give his life for another, like some poor man's messiah!"

"You have me. I'll not resist anything you do. You can let the girl go now."

"You know, Mr. Tobin, I'm damned if I don't think I've never had a stranger night in all my life."

"Damned you very well may be, sir."

Flanagan's face twitched and his eye became flinty. "All right, you want to be my prisoner, my prisoner you'll be. What's the matter, Tobin? So sick you want to kill yourself but you're not man enough to do it alone? Want me to do the job for you? Is that it?"

"Mr. Flanagan, death is coming for me. I know it now. I can't run from it. But if I can make my death worthwhile to someone, even that poor young woman you have locked away, then why not? So here I am."

"Well, good for you. But you've caught me at a busy time. Upstairs with you. I'll put you in the room where the girl is—and don't worry, I'll not offend your fine Christian morality by leaving her in there with you. With you in hand I certainly don't need her now. Come on. Up the stairs."

She was gone. Flanagan stared into the dark and empty tower room, unable to believe it. The window was open, a cold wind, laden with snowflakes, blowing through.

"Inside with you!" he said to Tobin, grabbing his arm

and pulling him in, even though Tobin clearly was going to give no resistance. "The cursed little trollop has gone and escaped me!"

Flanagan found the cranked-down lamp and fed it more wick. Light filled the room. He went to the window and looked out and down. The bedsheet rope Carolina had made flapped loosely in the wind. He shook his head.

"Enterprising little harlot, that girl! I would never have guessed she'd try such a thing." He felt of the flimsy fabric rope and wondered if he should remove it, just in case Tobin tried a similar escape. But that was absurd. The man was far too ill and weak to climb down a high, sheer wall. Besides, he'd come here willingly and surrendered himself. He wasn't going to go climbing out of windows.

"Well, it seems you've made a show of nobility for no reason at all, Mr. Tobin! But this does save me the trouble of freeing her," Flanagan said, closing the window. "I'm afraid the room is a bit cold, especially for a man in your condition. Build yourself a fresh fire if you want. I'll be back later to deal with you." Flanagan walked to the door, paused there, and said, "You are quite a fool, sir. I'm sure you have the notion in your head that I'd never *really* do away with you, not with you making such a noble display of selflessness as this." Flanagan smiled. "I may, however, surprise you on that one." He closed and locked the door.

Tobin went to the fireplace, shivering and coughing. He knelt, slowly, and added wood to the nearly expired fire. As it caught, he let the heat bathe and soothe him.

Then he rose, as slowly as he'd knelt, and went to the bed, throwing himself in and pulling the covers up to his chin. There he lay, weak, coughing, and exhausted.

He wouldn't make it much longer. In the last day alone he had declined severely. He'd watched his grandfather die in this same way, of this very disease, and knew how fast he could fade away.

If Flanagan wanted the chance to take his life with his own hand, he might have to hurry.

When Flanagan opened the door to his little office, he found Blessed standing backed up against the desk, staring at a small, low doorway that led off the opposite wall into the attic.

"Why aren't you working?"

"There's someone in there," Blessed said, nodding toward the attic door.

"Hell, man, that's nothing but an empty attic! Why would anyone be in there?"

"I don't know, but there is."

"You heard a rat."

"It didn't sound like a rat."

Flanagan heard something, too, right then. Quiet, stealthy, but definitely there. It might have been human footsteps somewhere on the other side of that door.

"Did you hear it?" Blessed said.

"Yes," Flanagan whispered, his mind filling with images of sneaking Red Band assassins.

"Do you have a weapon on you?" Blessed asked.

Flanagan thought of his missing shotgun. *Dear Lord,*

might whoever was in the attic be the one who had taken it?

Without answering Blessed's question, he said, "Get in there. See what it is. It's probably some kind of creature."

"You want me to go in *there*?"

"What are you? Some cowardly schoolboy? Go on with you! Take that candle there."

"Why don't *you* go investigate? It's your house!"

"What? And then while I'm gone you take the letters and flee? No deal there, sir."

"You left me alone just now."

"I was only in the hallway below. If you had come down, I would have seen you. Now take that candle and get in there."

"If something happens to me, who will decode those letters?"

"You let me worry about those letters. Just get in there and see what kind of creature is fouling up my attic space!"

Once he'd crawled through the little square door into the attic, Blessed rose and stepped forward slowly, the candle shaking in his hand, the flame wavering and casting eerie shadows around the attic. The wind howled outside and cut its way through gaps in the wall and cracks beneath the eaves of the roof. Blessed looked around, hoping he was alone but feeling that he wasn't.

"Who's there?" he said weakly, hoping that no one replied. And no one did. "Is anyone there?" he asked again. Still no reply. Relief came. The candle didn't shake so badly now.

He was alone. Whatever he and Flanagan had heard must have been a rat, or mice, or even a high-climbing cat or squirrel. Exhaling slowly, he turned back toward the little door through which he'd come. He stooped and called out to Flanagan, "Nobody's here."

"How far in did you go? Explore it completely!"

Blessed had been afraid he would say that. He knew better than to argue, though. Rising, he turned and walked farther back into the cold, cavernous space.

He looked this way and that, lifting the flickering candle and ducking cobwebs. Something scurried past his feet and he dropped the candle, plunging the attic into darkness. *Just a mouse*, he thought, and cursed himself for his nervousness.

He knelt, found the candle, and with a match broken from a matchblock in his pocket, lit it. He rose.

A figure stood before him. Strangely dressed, and his face was painted. Blessed sucked in his breath and held it, eyes growing large.

"You are one of Flanagan's men?" the painted figure asked in a low, growling whisper.

"No!" Blessed replied, his voice gone hoarse and weak. "No, I'm not."

"Then who are you? Why are you in this house?"

It was a question Blessed would have asked of the figure itself if he had dared. But this figure was far too fearsome and strange to be questioned. Blessed was actually thinking thoughts of vengeful ghosts. "He's forcing me to . . . translate some documents for him."

"Then you aren't here willingly?"

"No. No, not at all."

The painted man pointed over Blessed's shoulder. "There is another way out of this attic, that way. The way I came in. You can go out that way. Leave this house."

Blessed looked back. A second way out of the attic! Flanagan must have forgotten it.

He heard Flanagan call through the doorway again. "Blessed! What have you found? Who are you talking to?"

Blessed thought of those letters, those precious, long-sought letters, lying on the desk. Out of reach. If he left this house he would lose them, and he might never find Kane again to re-create them. But if he stayed here and finished his decoding, he would be eliminated. Of that he was sure.

"Go!" the painted man said.

"I will," Blessed replied. He turned and headed away from the door through which he'd entered.

"Blessed!" Flanagan called in. "Blessed, where are you?"

Blessed did not answer. He found the second door and opened it. It led into a small loftlike room, stacked with old boxes and furniture, with an opening in the floor through which extended a ladder. He put hands and feet on the rungs and descended. He could still hear Flanagan's voice, but distantly now, and muffled, angrily calling for him. Soon he could not hear it at all.

He reached the bottom and found another door, exiting into a dark hallway. At the end of that hall, a final door opened onto the yard.

Robert Blessed slipped out of the Flanagan house

and ran across the snow as hard as he could, not even bothering to close the last door behind him.

Kane shook Trumbling's shoulder. The big man jumped, rumbled, sputtered. "What the devil!"

"He's gone, Mr. Trumbling. Yancey is gone."

"What? Where?"

"I'm not sure . . . I'm afraid he's gone to the Flanagan house. I left him about an hour ago, and when I looked in again just now, he was gone. I found his tracks in the snow, heading toward Flanagan's."

The big man sat up, running a ham of a hand across his stubbled face. "What did you just say? He's gone to Flanagan's? Why the devil—"

"Because he's not willing to let a young woman be hurt or killed by Flanagan when it's really him that Flanagan wants. It's a long story and I can't tell it all now. Just hurry! We have to find him. Flanagan will kill him. There's no time to lose!"

Trumbling shook off the sluggishness of sleep with one great effort and rose out of bed. He reached for his trousers and shirt and began to dress at once.

Chapter 26

Flanagan lit the lamp and cranked the wick high. His throat was dry and raw, and his heart was hammering in his chest.

Blessed would pay for this! What kind of game was the man playing, hiding silently in that attic while he was being called for? What was he up to?

Flanagan ducked his head and passed through the low doorway. Light from the lantern spilled into the cobweb-strung attic space. The wind-pounded roof, heavy with snow, creaked and groaned above him. Flanagan straightened, holding the lamp high.

"Blessed!"

No one replied. He remembered, then—there was another way out of this attic. Damnation! Had Blessed fled?

Flanagan strode across the attic toward the other side, trying to remember just where that other door was. Ah, yes, now he saw it. Stooping, he let the light of the lamp play over the floor. In the dust he saw footprints leading straight to that door. Had Blessed escaped him?

Flanagan frowned. There were other prints here, too.

Many of them. Smaller than Blessed's, and made by a different shoe. Who else would have been up here? He remembered that the opposite attic door led to a ladder, which reached to a hallway with an exterior entrance. He'd regretted allowing that design to stand almost from the day he'd finished this house; such a setup invited some thief or prowler to gain access to the house by way of the ladder and attic. It seemed to him that exact event had finally come about.

He swung the lamp around, letting its light expose every corner. "If there's anyone in here, then he'd damned best show himself, or there'll be hell to pay for it!" he bellowed. "Who's in here? Show yourself!"

Even though he'd just made the demand, Flanagan was stunned to see a man step from behind the center chimney. He backed away, gasping, when he saw that the man's face was painted in a bizarre, ghastly fashion. He looked for all the world like some old picture of an Indian painted out for war.

"Who the hell . . ."

"Flanagan!" the painted man said, coming toward him. "Flanagan himself! The very man I've come to find!"

"Who are you? *What* are you? Get out of my house!"

"My name is Tsani, though I'm known among the white men here as John Ridge. I am Cherokee. You don't know me, Flanagan. I'm the kind of man who is nothing and no one to you. But I had a brother, a fine and good man named Aganstati. He died at the hands of some of your hired killers. He died because he was bold and good enough to refuse to stand by and watch your hired men murder an innocent man. And now, Flanagan, I have come to avenge my brother's death, as I have already avenged him several times over with the lives of your men."

"I'll see you jailed for this! I'll have you *killed* if I choose!"

"There are no more choices for you, Flanagan, but to die." Tsani brought out his hatchet and advanced, beginning to chant. The words, spoken in Cherokee, were the same ones he'd written on the inner walls of the cabin he and his brother had shared, in a wild explosion of fury and grief.

Flanagan, his chest suddenly hurting terribly and sweat bursting from every pore, staggered back and fell to his knees. He dropped the lamp from a hand suddenly gone numb. He groped at his chest, which felt like a band was constricting around it, very hard.

"No . . ." he said to the living nightmare before him. "No . . . I am Eiler Flanagan! You cannot—"

The hatchet rose and fell, many times, the terrible sound of every impact echoing inside the attic, while the wind howled louder just outside.

At last, Tsani stopped the blows and looked down at what remained of the mortal flesh of Eiler Flanagan. The terrible sight was easily visible, because the lamp had broken and flames were spreading across the attic floor, brightly illuminating the interior. He stared at the corpse and decided there was no point in taking the scalp this time. There really wasn't enough left of the head to make it all that feasible, and besides, the fire was spreading fast.

Tsani descended the ladder to the hallway and walked slowly out the still-open doorway, into the night. He walked away, toward the mountains, as the first flames began to lick out beneath the eaves of the house.

He was satisfied. Aganstati was avenged.

Tobin, awakened by some inner alarm, watched the smoke billowing up under the door of his room and knew that flames would soon follow. Though he was a brave man and knew it, he was terrified of fire, and the thickness and toxicity of the smoke coming under that door told him that flames were already spreading below. Even if he managed to hammer down the door somehow, he would probably be cut off from descent.

He decided that if he was meant to die tonight, then die he would ... but *not* by fire and smoke. Anything but that!

Tobin, coughing and spitting up even more blood than usual, opened the window and looked down at the makeshift rope that Carolina Railey had strung. Whether consumption had left him the strength to take such a perilous route to freedom he didn't know, but even if he fell, that alternative seemed far better than the fate of death by fire.

Tobin saw people below, running up the hill, and heard yells, the clanging of the fire bell, and the barking of many dogs.

Perhaps he should wait ... perhaps they would reach him, rescue him ...

Flames slipped under the door behind him and began

creeping up the panel. The smoke grew thicker, more choking.

Tobin genuflected and said a prayer, committing himself to God, whether he lived or died. Then he put his hands on the rope and edged his body out the window.

He made it almost halfway down before the fabric tore in his hands. His heart jumped to his throat as he fell, but he did not cry out.

Yancey Tobin hit the snowy ground very hard, almost at the same spot where Carolina had fallen. He moved, just a little, and groaned, and then lay still.

He heard men yelling, felt the vibration of running feet drawing near. Someone touched him. "It's Tobin!" a voice said. He felt himself being dragged away, through the snow . . .

And then he felt nothing at all.

Kane stood in the yard, staring at the house as flames engulfed it. His eyes were locked on the tower, fully in flames now, but he did not see it clearly. The tears in his eyes prohibited it.

Carolina. Poor, poor Carolina! He thought of her, bravely saving her father from a terrible fiery death in the hotel in Dodge City. And now, for her . . . this.

He wanted to turn away, to become sick, to scream and rant at the sky and land and heavens for letting her be taken in this awful way, but he didn't have it in him.

All he could do was stand and stare while the house of Eiler Flanagan burned to the ground.

* * *

Most would blame the Red Bands for the fire that destroyed Eiler Flanagan's house. It made sense. The Red Bands had often publicly threatened to burn down Flanagan's house, and at the time the fire broke out, a gang of Red Bands was engaged in vandalism at the Flanagan Hill Mine. Quite likely the mine vandalism was merely a deliberate distraction to draw Flanagan's personal guards away from the house so that the arsonists could move in quietly.

It could have gone much worse in terms of the loss of life. Flanagan himself was dead; his body was found burned, battered, but still recognizable, amid the rubble. As best the events could be re-created, it appeared that he'd died somewhere in the upper levels of the house, hacked to death with a hatchet. The fire had probably been set to cover the crime, but a falling timber had shielded Flanagan's body and enough of him had survived the flames to leave evidence of the way he'd truly died.

Flanagan's house staff, other than his guards, had consisted of a couple of cooks, a scullery girl, and a longtime black servant named Edgar. The cooks and scullery girl, who lived in a small house behind the main structure, had come through safe and sound, but Edgar, whose room was near his employer's in the big house, was missing and presumed lost in the fire. In all the hubbub, nobody noticed him, very much alive, slipping onto the first outbound train that left Three Mile the morning after the blaze. He'd bought the ticket under an assumed name after watching the Flanagan mansion burn down from a hiding place on a hillside overlooking the train station. The fire had mystified and troubled him. That poor girl, locked up in the tower! He hoped they'd gotten her out!—but he wasn't troubled enough about it to go back there.

His life in the shadow of Eiler Flanagan was over.

Kane remained at Yancey Tobin's bedside for days. The man was unconscious, and no one expected that he would regain his senses before death took him. Still, Kane lingered nearby, hoping that somehow Yancey Tobin would come back around, at least long enough to tell him anything at all he might know about what had become of Carolina.

They'd found no corpses in the house except that of Eiler Flanagan—though, surprisingly, one of the firemen stumbled across the snow-covered, frozen corpse of Ves Snowden in the yard. The speculation was that the man had drunk himself into a stupor, passed out, and died of exposure. He was no more grieved for than Eiler Flanagan himself.

Kane was warned not to make too much of the fact that Carolina's body had not been found in the house. The fire had been intensely hot, especially in the higher parts of the structure. Perhaps any other bodies inside the house had been consumed so thoroughly that no one had yet spotted the meager remains in the smoldering heap of rubble.

Kane wondered how that could be, though. No burned-down house in the nation was ever so thoroughly explored, for everyone knew of Eiler Flanagan's hobby of gemstone collecting, and went prospecting in the ashes in the slim hope that they might find a stray jewel here or there.

Kane not only worried about what had befallen Carolina, but wondered about Robert Blessed as well. Had he gotten away, or was he, too, dead in the fire? If he'd escaped, had he taken the re-created letters with him, or had they burned up?

He even wondered if it was Blessed who killed Eiler Flanagan and set the fire. He supposed he would never know.

Ironic, Kane thought, how he was left in almost the same situation as when he first went to Dodge City, not knowing whether his enemy was alive or dead.

Kane was dozing at Tobin's bedside the day Frederick Railey showed up. Kane had wired him in Dodge City, telling him about the fire, and that Carolina had purportedly been in the house and was now missing. He hoped the return wire would tell him that Carolina had never been in Three Mile at all and was still safe in Dodge. But the derringer that Flanagan had showed him was evidence that she had indeed been there, and the return wire confirmed it: Carolina had left Dodge City to find Kane, via contact with Eiler Flanagan, to warn him that she had spotted Robert Blessed alive in Kansas.

Frederick Railey, still weak from his ordeal in the Dodge City fire, looked almost as deathly as Yancey Tobin. He hung his head and wept on Kane's shoulder while Kane did the same on his. They had both loved Carolina, and she was gone.

When the initial grieving was done, Frederick told

Kane that he had come to Three Mile in the company of Ben Flanagan and his assistant, Grossett. Not only had Ben Flanagan come to claim and bury the remains of his unlamented late brother, he was also going to take over the ownership and management of the Flanagan Hill Mine.

"He intends to settle this strike forthwith, by giving the miners exactly what they want and deserve—better pay, greater safety . . . almost every demand. He's a very different man than his brother was. The miners of Flanagan Hill are at last going to have a superior they can trust and respect, and working conditions second to none."

Kane was glad to hear it. He leaned over and repeated the information, slowly, to the unconscious Tobin.

Probably a vain effort, he knew, but when he was finished, he was surprised, and touched, to see one tear emerge from beneath Tobin's closed eyelid and slide slowly down his face.

Chapter 27

When they buried Yancey Tobin on a snow-blown, bitterly cold day, all of Three Mile turned out. The graveyard was crowded to and beyond the fence that surrounded it, the crowd becoming so intrusive that the fence finally was simply trampled down and forgotten.

Many eulogies were given; even Caleb Creede, chief critic of the peace-minded Tobin and leader of the radical Red Bands—who were strenuously denying any involvement in the burning of the Flanagan mansion—spoke kind words, going so far as to declare that just maybe the man had been right to take the approach he had. If not for the calming influence of Tobin's turn-the-other-cheek philosophy, the Flanagan Hill "war" might have become a true war long before, with dire results for many.

The speaker who received the strongest response, however, was Ben Flanagan. He stood beside Yancey Tobin's grave and declared that the man had not died in vain. The goals he had sought would, under the ownership of a different Flanagan, be attained, and quickly.

The strike, he declared, need not go on. What was right and needful would be promptly done.

Kane looked down at Tobin's coffin and smiled at the thought that Tobin's twin desires to live a meaningful life and die a meaningful death had both been achieved.

Kane and Frederick Railey remained at the grave-yard after the coffin was covered, each knowing the thoughts of the other. They were wondering if ever there would be a gravestone to mark the resting place of Carolina Railey, or if she would remain lost, forever unfound.

Memorial or no memorial, Kane thought, he would never forget her. Never.

He and Railey were turning away from Tobin's grave when they noticed the tall, broadly built young man standing about the place the fence had been. He watched them quietly, and nodded a greeting when they looked at him.

"Who is that?" Railey asked softly.

"I don't know," Kane said. "But I believe he's waiting for us."

They walked toward the young fellow, who looked even younger the closer they got to him.

"Hello, sir, and you, too, sir," he said, yanking off his hat. His brogue was distinctly Irish, much stronger than Tobin's had been. "Might I have a word with you, if you're Mr. Kane Porterfell?"

"I am Kane Porterfell. And yes, you may."

"My name's Rich Clancey," the youth said, crumpling his hat nervously in his hands. "I've been sent to fetch you."

"Sent by whom?"

"By the young lady, sir. By Miss Railey."

Kane and Frederick Railey looked at one another, then at Clancey. "Carolina Railey? She's *alive*?"

"Oh, yes, sir. She's alive, though her ankle bone was hurt rather nicely when she took that fall from the tower at the house of the late Mr. Flanagan. And it helped her not at all that she nigh froze to death in the yard before I happened in God's providence to find her while I was searching for my mother's lost cat. She was passed out cold for days, she was, but thanks mostly to Mr. Colby's care she's since come around and is faring real nice, and calling for you, Mr. Porterfell."

Railey was about to burst into tears. "Good Lord, son, are you telling me that my daughter is alive, and lucid, and—"

"I don't know what you mean by 'lucid,' sir, but I can tell you she's alive and well. You be her father, do you?"

"Yes, yes, indeed."

"Take us to her," Kane said. "Please."

The house was nothing but the smallest and simplest of cabins, tucked away at the edge of town in the literal shadow of Flanagan Hill, high above. A hand-lettered slab sign outside bore the words: LAWNDRY SERVICE.

Rich Clancey's mother was a stoop-shouldered, wrinkled woman who might have qualified for the description of "hag" but for a certain gentle, warm sparkle in her drooping eyes. She welcomed Kane and Railey into her plain, very humble dwelling, which despite the evidence of poverty it displayed, was as neatly kept as a queen's castle.

"The young lady is waiting for you in yonder back room," she said, pointing toward a "back room" that was really no more than a curtain stretched across a rear corner of the cabin.

It was all Kane could do to restrain himself from rushing to that curtain and yanking it aside. He held back, though, and let Frederick Railey take the lead.

It *was* Carolina! Kane lowered his head and wept in relief as he watched daughter embrace father. When Carolina looked at him over her father's shoulder, her eyes were wet too.

Railey hugged his child for the longest time, but at last Kane had the same privilege. To feel her alive and warm and safe in his arms seemed to him at that moment the greatest joy he'd ever known.

He pulled back just enough to look at her face. "Carolina, I think we both have many stories to tell one another."

"Yes, Kane, but not now . . . Kane, I need to tell you—I've seen him. I've been with him."

"Who?"

"Your father, Kane. He was here."

"Here?"

"In this house! Kane, he took care of me. He bound up my ankle for me. He treated me for frostbite—I think he may have saved me from losing some of my toes. He wasn't using his real name, but it was him. He was a kind, gentle man. And very good at drawing. He drew sketches for me. Beautiful pictures, portraits of myself, of Mrs. Clancey, of Rich and the other young ones."

"But how do you know it was my father?"

"We talked about you, Kane. After I realized who he was, I told him about you. He never directly admitted he was who he was . . . but it was *him*. I know it was, from the things he told me. And from his face, his eyes. They were *your* eyes, Kane. When I looked in his face, I saw you."

"But why would he be here?"

"Mrs. Clancey—oh, she's a fine woman, Kane—can tell you more, maybe, but Mr. Colby—that's the name your father was using—told me enough on his own for me to be sure of him. Long before he knew anything about my background, where I'd come from, and that I knew you, he told me how he'd come to Three Mile from Kansas to work as a guard for Eiler Flanagan during the strike. But he left Flanagan's hire after he was asked to do wicked things, cruel things, and after he became suspicious about Flanagan himself. He never would say what he meant by 'suspicious.' But he fled Flanagan, and came to this house almost by accident. He might have left Three Mile completely, but he stayed on because he saw that Mrs. Clancey needed help. Her husband died, you see. And she was sick at the time. He actually did laundry for her, Kane! So that she could continue to have money coming in until she was well enough herself to work again."

"You told him . . . about me?"

"Yes. After I understood who he was, I did. And when I said the name Porterfell, he looked like he might faint. He was shocked. And Kane . . . I told him everything. Your capture, the death of your mother, Blessed and his pursuit, how you were looking for him . . ."

Kane closed his eyes, absorbing it all. He was shaking and couldn't stop. "And what did he do?"

"He . . . he left, Kane. He refused to answer when I asked him if he was William Porterfell, and then he left."

Kane looked away, fighting against tears. "So that answers the question. He doesn't want to know me."

"No, Kane. I don't think that's true. It's just that he was so overwhelmed by it all. It frightened him, I think."

"But he left. He went away. And now I'll never find him."

"Yes, Kane, I think you will. He left me this. He said to give it to you."

Carolina handed him a folded paper. Kane took it, opened it, and what he saw made him blink fast and swipe at his eyes with the back of his hand.

The sketch was of his mother, as she'd looked in his earliest memories of her, when she was young. In her arms was a sleeping baby, tightly wrapped in a blanket.

Below was a map of sorts. Nothing but one small dot with the words "Three Mile" written below it. A line extended up and to the left, to another dot. Below that dot were the words "Helena, Montana."

Carolina smiled. "He's telling you to come to him, Kane. To follow him to Montana. Can you see that?"